Unexpected Reality

USA Today Bestselling Author

KAYLEE RYAN

Cover Design: Perfect Pear Creative Covers
Cover Photography: Marc-André Riopel & Josée Houle
Cover Model: David Juteau Marineau
Editing: Hot Tree Editing
Proofreading: Masque of the Red Pen
Formatting: Integrity Formatting

Prologue

Melissa

This bar looks as good a place as any to take a break. I've been driving for hours with no destination. I have nowhere to go, nowhere to be, and no one who will be looking for me. That is my reality.

I've always tried hard to be positive with the life I've been given. I always had three hot meals and a safe place to lay my head at night. I'm one of the lucky ones who landed within the system that didn't have to sleep with one eye open. Jeff and Maggie were great foster parents and even better adoptive parents. They made sure I had everything I needed, and in turn, I did what was expected of me. I did my chores, my homework, and never broke the rules.

Rebel, I know.

My chest literally aches at the thought of Jeff and Maggie. Did I tell them thank you enough, show them how grateful I was for bringing me into their home? My eyes start to burn with tears.

I've lost the only family I've ever known.

I was blissfully happy, one week from graduating college, moving back home to help Jeff and Maggie at their law firm. I chose paralegal because of them.

1

It's been a month since I got the phone call. Thirty days since my world came crashing down.

"Home invasion."

"Two fatalities."

"You need to come home."

Those are the details of the call that I remember. The night I lost the family that chose me. Jeff and Maggie's family were not as open to me as they were. They felt it was silly that they were able to conceive their own children, but decided to adopt me instead. I was the only one. They said they didn't want to have to share their love. Needless to say, now that they're gone, it's just me. I'm alone in the world once again, no family and no close friends. I have acquaintances, but I spent all my free time in the library. I didn't go to parties or football games. I studied. I wanted to do it for them to show them how much I appreciated all they had given me. Everything I've ever done in my life has been for them.

Now they're gone.

Where do I go from here?

The neon sign flashes in the window advertising different kinds of beer. I don't care what kind it is; I just need something to help take the pain away. Across the street is a motel. *Good. I plan to drink until I forget.*

Quickly, I cross the street and reserve a room. It's actually perfect that I won't have to drive. I pull out my debit card and pass it to the young receptionist. I have money, lots of it. Jeff and Maggie left me everything, just something else their families didn't approve of. I was about to give it back, tell them they could shove it. That money won't bring back the only parents I've ever known. It won't bring back my family. It wasn't until the attorney handed me a letter from them, my parents,' that I changed my mind. The letter said that I brought joy to their lives, that I was their greatest accomplishment. I have that letter memorized.

"Take it, Melissa. We want to know that you will always be taken care of. Live your life and follow your dreams. Live for you, sweet girl. No one else."

They were always telling me that. "Pick a career you love, Melissa. Not for us but for you."

I lived for them, and because of them, my life wasn't the hell that it could have been. How do I learn to live without them? Learn to live for me?

"Sign here." The receptionist hands me a pen.

I scrawl my name on the receipt, take my key, and head back outside. I don't want to feel this pain anymore. I just want the pain to go away. The flashing neon sign calls to me. Maybe I can drink it away.

Opening the door, the smell of smoke and alcohol invade my senses. The place—Danny's, as according to the sign, is packed for a Thursday night. I make my way to the bar and spot an empty stool at the end. Perfect, it's just me. I'm good with being tucked away, as long as the bartender keeps the drinks coming.

My ass hasn't even hit the chair before a woman in her late fifties or so is asking for my order. I'm not much of a drinker, but Maggie used to drink cranberry and vodka, so I go with that.

"Coming right up." She smiles causing the laugh lines around her eyes to be more prominent. "Here you go, sweetie. You want to start a tab?" she asks, wiping down the bar.

"Yeah, keep them coming." I tilt back the glass she just set in front of me and drain it.

She studies me. "You driving?"

"No. I have a room across the street."

She nods, accepting my answer, and then gets to work making me another drink.

I take my time with this one. I've got nowhere to be.

I've lost track of how long I've been sitting here, lost in thought, waiting for the alcohol to dull the pain. I don't know how many drinks I've had, having lost count of that too, but my mind is finally starting to turn off.

"Can I get another round for our table," a deep voice says beside me.

Glancing over, I take him in. Tall, dark hair, tattoos. Not someone a good girl should be attracted to, but I am. He's wearing a tight shirt that shows off his ribbed abs. Holy hell, he's sexy. Turning back to my drink, I try to shake off the thought.

When he reaches back for his wallet, his elbow bumps mine. "Nothing like rubbing elbows with a beautiful woman." He winks.

3

I smile shyly. "Lucky me," I say, facing forward and going back to my drink. I can't believe this guy is actually flirting with me. I'm sure he's just being friendly. I'm just as surprised that I gave it right back to him. That's not something I've ever done.

"What's a pretty little thing like you doing here all alone?" he questions.

"Just passing through," I reply. Again, I face forward. I'm afraid if I don't I'll start drooling over this guy. I'm out of my element here.

"I thought so. I would have remembered you." He winks again. "We've been here a lot the last couple of months."

"You think so?" Holy shit. I fight the urge to wipe my sweaty palms on my jeans.

"Definitely." He takes his time running those chocolate brown eyes over my body. "Listen, why don't you join my friends and me? No sense in drinking alone."

Sober Melissa would decline such an offer. Buzzed Melissa doesn't want to be alone. *This guy seems interested; what harm can come from sitting with them? It will serve as another distraction, help me forget.* "Sure." I grab my drink and my purse, sliding off the stool. I stumble and the sexy stranger catches me. "Thank you . . ." I don't even know this guy's name.

"Ridge." He grips my arms to steady me. "You okay . . . ?"

"Melissa." I pull away from him. "I've just been sitting there for a while, sorry," I flush with embarrassment. I'm not that drunk, so it has to be him; he has me off-kilter. I don't know that I've ever talked to anyone who looks like him before. In college, I kept to myself and the guys didn't even bother. Why go after the one you have to work for when the others are willing to give it for free?

I've been with two guys. The first was a means to an end. A 'get it over with' kind of deal. Guy number two was a friend of my roommate. It was the first and only time I've ever been sloppy drunk. I don't even remember it, really. Pathetic, I know, but that's my life. The irony is not lost on me that tonight, I want to be that drunk again, if not more so. I want to forget the pain, the loss, the feeling of being alone. Lucky for me, my new friend Ridge seems like he's willing to help me out.

"Guys, this is Melissa. I found her drinking alone, so I asked her to join us," he says once we reach the table.

Four guys, all of equal hotness as my new friend Ridge, appraise me. I feel my face heat under their gaze. Attention is not something I'm used to. They all offer me some sort of greeting, and I stupidly wave at them in return.

"You can sit by me," Ridge says next to my ear.

The warmth of his breath against my skin sends shivers down my spine. Awkwardly, I take the seat he pulls out for me, clasping my hands together on the table.

"All right, so we've got Seth, Tyler, Mark, and Kent." Ridge points to each guy as he says their name.

"It's nice to meet you," I say politely, barely glancing at each of them, still embarrassed by their attention.

"So, missy, you live around here?" the one on my right asks—Kent . . . I think.

"No, I'm just passing through. How about the five of you? Locals?" I take a sip of the fresh drink that was just set on the table in front of me.

"No," Ridge says, throwing his arm over the back of my chair. "We're in town for a job."

I take note of the Beckett Construction T-shirts they all seem to be wearing. "Construction," I say like an idiot. These men are sexy and intimidating.

"Yep." Ridge tips his beer back, and I get lost watching his throat as he swallows. Like I said, he's sexy.

"We grew up together," one of the guys says.

I can't remember what Ridge said his name was. Mark, maybe?

"So, just living it up after a long work week?" I wonder what it would be like to have friendships you formed in elementary school. I feel a pang of envy and sadness in my chest so I tip my glass and drain it, wanting to forget.

The five of them chuckle. "Something like that," the one with longer hair replies.

And that's how this night goes. The guys are funny, charming, and flirting. A few other women join us, but Ridge continues to stay close to me, ordering me drinks. I even buy a round or two, and relax into his touches. Simple ones like rubbing my shoulder, his hand on my arm and of course, whispering in my ear. I quit trying to hide the shiver it causes in me about three drinks ago.

I'm attracted to him, and he knows it.

One by one, the guys pair up, leaving just Ridge and me. "Where are you staying tonight?" His hand rests on my thigh.

"I . . . I, uh, got a room across the street."

"Hmmm, that's where we've been staying too." Leaning in close, his breath mingles with mine as the bartender announces last call. "I'll walk you home."

Ridge stands and offers me his hand, and I take it without hesitation. There's something in his eyes, the way he's been by my side all night. I trust him. I don't know how to initiate it, but I want him with me, in my room, tonight. I'm not ready to let go of the way he makes me feel.

Ridge keeps his arm around my waist as we head to the bar. I pay my tab, after much protest from him.

The cool night air feels good against my heated skin. He pulls me into his chest and again, I go willingly.

"Which room is yours?" he asks.

"119," I say, so softly I'm surprised he heard me. His touch has my body craving him. We reach my door and I slip the key from my back pocket. "Would you like to come in?" I'm looking at my feet, my back turned to him. I grip the door handle, bracing myself for his rejection.

Stepping closer, he aligns his body with mine. One hand rests on my hip while the other moves my hair to one shoulder. "I don't know if that's such a good idea." He kisses my neck.

"Oh," I say, dejected.

"I won't be able to keep my hands to myself," he continues, pressing his erection into my ass.

Oh, my. Excitement rushes through me. *I'm doing this.* I passed my comfort level hours ago, and it's scary, but my gut tells me that Ridge is a good guy. That, for a one-night stand, I couldn't have picked anyone better. Well, except maybe for his four friends. They all seem like great guys.

"What if . . . What if I don't want you to?"

His lips trace my neck. "Open the door, Melissa."

Fumbling with the key, I do as he says. Suddenly, the buzz of the alcohol is gone and in its place is pure lust. I want this. I want one night with him. One night to feel wanted by this Adonis of a man.

Once in the room, Ridge rips off his shirt and throws it in the chair. I take him in—his firm, ridged abs, the tattoos I want to trace with my tongue.

"You keep looking at me like that and this is going to be over before it starts," he warns me.

I shift my gaze to the ground, embarrassed to have been caught ogling him.

"Hey." He steps close, lifting my chin with his index finger to face him. "You didn't do anything wrong; I just meant that the look you were giving me alone has me ready to blow." He studies my expression once his words sink in. "Have you done this before, Melissa?"

Shit. Not exactly one-night stand conversation. "Twice," I blurt out.

Ridge closes his eyes and takes a deep breath. "You want this?"

"More than I could ever explain."

His hands land on my waist and pull me close. "I'll take care of you." His lips softly cover mine.

And then he does. He shows me passion like I've never known. He soon has my body singing his praises, and I loudly call out his name.

Afterward, he doesn't leave like I expect him to. Instead, he curls up beside me and drifts off to sleep. I lie there for hours until the reality of what I've just done hits me. I had a one-night stand with no regrets. I wanted it. I wanted him. However, I don't relish doing the walk of shame. The awkward morning after I've read about so many times. I don't want that. I don't want to give him the chance to ruin this high I'm on. I won't give him the chance to reject me.

Quietly, I slide out of bed, gather my things, and slip quietly out the door. I didn't even bring in clothes, just rented the room and went straight to the bar.

Ridge gave me a night to remember, and a night to forget. I will forever be grateful to him.

Chapter 1

Ridge

"Another round?" the waitress asks.

"Keep them coming, sweetheart." Kent winks.

I watch as her face flushes red, and she saunters away. The guys and I are having a much-needed drink after the long workweek. We've been coming to Bottom's Up for a few years now. It's a small little place, with a jukebox full of classic tunes. The atmosphere is laid-back and the waitresses are always a nice distraction. Not that I've taken advantage of that; I've been going through a small dry spell the past several months.

My eyes are glued to the makeshift dance floor when Seth speaks up. "You picking out your after-party?" He smirks at me.

"Haven't decided yet. You?"

"Like you need to even ask," Mark chimes in.

"What I want to know is why haven't you decided," Tyler adds.

I shrug. "Just not feeling it," I say honestly.

"Who are you and what have you done with Ridge?" Kent remarks.

"You worry about your cock, and I'll worry about mine." I give him the look that says back off.

"Little Ridge has to be feeling neglected. What's it been—four, five months?" Seth asks.

Fuck! That's the downfall of being friends your entire lives; they hold nothing back, and they can read you like a book.

"About that," I say, grabbing the beer the cute little waitress just sat in front of me. I tip it back and drain half of it.

"Not since what's her name . . ." Tyler places his finger on his chin.

"Shit. That's right, the job we did out of town. Cute little thing. What *was* her name?" Mark says.

"Melissa," I mumble.

"Yes!" all four of them say in unison.

"Was it that good?" Kent asks.

Yes. There was something about her, like she was desperate for the connection. She was definitely not like my usual hookups, but her sneaking off in the middle of the night? Well, that does something to a man. I'm used to the stage-five clingers, the ones who beg to get together again and plead for your number. The ones who frequent Bottom's Up just to get the chance to come home with you again. The ones who will latch on to you and fake being asleep just so they can spend the night. That's what I'm used to. Waking up alone in a hotel room? That doesn't happen.

At least not to me.

No note, not even a trace of clothing for proof that she was there. It's as though she were a figment of my imagination.

"It's all right, bud." Seth places his hand on my shoulder. "We've all gone through a dry spell." He's trying hard not to laugh.

"We got you," Mark chimes in.

"We'll make sure our flavor of the night has a friend. And we'll get her all liquored up so she wants to be with you," Tyler says.

"Surely, we can convince her," Kent adds.

"Fuck off."

"Ooh, I think we hit a nerve," Seth taunts.

"I don't need help finding a willing female," I grumble.

"Really?" Kent questions.

"Gentlemen, I think we have a challenge on our hands." Tyler rubs his hands together in excitement.

"Yep. We pick the girl." Mark smirks.

I grab my beer and bring it to my lips, just letting them talk. I've never had trouble with the ladies. It's the dark hair and the tattoos. They all have a fantasy of being with the bad boy, the rebel who will make them feel dangerous and lively. The guy their mothers warned them about. Then, there are woman who simply see what they like and want to experience it. They think that's me, but looks can be deceiving. Yeah, I have the dark, mysterious look—black hair, dark brown eyes, and the ink. Doesn't mean I'm a bad guy. Sure, I've been with my fair share of women, but I'm a young, single guy. No harm no foul.

"Any requests?" Seth asks.

I look around the table at the four of them. "Nope," I snap, tipping my beer to my lips.

"Time to set the terms," Marks says.

"None needed. Pick the girl, and I'll seal the deal," I tell them with confidence.

"Well now, cocky much?" Tyler accuses.

"Fellas, I say we sweeten the pot. Mr. Cocky thinks he can seal the deal, so we just have to up the stakes." Kent sits up in his chair, leaning his elbows on the table.

I don't say anything, just sit back and watch them. I can practically see the little wheels in their heads turning, deciding my fate. We've always been this way, never backing down from a dare.

"I got it!" Mark exclaims. "Three months. We pick the girl and you keep her around for three months." He sits back in his seat, grinning wildly.

Fuck! Three months. That's relationship material, and that equals feelings and a mess of drama when it ends. At times, the one-night stands are hard to get away from, even though they know the score. Three fucking months. What? Just so I can have bragging rights?

"I'm digging it," Seth agrees.

A chorus of "Me, too" and "Hell yes" reaches my ears.

"What are the stakes?" I ask. "Three months is relationship status. I'll need more than bragging rights."

"Hundred bucks each," Kent suggests. "And you can only be with her, no others."

Seriously?

"I don't need the money," I say, signaling for the waitress to bring us another round.

"No, but if you win, we would have to pay up. Unless of course you're backing down already?" Seth goads me.

Four hundred bucks and bragging rights. Is it worth it? Four sets of eyes full of mischief watch me, waiting for me to turn it down.

What man would agree to keep some random woman, hand picked by his friends from a smoky bar around for three months? That would be crazy, right?

"Scared?" Mark heckles.

"Make your pick, boys." I smirk. Fuck it! It's three months, and they didn't say how much time I had to spend with her, just that she had to be around for three months. I've gone three months without sex, so that's not an issue.

Mark and Kent immediately begin searching the crowd for their suggestion. Seth looks confused, like he didn't think I would agree. Tyler is smirking.

Payback's a bitch, boys.

"Right, so we must consult. Ridge, my man, we'll be right back," Tyler says.

I watch as the four of them stand and head to the bar.

What the hell did I just get myself into?

The cute little waitress brings another round, even though the guys are standing at the bar. I quickly grab mine and pound it back, slamming the empty bottle on the table.

Game on.

"Ridge, this is Stephanie," Mark says as the rest of the guys take their seats. Turning to face the music, I see a blonde with long-ass legs and nice tits staring back at me. I prefer blondes.

Maybe this isn't going to be as bad as I thought.

Standing from my seat, I reach for her hand and pull it to my lips. "Nice to meet you, Stephanie. Can I get you a drink?"

"Hi." She blushes. "My friends are actually at the bar." She points over her shoulder.

I don't pull my eyes away from her, giving her all my attention. "You can sit by me." I wink, pulling the chair out for her.

"Thanks." She grins.

For the rest of the night, I focus on her. She seems . . . normal, not one of the crazies. Her friends are nice and otherwise occupied by mine. Everyone is having a good time, and I feel some of the dread slip away. Maybe, just maybe, I didn't sign myself up for three months of hell.

As the night carries on, my boys continue to drink, but I switch over to water. It's go time, so I need to keep my wits about me, keep Miss Stephanie interested. As if she can read my thoughts, she yawns.

"I'm so sorry." She hides her mouth behind her hands. "I've been up since five this morning, and I'm worn out."

"What do you do?"

"I work in interior design. I had a final staging today for a house we just completed."

Beautiful and holds down a job. "Let me take you home," I whisper in her ear.

"I-I . . . um, would love to, but I have to be up again early tomorrow," she says while looking down at her clasped hands.

"As much as I would love to share your bed with you tonight, that's not what I meant. You're tired and have been drinking. Let me drive you home, make sure you make it there safe."

She hesitates. I'm sure she's trying to gauge if she can trust me. She looks around at our friends, who are obviously paired up.

"Steph, Mark is coming home with me. You ready to go?" her friend asks. I didn't bother to try and learn their names.

This could not have worked out better. I brought Mark, her friend brought her. She needs a ride.

"Just a ride," I whisper against her ear.

She nods. "Ridge said he could take me," she tells her friend, who is draped over Mark.

Mark grins.

I fight the urge to flip his ass off. Instead, I stand and offer Stephanie my hand. She takes it, any hesitation she may have had now gone. I wave to the table and lead her out to my truck.

Helping her inside, I wait until her seatbelt is on to shut the door, and then stop at the rear of the truck and take a deep breath. She seems chill, but who knows what the next three months will hold. This may be the first bet I ever lose. Shaking my head to remove that thought, I pull up my boxer briefs and make my way to the driver's side. "So, where are we headed?"

"It's not far from here, actually."

I listen as she gives me general directions before pulling out of the lot. "You lived here long?" I ask.

"No. The girls and I just moved here about three months ago. Carla's parents own the firm we work for. They've been planning to expand for a while, so when we all graduated, that's what they did. The three of us had instant jobs right out of college."

"That's a pretty sweet deal."

"We were lucky, that's for sure."

The cab of the truck grows silent. I'm pre-occupied with what I just agreed to and Stephanie . . . Well, I'm not sure what's going through her head right now.

"Second house on the right," she instructs, breaking the silence.

Pulling into the drive, I put the truck in park but don't kill the engine.

"Thank you." She reaches for the door.

Shit! I need to get with the fucking program here.

"Stephanie." I reach out and grab her arm. "Can I see you again?" My voice is soft; I don't want to make her think I'm some kind of fucking creeper.

"Yeah, uh, sure."

"Hand me your phone, darlin.'"

She hesitates before pulling it out of her purse and handing it to me. I quickly type in my number and send a text to myself. This act alone is against every rule I've ever had. I don't get involved—too much drama, too much . . . of the same.

I hand her phone back and smirk when mine sounds, alerting me to the message I just sent. Stephanie nods, then opens the truck door and hops out. I quickly do the same and follow her up to the door. I should be trying to seal the deal here, but fuck me, I can't not tonight. I need to wrap my fucking head around what I just agreed to. This has to be my stupidest agreement to one of our bets yet.

As she clears the final step to the front porch, I know time is running out. I have to say something, but she beats me to the punch.

"You want to come in?"

Do I? Of course I do. She's a looker. In my mind, I quickly try to play out the next three months. Maybe if I keep her as a casual hookup, I can pull this off. No strings. Fuck, worst-case scenario, I'm out four hundred bucks. That's not the part that bothers me, though. It's the bragging rights, and to not have to hear the ribbing of my boys over the next twenty years—or at least until another bet, better than this, one comes along.

"Lead the way, darlin.'"

Chapter 2

Ridge

Turns out, Stephanie was good with the 'friends with benefits' plan. She claims that her job keeps her busy and she doesn't have time for anything more serious, so we agreed to hook up when we both had the urge and the time, no expectations. She also insisted that we not sleep with anyone else during that time. I'm good with that.

It's been two months today that we met. We hook up about once a week, and so far it's working out great. I see my pocket being four hundred dollars richer very soon. The guys could not have chosen a better girl; she's just as detached as I am. Plus, the sex is good, so it's a win-win.

"You in for cards tonight?" Kent asks.

"Tonight's my night with Steph," I tell him.

"Oh, yeah, your girlfriend. She got you on a leash, brother?" Tyler chimes in.

"Fuck off. No leash, we've both been busy this week. This is our only night to get together." I need some relief, but I don't tell them that. Why fuel the fire?

"Bring her with you," Mark suggests.

"Maybe," I say, not committing. I'm running through my mind how to make it work. We need to grab dinner, spend a few hours with the guys, and still find time to rumple the sheets.

"What's it been—five, six weeks? She's already got you by the balls." Seth laughs.

"Eight. Laugh it up, boys, but I know my night is ending with getting my dick wet. Can you say the same?" I smirk.

"Ridge, come on, man. It's card night. Just bring her," Kent says, exasperated.

Card night has been our tradition for the last few years. We take turns having it at each other's house, bring snacks and beer and just chill. Missing is not something any of us has ever done without a family emergency, and certainly not for a hookup/bet.

"Fine, we'll be there. Now get back to work."

✦✦✦

I PULL INTO Stephanie's driveway right at six o'clock. I rushed home from work, grabbed a quick shower, and headed straight here.

"Hey," she says, opening the door.

"Darlin.'" I lean in and kiss her. "You all set?"

"Yep." She grabs her purse and keys and we're out the door. "How's your week been?"

"Busy, as usual. Finishing up the Allen job tomorrow, I hope. Just tying up some loose ends. Yours?"

She goes on to tell me about her day, and I listen as I drive us to the store.

"Uh, what are we doing here?"

"Card night. I need to pick up some snacks. I hadn't planned on going, but the guys guilted me into it. I'll be right back." I quickly hop out of my truck and make my way inside. I grab some chips, salsa, and one of those meat and crackers trays then make my way to the checkout counter. Total of five minutes and I'm back in the truck.

"Card night?" she asks, once we're back on the road.

Her arms are crossed over her chest, so I can tell she's not impressed. I should feel bad or something, right? So why is it that I don't? "Yeah, it's something we do once a month. Have been for years," I explain.

"And you picked tonight of all nights for us to get together?"

"I told you, I wasn't going to go, but they convinced me today. What's the big deal? We'll stop at Kent's, play a few hands, eat some pizza and snacks, and then be on our way." I reach over and grab her hand. "Then we'll see what we can do to relieve the stress of your week." I wink.

She's not impressed. "Ridge," she whines.

What the hell? This is new. I've not seen this side of her. Of course, it's usually just the two of us grabbing dinner and burning up the sheets. I've been able to avoid being out with her friends or mine until now. This is a first.

"Do you want me to take you back home?" I'm not dealing with the whining. If she wants to fuck, she has to endure card night. Simple as that.

"Ugh! Fine, but I don't want to stay long."

I grip the steering wheel tightly. I've never had a chick tell me what to do. Of course, I'm never around long enough for that to happen either. She's delusional if she thinks that just because she's the only one I'm fucking right now she can dictate what I do.

Not happening, darlin.'

Pulling into Kent's driveway, I grab the bag of snacks and wait at the front of my truck for Stephanie. I'm not a total dick. Knocking once on the door, I walk in since it's an open invitation at all of our places. We're family.

"Hey, hey!" I call out. A chorus of the same greets us as we walk into the kitchen.

"Stephanie, right?" Mark asks.

She looks surprised that he remembers. "Yeah."

"Welcome. You play poker?" Kent greets.

Fucker, he knows she doesn't. I bite my lip to keep from laughing.

"No."

The look on her face is priceless. She looks as though we just asked her to sleep with all five of us or something. That's something else that I've begun to notice about her. She's Miss Prim and Proper, never taking time to just relax—that is, of course, unless we are in the bedroom. All other times, she's so uptight. She needs to learn to let loose every now and then; life is too damn short to be so serious all the time.

"Don't worry, sweetheart. We can show you," Seth says, throwing his arm over her shoulder.

She looks to me—for what, I don't know. "I'm good," she says, shrugging off his arm.

"Suit yourself. We all set?" I ask.

"Yep," Tyler confirms, grabbing a bowl of chips and setting it on the table.

"Pull up a chair, or the living room is through there if you want to watch TV," I tell her. Her mouth falls open. What did she expect? I'm not going to coddle her. She's not my girlfriend, and frankly, I don't like this side of her.

She rolls her eyes and stomps off toward the living room.

"Whose deal?" I take my seat at the table.

"Trouble in paradise?" Mark asks.

"Paradise? You know the score, brother. Deal em.'" We spend the next two hours playing cards, eating, and shooting the shit. It's not until I hear Stephanie clear her throat that I remember I brought her. Shit!

"Are you ready?" she asks. Her arms are crossed over her chest and she's tapping her foot, a scowl on her face.

So it was a dick move to forget she was here, but come on. She chose to separate herself from us. Looking at the time, I see it's going on nine. "Yeah. This is the last hand."

She looks irritated that I don't just stand and leave, but we're in the middle of a hand. It plays out quickly, with Seth raking in the winnings.

"We're out," I say, standing and stretching. "See you ladies in the morning." I look over at Stephanie. "Ready?"

She doesn't reply, just turns and walks out the front door. The guys chuckle, and I can't help but laugh with them. She's being a diva. I wave over my shoulder as I follow her out to my truck.

"Just take me home, Ridge," she barks.

I don't dignify her bitchiness with an answer, just put the truck in drive and take her home.

I pull into her driveway and don't bother turning off the engine. She's pissed, and honestly, I don't care.

"I wanted to ask you something, but you were too caught up with the boys to spend any time with me."

That's a red flag. We don't really call it 'spending time together'—we eat and fuck, that's it. "Well?" I say, prompting her to continue.

She blows her hair out of her face and takes a deep breath. "There's a gala next week. It's a big deal, showcasing my designs. I don't want to go alone."

Well, fuck me. "What day?"

"Friday."

"Time?"

"We need to leave my place at seven. It starts at eight, but I want to be there early."

I think about the bet. Shit, it's the least I can do. I'm on the home stretch, and soon our time will end anyway. "Yeah, what do I need to wear?"

Her face brightens. "A suit?" she asks.

"Got it. See you then."

She hesitates. "You want to get together this weekend?"

No. "I've got a lot going on with finishing up the Allen job. I don't think I'll have time. I'll pick you up at seven on Friday."

She doesn't bother with a reply as she climbs out of my truck. I keep my headlights on her door and wait until she's inside to leave.

Four more weeks.

Chapter 3

Ridge

Today has been one disaster after another. First, the job we bid on over on Southern Avenue called to let me know we were underbid. I have plenty of work, but I still hate losing. Although, with that particular job, I was as low as I could get. Not sure how the winning contractor is going to make money without cutting corners. Something else I hate.

When I arrived at my current job site, I found the wrong materials were delivered. The Lumber Yard mixed up the Jefferson and Williams jobs. It took me two hours on the phone to get them to bring a truck to each site to switch everything out. Their mix-up cost me and my guys a day's work, putting us a day behind schedule, and leaving me the task of calling the customer to fill them in. Which led to my current situation. Did I mention that I hate to be off schedule?

I've spent my afternoon at the Jefferson job site, the final truck having just dropped off the correct supplies. Mrs. Jefferson was concerned that the materials would be wrong again, but I assured her they would be correct. In so many words, she insinuated that they better be or else. She's a tough cookie, and was insistent that the job be complete before her sister and brother-in-law visit from California next month. To appease her, I stayed until the truck arrived, and checked the contents of the order myself. A hazard of the job is keeping the customers happy.

I was supposed to be 'off,'—if that's really even possible for a business owner—by five, because I have the gala tonight with Stephanie. Several times today, I thought about calling to cancel, but I gave her my word, and that's not something I take lightly. Instead, here I am leaving the Jefferson site at six thirty, and to top off this fucktastic day, the skies open up and it starts to pour down rain.

The wipers are on high as they whoosh and skid across the windshield. I slow down when I see a car on the side of the road up ahead. As I get closer, I see a woman kicking what appears to be her flat tire.

Shit. I can't in good conscience not stop and help her. I doubt she even knows how to change a tire.

Turning on my signal, I pull off on the side of the road, parking behind her. She's wearing what looks like a nursing uniform and her hair is soaked. Reaching in the glove box, I grab two ponchos I keep on hand; you never know when Mother Nature is going to decide to open the floodgates. Working in construction, my supply has come in handy more times than I can count.

Tearing open one package, I slip the poncho over my head. Gripping the one I grabbed for her, I climb out of the truck. She's watching me, her arms crossed over her chest. I see her car keys sticking out between her fingers as if she's prepared to use them against me. Smart girl.

"Hi," I yell over the rain. "Looks like you could use some help." I hand her the poncho.

She hesitates, but the rain picks up and she relents, slowly reaching out to take the offering. I watch as she quickly unfolds the poncho and slips it over her head.

"I'm Ridge." I point back to my truck marked with the Beckett Construction logo. "Just left the job site and saw you looked like you could use some help. Do you have a spare?" I ask.

She still looks hesitant; again, I think she's being smart.

"I'm going to reach into my pocket and grab my wallet," I warn her. Slowly, I reach around to my back pocket and pull it out. Opening it, I pull out a business card that has my full name and contact information and hand it to her.

The rain continues to beat down, and I will her to decide if she's going to trust me so we can get this show on the road. I'm already late and can hear Stephanie whining already.

She studies the card, and then ever so slowly lifts her head and smiles warmly. Holding her hand out, she introduces herself. "Dawn Miller. Thank you for stopping. I have no idea what I'm doing."

"I got this." I wink at her. Even drenched, she's beautiful, with big blue eyes and long blonde hair. "Pop the truck and get inside the car. There's no need for both of us standing out here getting wet."

She waves off my concern. "I'm not going to melt. I couldn't sit in the car while you were out here, I'd feel guilty. I really do appreciate this, more than you know."

She pops the trunk and I make quick work of releasing the spare tire and jack. Just as I get the jack set, the rain lets up. I busy myself with taking off the flat tire and quickly replacing it with the donut version. "You're going to have to get this taken care of. I hope you don't have far to go. It's not safe on these wet roads to be driving on this thing." I point to the smaller tire.

"Not far. I'll get it taken care of tomorrow," she promises.

After making sure the lug nuts are tight, I place the flat and tools back in the trunk. "You're all set," I tell her, closing the trunk lid.

"Thank you so much. How much do I owe you?"

"Nothing, just drive safe. It was nice to meet you, Dawn." I offer her my hand.

She slides hers against mine and we shake. "It was nice meeting you too, Ridge. Thank you again, so very much."

With a nod, I release her hand and jog back to my truck. I watch as she settles back behind the wheel and drives off. Grabbing my phone, I send a quick text to Steph.

> **Me:** *Running late, been one hell of a day.*
>
> **Stephanie:** *Seriously, Ridge? You promised.*
>
> **Me:** *Couldn't be helped. I'll be there soon.*

I toss my phone in the cup holder and pull back out on the road.

Mother Nature decides she's not through torturing me today, as the rain once again unleashes. Huge, heavy drops hit the windshield and I have to slow to a creep, the visibility pretty much non-existent. I hope Dawn makes it to where she's going.

A gust of wind hits the truck and I have to fight to keep it on the road. This storm just popped up out of nowhere. Readjusting my position, I grip the wheel and lean forward, keeping my eyes glued to the road. My phone alerts me to a new message, but it's just going to have to wait. My gut tells me it's Stephanie wanting to give me a hard time about being late. If that were Stephanie or my sister Reagan on the side of the road, I would want a decent guy like myself to stop and help them. There are a hell of a lot of creepers out there, and it's just not safe. She'll get over it, and if not . . . Oh well.

Eyes glued to the road, I stare hard, making sure I don't hit stray tree branches—hell, even another car, for that matter. There's debris all over the road, so I slow down, knowing the Jacksons' curves are just up ahead. Old Man Jackson lives right in the middle of a hellish set of curves, and I've seen more accidents on this stretch of road than I care to count.

Just as I creep around the first set, I see lights. Lights that are coming from the other side of the small embankment. *Fuck! That's not a good sign.* Today is just not going my way.

I pull my truck over to the side of the road. Reaching into the glove compartment, I pull out a flashlight. I'm still wearing my poncho, not taking the time to remove it knowing Stephanie was already going to be pissed. Not knowing what I'm going to find on the other side of the embankment, I grab my phone and shove it into my pocket.

As soon as I open the door, the wind blasts me and almost knocks me over. I fight against the gusts to slam the door shut, then turn on the flashlight and check both ways before sprinting across the road. It's dangerous as hell, but my gut tells me that time is of the essence in this situation. I send up a silent prayer that I'm wrong.

What I find has me sprinting into action. A small SUV is turned on its side. Starting down the muddy embankment, I lose my footing. Slipping and sliding, I struggle to find my balance. I finally reach the front of the vehicle, but the headlights are blinding, making it impossible to see if anyone's still inside. I'm mindful not to lean on the car, not willing to take the chance of causing it to tip and roll further down the hill. It's too dark to assess the situation and the rain is still coming down in sheets. Better safe than sorry.

Very carefully, I make it to the driver's-side door. I shine the light through the window and can see a woman lying on her side. Her eyes are closed. Shit! I know enough that I shouldn't try to move her. Reaching into my pocket, I pull out my phone and dial for help. It takes me three tries, as my hands are trembling and wet from the rain.

"911, what's your emergency?"

"There's been an accident," I scream over the pounding rain. "I'm just off Anderson Drive, in Jackson's curves."

"Sir, are you hurt?"

"No, not me. I saw headlights, so I stopped. There's a woman trapped." I know I'm probably not making any sense, but my head is too jumbled. I need to help her.

"Stay with her, help is on the way. I have a team en route, less than five minutes out."

"What can I do?" I plead with her.

I'm crushing the phone to my ear so I can hear her. The rain makes it an almost impossible feat. "Just hold tight, help is on the way. Do not try to move her unless you feel she's in grave danger," she yells over the line, cool as a fucking cucumber. I guess that's why she's in that position.

After what I'm sure is the longest five minutes of my entire life, I hear the sirens. "They're here," I tell the operator.

"Good, please remember to allow them to do their job."

What the hell? Is this chick for real? "Got it," I say and end the call. Shoving my phone back into my pocket, I wave my arms in the air. "Over here!" I call out. The two paramedics carefully slide their way down the hill, carrying a board. Just as they reach me, a fire truck and a sheriff pull off to the side of the road. The cavalry has arrived.

Thank goodness. I hope this woman is okay.

"Sir, are you hurt?"

"No, I was driving by and saw the headlights. I've been here a little over five minutes. I didn't touch the car, just shined my light through the window. The woman behind the wheel seems to be unconscious. From what I can tell, she's the only passenger. I was afraid to move her or the car," I ramble over the roar of the rain, still falling in buckets from the sky.

"You did good," he yells back.

I step back out of the way and let them go to work. My phone vibrates in my pocket.

Stephanie.

She's just going to have to wait.

I stay rooted to the spot on the hillside just in case they need another hand. I watch as the firemen join us and survey the car, assessing the risk while they nod and use hand signals. They must say that all is safe, because they immediately get to work on trying to pry the door open. The paramedics are close by, waiting to get to their patient.

I don't move a muscle; I stand in my spot, soaking wet and wait to see if she's okay. I wish I could have done more. I make a vow to at least get my CPR certification. What could I have really done if she were awake, or if I had to try and drag her out of the car if there was more imminent danger?

My phone vibrates again, and I continue to ignore it.

My eyes are glued to the scene in front of me. I watch as the door—which will only open a fraction—is cut away from the car. The firemen are working carefully yet diligently. As soon as the door is removed, one of the men picks it up and throws it toward the rear of the car. I'm sure they're operating on pure adrenaline; it's their job to get to her as quickly as possible. You see this in the movies, hear about it on the news, but to be here and witness the determination and dedication these men and women have is awe-inspiring.

The paramedics swoop in and check on the driver. I see now that one of them is in the passenger seat. I guess that door opened just fine. Everyone works together assessing the situation. When they yell for the stretcher, my heartbeat accelerates. *Is she going to be okay? Can they get her out? Do they have to cut her out?* A million questions are running through my head, but I still keep my eyes glued to the car. To her. I need to see that she's okay.

Minutes, hours—I've lost track of time. It's not until I see them slowly and ever so gently lift her from the car and place her on the stretcher that I feel myself take a deep breath. From the ache in my chest, it's as if it's the first in a while.

The paramedics work on strapping her down. A fireman throws a big blanket over her body, followed by what looks like a tarp, an attempt to keep her dry in this torrential downpour. Mother Nature is relentless tonight. Tears from Heaven, as my mother always says.

Four of them flank each corner of the stretcher and begin the slow, slippery trek up hill to the ambulance. In the dark of night, I lose sight of them until they reach the headlight beams.

"Hey, man, are you good? You hurt?" One of the guys lays a hesitant hand on my shoulder.

I shake my head. "No, I just stopped to help," I try to explain.

He nods, letting me know he heard me. This rain makes it damn difficult to have a normal conversation.

Turning, he heads toward the car. Reaching inside, he pulls out a bag.

Her purse.

What if she wakes up in the hospital all alone? How long will it take her family to get here? She's going to be scared. It's that thought that has me climbing the hill. I'll go to the hospital and just make sure she's okay, that she's not alone. I'll wait until her family arrives. Maybe I can answer any questions she might have. I can at least fill her in from the point that I found her in her car.

At the top of the hill, they already have her loaded in the ambulance. I'm headed that way when the sheriff stops me.

"Excuse me, sir, do you know the victim?" he questions.

"No. I was driving by and saw the headlights over the embankment," I explain.

He nods. "I'm going to have a few questions." He looks up at the rain still falling from the sky. "Can you come down to the station?"

"No. I'm following them to the hospital."

Tilting his head to the side, he studies me. "I thought you didn't know her?"

"I don't. However, I do know what happened here tonight—after I found her, at least. I don't want her to wake up alone. I'll stay until her family arrives." I give him the details of what I just decided only minutes before.

Understanding crosses his face. "I'll meet you there."

I give him a quick wave and hustle across the road to my truck. Cranking the heater, I pull out my cell phone. Several missed calls and one text from Stephanie.

Stephanie: *I can't believe you stood me up.*

Really? Does she not know me any better than that?

Me: *Drove up on an accident. Stopped to help. Headed to hospital now.*

I'll make it up to you.

After I hit send, I drop the phone in the cup holder and reach for my seat belt, securely fastening it. I wait for the ambulance to pull out, because I'm going to follow them, not knowing for sure where they're taking her. I don't have to wait long before the siren sounds and they're moving. The sheriff pulls out behind them, sticking his hand out the window for me to follow.

Thankful for the escort, I put the truck in drive and follow close behind. The entire way, I pray she's okay. I'm not really a praying man; I've done it, but don't make it a habit. But something inside me needs her to be okay.

Chapter 4

Ridge

The drive to the hospital is a blur. My grip on the wheel is so tight my fingers start to ache. Thankfully, the rain has started to ease a little; however, it does nothing to calm my nerves. I follow the sheriff into the emergency room parking lot, and he parks behind the ambulance. I find the first available spot, throwing my truck into park. I tear off the poncho and throw it in the backseat of the truck, then grab my phone and keys and head toward the entrance.

By the time I reach them, they've already wheeled her back to an exam room. The sheriff is waiting for me just inside the door.

"Simpson." He holds his hand out for me.

I take it. "Ridge Beckett," I introduce myself.

"They have a room we can use. I turned over her belongings, so they're going to try and contact her family."

"Do we know who she is?"

He gives me a sad look. "She had her ID in her wallet. Unfortunately,

I cannot divulge that information."

I run my hand through my hair, frustrated at the situation. I understand that she has rights, confidentiality and all that, but I just . . . She needs to be okay. "Yeah," I finally say, following him to the room he just mentioned.

"Have a seat." He points to the row of chairs in what appears to be a private waiting room. "Now, tell me what happened tonight."

I spend the next several minutes going over the evening. Hell, I even started with stopping to change Dawn's tire. He doesn't say a word, just listens and takes notes.

"So, you don't know either of them?" he asks.

I shake my head, just as my phone vibrates in my pocket. I'm sure it's Stephanie. I need to explain to her what's going on. Glancing at the screen, it's a local number, but one I don't recognize. I nod toward the phone, letting him know I'm going to answer before swiping the screen and holding it to my ear. "Hello."

"Hi, is this Mr. Beckett? Mr. Ridge Beckett?" the lady asks.

"Yes, who is this?"

"Mr. Beckett, my name is Alice and I'm calling from Mercy General. Sir, we need for you to come in right away."

My heart drops. Something's wrong. "Who?" I grit out, my mind racing. Mom and Dad are home, or should have been. Reagan, she would have been on her way home from work. One of the guys? Fuck!

"Mr. Beckett, it would be best if you come on in. Come to the emergency department and ask for me, Alice. I'll be at the reception desk."

Swallowing the lump in my throat and taking a deep breath, I answer her. "I'm already here. I was . . . I'll be right there." I hit end and grip the phone tight in my hands.

"Mr. Beckett?" Sheriff Simpson is watching me closely.

"That was the ER," I tell him. "They need me to come in right away."

His face pales with what that simple request means. I'm sure he sees it all too much in his line of work. "I'll go with you."

Standing on trembling legs, I let him lead the way back to the reception desk. I'm numb with fear and completely over this day. I send up another silent prayer that whoever it is, they'll be okay.

"This is Mr. Beckett." Simpson points over his shoulder. "He was the Good Samaritan who stopped to help an accident tonight. Someone just called him, stating he needed to come in right away, but he was already here," he goes on to explain.

Alice stands from her chair, a folder in her arms. "That was me who called. We can actually go back to that room you were just in to talk." She doesn't say anything more, simply starts walking. Sheriff Simpson gives my shoulder a tight squeeze before following her. It's as if my body is on autopilot, my legs carrying me down the hall on their own accord.

Alice holds the door open for us. "Have a seat," she says calmly.

"Who?" I grit out again. I'm over waiting for her to tell me.

"Mr. Beckett, I'm a little confused at this, so maybe you can help me understand." She opens the folder in her hands. "The victim in the car you stopped to help tonight, she has you, Ridge Beckett of Anderson County, listed as her next of kin."

My mouth drops open. "How is that possible? Who is she?" It was dark and the rain was pouring down. The car . . . I didn't recognize the car. There has to be some kind of mistake.

"Her name is Melissa. Melissa Knox."

My mind races. *Melissa Knox. Do I know a Melissa Knox? Could it be Melissa from a few months ago? The one who ran out on me in the middle of the night?* She's the only Melissa I can think of. "I know a Melissa, met her several months ago. I don't know her last name, though. It doesn't make any sense. There has to be some kind of mistake."

"It's all here in her records. She has you listed: Ridge Beckett, Beckett Construction."

Holy fucking shit! Is this real? There are so many emotions rolling through me right now. Relief that it's not my family or friends, confusion as to why Melissa—if she is even the same Melissa—would list me as her next of kin, fear that she's not going to be okay. Regardless of that fact that I now could have a connection with her, I still have this strong urge, a feeling deep in the pit of my gut, that I need her to be okay.

"What does that mean? Is she going to be okay? Can I see her? See if it's the same person?" I fire off questions one after the other.

"Yes, you can see her, but just for a few minutes. She's still in critical condition. And being her next of kin means you'll be the one making medical decisions for her until she wakes up."

No fucking way. "I need to see her, see if I know her. This has to be a mistake."

"Sure, but like I said, it can only be a few minutes. We're monitoring her closely."

"That's fine, I just need . . ." I swallow hard. "I need to see if it's her, if it's the same Melissa."

"Of course, right this way."

"I'll wait here for you," Sheriff Simpson says. "Anyone you want me to call for you?"

"Not yet. I don't know if . . . Not yet." I stand and follow Alice out of the room.

The hallways are bustling with activity—doctors, nurses, even patients walking around. Alice leads us to the end of the hall and through a set of double doors marked Critical Care Unit. There are patient rooms surrounded by glass and doors, unlike the other that are only separated by curtains.

Stopping in front of Room 3, Alice turns to me. "She hasn't woken up yet. I'll leave you, but just a few minutes." I watch her walk to the small nurses' station, seemingly to give me a sense of privacy.

Squeezing my eyes closed, I take in a deep breath and hold it. Slowly, I release the air from my lungs, willing my heart to slow its pace. I repeat this at least three times, probably more before I grip the door handle and walk into her room. The privacy curtain is pulled around the bed. When I slowly walk around it, I freeze.

It's her.

Melissa.

Melissa from the bar all those months ago, who left me in her bed in her motel room after our night of hot sex. The Melissa I've thought about often and wondered what made her slip away in the middle of the night. What would've happened if I had woken up with her lying beside me? Would she be here now? Lying in the hospital bed fighting for her life? I think back to that night—she said she was just passing through. What is she doing here now, so close to me and my company? Why would she list me as her next of kin?

Her face is bruised and she's bandaged over one eye. Her eyes are closed, and she appears to be sleeping peacefully. Except that's not the case at all. She has yet to wake up.

Will she ever?

"Oh, I'm sorry I didn't know she had company. I'm Dr. Ellis. I just came by to check the baby's vitals."

Wait? What did he just say? "Umm, the baby?"

"Yes, it appears as though Miss Knox is eight months along." He gives me a look like I must be crazy. Why wouldn't I be? Who lists someone they met briefly, had hot sex with and runs out on them as their next of kin?

That's when it hits me. Eight months ago. I count back in my head. *No. It can't be.* I try to breathe, but I can't seem to suck in any air.

"Sir, you okay?"

Bending over, I place my hands on my knees and fight like hell to catch my breath.

Is this really happening?

"Sir?" the doctor tries again.

"Why don't you sit down?" a soft, feminine voice says from beside me.

I don't know who she is or where she came from, but when she and the doctor each take an arm and lead me to a chair beside the bed, I don't fight it.

"Slow, deep, even breaths. That's it, in and out," she coaches me.

I focus on her voice, blocking out the white noise bouncing around in my head. Another slow, deep breath and I feel some of the pressure release from my chest.

"Good," the woman says. Looking up, I see that it's Alice. "I take it you didn't know she was expecting?" she asks.

No shit, Sherlock. "No. I met her once, briefly." I'm barely able to croak the words out around the lump in my throat.

Confusion crosses her face.

"Is the baby . . . okay?" I can hear myself speak, but it doesn't even sound like me.

"I've been monitoring the baby closely and everything is fine," Dr. Ellis replies.

Slumping back in the chair, I stare at Melissa, trying to make sense of all this. Why me? Unless . . . Is this baby mine? Is that why she was here, to tell me that I'm going to be a father? My mind races with different scenarios, and that's the only thing that makes sense.

"I found this in her personal belongings." Alice keeps her tone soft and soothing.

Looking up, I see her holding an envelope with my name scrawled across the front.

Fuck!

"We'll give you a few minutes," Dr. Ellis says.

I grasp the letter in my hands, staring at my name. I want to open it, see what it says, but then again I don't. I just want to wake up from this nightmare. I want a do-over on today. Squeezing my eyes closed, I lean my head back against the chair. I feel it deep in my soul that these words, this day, are going to change the rest of my life.

Expect the unexpected, isn't that what they say?

Steeling my resolve, I rip open the envelope and begin to read.

Ridge,

If you're reading this, that means I chickened out. That's the coward's way, I know. I have a tendency to run, but you already know that. First, let me start by saying how sorry I am about leaving you that night. No excuse is a good one, but here's mine.

A few weeks before I met you, I lost my parents. My adoptive parents. Growing up, I was in and out of foster homes until I met Mr. and Mrs. Knox. They adopted me and gave me my first real home. I wanted to show them how grateful I was, so I studied hard, kept my nose buried in a book, and didn't cause problems. They missed me graduating from college. I chose to be a paralegal to work in their law firm. Needless to say, the day I lost them, I lost my entire world.

The night I met you, I just wanted to forget. I'm not a drinker, but I was willing to do anything to numb the pain. Then I met you and the guys. It was nice to be included in the conversation, to feel like I was a part of something more. I was instantly attracted to you and have no regrets about our night together. You were the first real thing I ever did for myself. I wanted to know what it would feel like to be spontaneous and feel wanted. You gave me both. When I woke up, I was ashamed. Not because of you, but because of the feelings you brought out in me. I still replay every minute of that night in my head. Even through my drunken haze, I remember everything like it was just yesterday. For many reasons, that is, to date, the best night of my life.

I finally lived for me, with no regrets.

Now, here's where things get interesting. Not only did you give me the greatest night of my life, but you gave me my own little miracle. Not even a month later, I started to feel ill. It just wouldn't go away, so naturally I broke down and went to the doctor. Turns out, I wasn't sick at all——I was pregnant. I am pregnant. I know we used protection, but you were still able to give me my little miracle. I refuse to call him an accident. I believe in fate, Ridge, and I believe our night together was supposed to happen. In just a little under a month, I will give birth to a little boy, who I already love more than words could ever express. You gave me a real family, something I had for a small time before it was taken away from me. I was lost in the world, until the minute I heard those two words: 'You're pregnant.'

Since you're reading this, you know that I am again taking the easy way out. I know that you have a right to know about your son, but I'm scared to death that you will reject him, or worse, take him from me. You seem like a great guy, but honestly, I don't really know you. I know it's still possible, but then again, will I chicken out and not send this letter? I hope not. You deserve to know. I want you to know that I do not expect anything from you. My parents' left me set for life, so money is not an issue. I don't expect you to play a role in his life, unless you want to. All I ask is that if you do, make sure it's what you want. I don't ever want my son to know the rejection of a parent like I did. At least that is my hope.

I do plan to list you as his father because, should something ever happen to me, you will be all he has. It will then be your choice to make. I pray that you would not reject our son. I have a trust set up for him as well—like I said, my parents' left me financially stable. I've tried to prepare for every scenario. I had to put an emergency contact in my medical records. After discussing it with my OB/GYN he suggested that since I was listing you on the birth certificate that I put you for the contact as well. That way, if something were to go wrong in the delivery, they would know how to reach you. So I did that. I don't anticipate that you *will ever be called, but I felt obligated to tell you.*

I love this baby, Ridge. I will give him a life full of love and happiness. I am leaving the ball in your court as to how much or how little you would like to be involved. Below, you will find my contact information. I hope to hear from you soon.

Best Regards,

Melissa

My hands are shaking. I'm going to be a father. I cast my gaze on Melissa, who still looks as though she's just sleeping soundly. I take her in until I reach her swollen belly.

I have a son.

Fear like I've never known before races through my veins. *Is he okay? What does Melissa's condition mean for him? What if she never wakes up? Can I raise him?* Slowly, I stand and walk to the side of the bed. I rest one shaking hand on the bed to hold me up and gently place the other over her swollen belly. Tears prick my eyes.

This situation is ten kinds of fucked. I want to be mad at her, but she was coming to tell me. At least, I hope she would have made it; she was close, a few miles from the shop.

I'm lost in my thoughts when I feel a bump against my hand. I pull it back quickly, just as Alice and Dr. Ellis walk back into the room.

"It's okay," Alice says in her calm, soothing voice. "The baby kicked." She gives me a soft smile.

"Are you her nurse?"

"Yes, I've been with her since they brought her in."

"And you?" I point to Dr. Ellis. "Are you her doctor?"

"I'm the obstetrician on call. The baby is my patient, and Ms. Knox is being treated from the staff physician on call. He and I are working together for the best possible outcome for both."

"Is the baby . . . Is he okay? I mean, what happens if she doesn't wake up? Are you sure he's fine?"

"I'm sure. I'm watching his vitals, and I performed an ultrasound as soon as they were brought in. I think you should speak to her physician about her condition."

"I'm the father." I point to the letter that I set on the end of her bed. "That's what the letter says, that I'm the baby's father."

"How about I do another ultrasound? That way, you can see your baby, see for yourself that he's okay," Dr. Ellis suggests.

That lump is back. "Please," I croak out. "I would also like to speak to her doctor and you, if possible. I just . . . need to know what to expect."

"I can page him while you're performing the ultrasound," Alice offers.

"Thank you, Alice," Dr. Ellis says.

I watch as she leaves the room and comes right back in, pushing a machine. She sets it next to the bed, gives me a soft smile, and scurries back out the door.

I watch with rapt attention as Dr. Ellis carefully pulls back the blanket covering Melissa's body and lifts up her gown.

"Wait, what are you doing?" I ask.

"I need to have her belly bare. I place this gel on her abdomen and then this—" he holds up a small piece of equipment that appears to be hooked to a screen "—will let us see your baby."

I've see this done on TV, so I get the concept. But she's just lying there, unable to speak for herself. I need to protect her—that's my job, right? As her emergency contact, it's my job to look out for her, and as the . . . father. I swallow hard.

I'm going to be a father.

Dr. Ellis continues, placing the gel on her swollen belly and the small handle. "Watch the screen," he tells me.

Stepping as close to the bed as I can get, my eyes lock onto the little black screen. I'm just about to ask what I'm looking for when the screen turns to black and white. And there, in a tight little ball, is my son.

I have a son.

"Ten fingers." The doctor points to the screen. "Ten toes." He points again. "This is his heartbeat, steady and strong. He's a fighter."

I grip the side of the bed to keep from falling over. It's all too much to take in. There he is—a part of me, on that tiny, little black and white screen. I have so many emotions running through me I can't even identify them all.

Without thinking, I lean down and whisper in her ear. "Hey, Melissa. You need to stay strong, fight. He needs you."

Dr. Ellis, takes some measurements and points out different things. The baby starts to suck on his thumb, so he zooms in on that. I'm enthralled with watching him. All too soon, the screen goes black and Dr. Ellis is wiping off her belly.

"Here." He hands me a CD. "I recorded it for you. I also have these." Reaching beneath the machine, he tears off a long, thin strip of paper.

Pictures.

Of my son.

"Thank you," I rasp.

He leaves the room, taking the machine with him, just as my phone vibrates in my pocket. Pulling it out, I see 'Dad' flash across the screen. I don't know if I can even have my phone on in here; will it mess with all these machines? I let the call go to voicemail and step out of the room.

"I need to make a call. Am I allowed to use this here?" I ask Alice once I reach the nurses' station.

"Yeah, we just ask that you leave it on vibrate, and of course end any calls when the physician is in the room," she tells me.

"Thank you. Can I stay?" I point over my shoulder.

"Yeah, she's stable for now. But if anyone asks, I told you no." She winks at me.

I nod since smiling back would take too much effort at this point. I walk back to her room and take the chair next to the bed, swiping the screen to call my dad back.

"Ridge, how was the gala?" He chuckles. Dad knows that's not my thing.

"I didn't make it. Tonight has been . . . one for the books," I confess.

"What's going on, son?"

My parents' are awesome, always there for Reagan and me growing up, and even now as adults. I know I can go to them with anything. Looking at my watch, I see that it's after ten at night. "It's a long story. I'm not hurt, but I'm still at the hospital."

"Hospital?"

I can hear the worry in his voice. "Yeah, would you be able to . . . ?"

"I'm on my way. Your mother?"

I love that he gets me. He wants to know if he should bring Mom or if this is a 'guys' conversation. At this point, I need all the support I can get. "Yeah, if she's not already asleep. Just ask the nurse at the reception desk to get me. I'll let them know I'm waiting for you."

"We're leaving now."

Just like that, no questions asked. I should probably call Reagan and the guys, but I just can't find the strength to do it. I will also have to deal with Stephanie at some point. She's obviously pissed, hence the reason I haven't heard from her since I told her I wasn't going to make it to the gala.

There are more important things in life.

When Alice comes in to check Melissa's vitals, I inform her that I'm waiting on my family.

"I'll let the receptionist know where to find you."

"Thank you." I spend the next fifteen minutes studying the pictures of my son. I'm glad that I have them; it makes this more real. It will be easier to explain with proof.

A little while later, Alice peeks her head in the door. "Your family just arrived. I had Kate put them in the private room you were in before."

"Thanks." I stand and grab the letter and with one last parting look at Melissa, I leave the room to fill my family in on the events of the evening.

Chapter 5

Ridge

"Knock, knock." Dr. Ellis peeks his head into the private waiting room.

I just finished giving my parents' and Reagan the condensed version of my day. Telling them that I was going to be a father was the hardest part. By the time I was finished, there were lots of tears for Melissa, the baby, and just the entire situation.

"Ridge, this is Dr. Robbins. He's treating Melissa," he introduces us.

"So, how is she? How's the baby? What's next?" I rush through questions that have been bouncing around in my head since I first found out.

"Baby is good, vitals are strong," Dr. Ellis states, looking at a tablet in his hands. "Her vitals are good, now we just wait for her body to decide to wake up. Medicine is not an exact science. We have to let her body heal and decide when she wakes up; it's a waiting game."

"Mom is stable for now. Her body is protecting her from her injuries. It's now just a waiting game to see if and when she wakes up," Dr. Robbins tells me.

"If?"

He nods slowly. "If. Medicine is not an exact science, and it's hard to know how the body is going to react to trauma. We are hopeful, but she's been out for a long time."

"And the baby? What does all of this mean for him? What happens if Melissa doesn't wake up?" I ask, even though I'm fearful for the answer.

"In situations such as this, we will continue to monitor the baby and do a cesarean delivery when the time comes," Dr. Ellis answers.

"Is that safe for Melissa? How does that affect her?"

"As safe as it can be. We would provide her with the same anesthesia we would any mom in this situation."

"So, we just wait?" I scoff, thinking there has to be something else.

"At this time, yes. That's all we can do. Dr. Ellis will monitor the baby closely, and if there are any signs of distress, we will deliver without question," Dr. Robbins states.

Resting my elbows on my knees, I bury my face in my hands. I hate that I can't fix this. I can't help Melissa, and I can't do anything but wait and pray that the baby is okay.

More prayers. I've been calling in a lot of those in the last several hours.

"We'll keep you posted should things change."

They both turn and leave the room, leaving me with 'all we can do is wait.'

"Ridge, is there a chance . . . ?" Reagan stops.

I know what she was going to ask me. "I don't really know her, I explained that, but this letter, and just the few hours I spent with her . . . She's not the deceiving type. At least, I don't think she is."

"I'm sure the hospital will do a test once the baby is here, just to make sure," Mom assures me.

"Yeah, but I still can't leave them. If the baby *is* mine—and I feel like it is—I can't just leave them here. She has no family. What if something goes wrong?"

"You do what you need to do. I have the office covered," Dad says, placing his hand on my shoulder. "Retirement is getting boring anyway." He winks at me, trying to lessen the somber mood.

"You tell us what you need, and we'll do it. We're here for you," Mom adds.

"Thank you. Reagan, can you call the guys and let them know what's going on? That saves Dad the hassle of going out to the job sites tomorrow."

"Consider it done, big brother. Do you need me to bring you anything?"

"It would be nice to have some dry clothes and maybe my cell charger."

"Hey, why don't you run home, take a hot shower, change, and grab what you need? I'll stay here in case she wakes up. If anything happens, I'll call you, promise," Reagan suggests.

"Not tonight, maybe tomorrow. I just . . . want to be here." I can't explain it, but I feel like this is where I need to be.

"Okay, well, the offer stands for whatever you need. I'll run to your place and pick up some clothes and your charger and be back in no time."

I stand and pull my little sister into my arms, hugging her tight. "Thank you. Please be careful. Take your time," I stress.

"Always," she says with shimmering eyes. "I'll see you in a little while."

"We'll sit with you for a bit," Mom says.

"No, you guys go on home. I'm going to go sit with her. They're moving her out of the ER and into the ICU. I'll call you tomorrow. Dad, thanks for taking care of things at the shop."

"You don't worry about a thing. I got it. If there's something I need, I'll call you. You remember to do the same." He pierces me with his 'listen to me, I'm your father' look that I used to get more often than not as a teenager.

I nod, hug them both, and head back to Melissa.

It's after midnight by the time they get her moved to the ICU. The nurses pitched a fit when I said I was staying in her room—apparently guests aren't allowed to stay overnight. I don't know what she said to them, but Alice spoke to the nurses and then the doctors. I have strict rules to stay out of the way, but I'm allowed to stay.

I settle into the chair that flattens into a not-so-comfortable bed. The pillow that Alice gave me is so flat I can hardly call it one. Sleep evades me. My mind is racing and as soon as I do start to drift off, someone is in the room, checking on Melissa. I drift off again and they're checking on the baby. I'm not going to complain, though; it's reassuring to know they're getting such good care.

I finally give up at around six in the morning, when Dr. Ellis brings in the ultrasound machine.

"Is something wrong?" I ask, trying to keep the panic out of my voice.

"No, but I want to make sure I get a good look at this little guy at least once a day."

I sit up to watch him set the machine up and place the gel across Melissa's abdomen. He's quiet as he takes his measurements.

"She's measuring at thirty-seven weeks."

"I don't know what that means," I confess.

"Full term is forty weeks. If we had to deliver from this day moving forward, I feel confident on the outcome. She's been getting IV steroids, which will help strengthen the little guy's lungs."

"Will that hurt her?"

"No, it's safe for both of them."

"Good."

The morning nurse stops in for dressing changes and I step out, hitting up the vending machine for a stale coffee and a pack of donuts. I haven't eaten since yesterday at lunch. I take a walk out to the garden in the center of the hospital. It's a safe place for patients who are not in the ICU to walk outside and get some fresh air. The morning air is crisp and I relish it, sucking in a slow, deep breath, thinking maybe I can catch a quick cat nap.

My phone vibrates. No such luck.

Stephanie: *Where are you?*

Me: Hospital.

Stephanie: *Call me.*

Here we go. I tap on her contact and wait for her to pick up.

"Hello."

"Hey, it's me."

"Everything okay?"

"No."

"Oookay. Are you hurt?"

"No."

"Care to fill me in?"

"I don't really want to do this over the phone," I tell her.

"I have a busy day today, Ridge. Just tell me what's going on."

So, I do, giving her the condensed version. Only I leave out the fact that Melissa was just a one-night stand because, at this point, it's no longer relevant. After I explain the flat-tire girl and the accident, I pause. I know she's not going to take this well. "And . . . uh, Melissa . . . She's pregnant."

"Good for her. What does that have to do with you?"

How have I put up with her for this long? "It's mine. We were together before I met you. About eight months ago was the last time." I don't know why I don't want her to know, I just don't.

"So, you're having a baby?"

"Yes. He's due in three weeks."

"He? I guess you all are going to be a little happy family, huh?"

Bitch! "What part of 'she's still in a coma' did you not understand?" I seethe.

"Look, I have to go. Can we talk about this later?"

"Whatever." I end the call. I don't have the time or the energy to deal with petty drama. I have an unborn son and his mother, who is fighting for her life that I need to take care of.

Chapter 6

Ridge

It's day three and so far, no change. Melissa still continues to slumber on, but her vitals are holding strong so her doctor is hopeful. The baby's also proved to be a fighter. His vitals are strong, as is his heartbeat, which I get to hear a few times a day. I've come to crave the sound.

"Good morning," Lisa, the day nurse, greets me.

"Morning," I mumble, sitting up in my chair. "I'm going to get some coffee," I tell her then leave the room. I feel like I need to give them privacy to change her.

I decide to head to the cafeteria to grab a bagel and the largest coffee they offer. I can't do any more vending machine coffee; surely this has to be better. I sit at a small table in the corner and scroll through my phone. I have text messages from the guys, Reagan, and my parents.' They've all been great, stopping by to see me, keeping me company, and bringing me food and clothes. I have yet to run home to shower, using the one in Melissa's room instead.

When I get back to her room, both Dr. Ellis and Dr. Robbins are there. This is the first time I've seen the two of them together since that first night.

"Something wrong?" My heart drops when I see the intense expression on both their faces.

"Ridge, the baby's vitals have been dropping slowly overnight. I think it's best if we deliver today," Dr. Ellis says.

"Today?" I repeat.

"Yes."

"Is he okay? It's too early."

"He's good, but I don't want to wait until there's a chance that he won't be. Melissa has had the steroids, and I have full faith that he'll have no complications. Babies are born at thirty-seven-and-a-half weeks every day. I do feel like this is the best decision."

"What do you think?" I ask Dr. Robbins.

"I agree with Dr. Ellis. This is what is best for the baby."

"What about Melissa?"

"Her vitals are strong, and I'm confident that the cesarean will be a smooth process."

"So, when?" I ask.

"Now. Like I said, I don't want to let his vitals get down to the risk stage. The sooner we deliver, the less strain it will be on both of them," Dr. Ellis explains.

"W-What do I do?"

"The nurses will help you scrub in. Get ready to meet your son."

"I know she says that he's mine and I'm not disputing, but I haven't seen her in over eight months. Can we do a test? You know, just to make sure. I feel like he is, but you know, I just . . . Yeah, can we do that?" I ramble. It feels like I'm betraying her by even asking, but it's something I need to do for my own peace of mind.

"Of course. It takes anywhere from two to five days to get the results, but I'll put a rush on them," Dr. Ellis says.

"Thank you."

"We're going to take her to the OR. Contact your family and then have Lisa escort you and help you get scrubbed in."

I nod and watch as they wheel her out of the room. *I guess I better do what he says; I don't want both of us to miss his birth.*

I decide on a group message.

> **Me:** Baby's vitals are dropping. Delivering today. Now. Will text when I know more.
>
> **Mom:** *On our way.*
>
> **Dad:** *What she said. Be strong, son.*
>
> **Mark:** *We got you.*
>
> **Seth:** *Good luck, Daddy.*
>
> **Kent:** *Closing up shop early.*
>
> **Tyler:** *You got this.*
>
> **Reagan:** *I love you, big brother.*

Their words ground me. I have to stay strong for my son. Yes, *my* son. I feel it deep in my soul that he's mine, and right now, he needs me. It's time to get my shit together and be what he needs.

A father.

I power my phone off and slip it into my pocket just as Lisa opens the door. "You ready?"

"As ready as I can be."

She smiles. "Follow me."

I do as I'm told, and after an elevator ride and several hallways, we make our way through a set of double doors marked Operating Room. We stop at a large, very sterile room with sinks.

"You need to put scrubs on over your clothes and booties over your shoes. After that, we'll scrub your hands and put gloves on you, as well as a facemask. You need to be just as sterile in the surgical environment as the medical staff," she explains.

After getting myself set up, Lisa opens the door to what I now know is the actual operating room. "There is a chair by Melissa. Hold her hand and talk to her. Some say that even though they're not awake, they can hear you. Some patients say they remember."

"Do you believe it?"

Lisa shrugs. "I've been a nurse for twenty years, and I've seen a lot. I'm not sure I'm a firm believer, but I do know that if I were in your shoes I would want to believe it. Help her be here in this moment. Maybe she'll remember, maybe she won't, but either way, you'll have no regrets." With those parting words, she shuts the door, closing me in.

"You must be Dad," a cheery nurse greets me. "We have a chair for you, right beside Mom. I'll help answer any questions you may have during the procedure."

Swallowing hard, I nod and take the seat next to Melissa. Reaching out, I grab her hand and lace her fingers through mine, mindful of her IV. "Hey, Melissa. So, little man is having some trouble. It's nothing serious, they tell me, but his vitals are dropping. The doctors think it's best if they deliver him today. We're here now in the operating room. I'm here with you, and I'm not going anywhere." I ramble on and on, my nerves getting the best of me.

I continue, telling her about the daily ultrasounds and how he seems to like to suck his thumb. I tell her that my family is here for all three of us, waiting to meet our son. I tell her how great she's done, doing this all on her own, and how sorry I am that she's missing this moment.

"He's out," the doctor says, but his voice is tense.

The room is quiet, no cries. *Aren't there supposed to be cries? Come on, baby, one breath. One breath at a time.*

Then I hear him.

"Is he . . . ?" I'm overwhelmed with the sound of my son's first cries. I'm a father.

"They're going to get him cleaned up, run a few newborn tests, and then you can hold him," the cheery nurse explains.

"She's doing great, Ridge," Dr. Ellis assures me. "Just closing up and then we'll send her to recovery."

"You hear that, Melissa? Did you hear him? His lungs sound strong and healthy. They're checking him over really well and then I get to hold him. Open your eyes for me. I hate that you're missing this. He's your family." My voice cracks when the last few words fall from my lips.

His cries suddenly quiet, causing me to whip my head around. There, standing behind me, is the cheery nurse holding him. He's all bundled up in a blanket. My hands start to shake, and my heart beats wildly in my chest.

"He passed with flying colors. He's already had his bath, and we even did the swab for the paternity test. He's ready to eat, Dad. What do you say?"

I look back at Melissa, willing her to wake up. She's missing this. Turning back to the nurse, I answer with, "I-I don't know what to do."

She smiles. "How about I take him to the nursery while you change out of the scrubs, and you can meet me there? Mom will be in recovery for a few hours at least before we can move her back to her room."

"Okay." I stand and lean over, kissing Melissa on the forehead. "I'll take good care of him, and we'll see you soon. Fight, Melissa. We need you." Rising to my full height, I wait as the nurse places my son in an incubator-looking contraption and motions for me to follow her.

In the nursery, I'm pulled to the side and told that I need to go to the lab for my part of the paternity test. With directions in hand, I head that way. I'm speed-walking, because I want to get back to him. My hearts tells me he's mine, so I just want to get this over with so we can get the results and move forward.

The test is a simple swab to the cheek. They get me in and out, confirming that the doctor has requested the test to be performed STAT. I make quick work to get back to the nursery. The same nurse from the OR greets me with a smile. "I'll be your nurse until the shift change this evening. Have a seat in one of those rockers, and you can hold and feed your son."

My son.

On shaking legs, I take my place in the rocker, wiping my sweaty palms on my jeans. I'm scared as hell that I'll drop him, or hurt him, or . . . I don't know what, but I'm nervous.

"Here you go, Daddy," the nurse says. "Cradle your arms. There you go," she cheers then gently places him in my arms.

He's sleeping, all wrapped up in a blanket. Suddenly the nerves are gone, the need to make sure he's okay overtaking me. "Can I unwrap him?" I ask.

"Sure! We actually suggest skin-to-skin contact, especially for those babies who are born early. It helps regulate their breathing," she explains.

Skin-to-skin contact? "Uh, what does that mean exactly?"

"You take off your shirt, and we unwrap him. You lay him on your chest, skin to skin."

"Okay," I say hesitantly. However, if it helps him, I'm all in.

"Let's try to get him to eat first." She hands me a tiny, odd-shaped bottle. "Hold him up a little, like this," she demonstrates. "Good, now place the bottle to his lips. It's instinct for most babies. Some of them can be stubborn, but looks like your little guy is a natural." She beams down at him.

And he is. As soon as the bottle touches his lips, he knows what to do. "How much does he eat?"

"We'll start with a few ounces every few hours. You need to make sure you burp him after no more than an ounce at a time. The amount spreads out as he gets older. It's extremely important during the early stages of life to make sure he burps several times throughout the feeding."

I mentally catalog everything she's saying. I wish Melissa were here, or my mom.

Shit! I forgot to call them. I'm sure they're here by now. I'll text them once he's done eating.

"Let's try that burp now, Dad."

I pull the bottle from his lips, and he whines. I immediately start to give it back to him.

"No, he has to burp first. You'll learn his whines and cries. He's just hungry, but this is an important step in the process.

I nod and listen to instructions as she walks me through how to care for my son. If I weren't so mesmerized by him, I'd feel like a tool. Who doesn't know how to take care of their own kid? Maybe someone who didn't have nine months to prepare like most parents.

I bite back that train of thought. I can't be mad at her, not when she's lying in a hospital bed fighting for her life. Besides, she was coming to me.

I can't take my eyes off him as he eats. He has my nose and my chin. It's surreal.

"Looks like he's done. You want to try skin-to-skin?" she asks.

"Yeah, but I need to notify my family first. I'm sure they're pacing the floors by now." She takes my son from my arms so I can step out in the hall and make the call.

"Ridge," Mom says in greeting.

"Hey, he's here. Little boy, cute as hell," I gush.

"How much did he weigh? How long? I need details."

Damn, I should know this shit. "Uh, I don't know exactly. It's been crazy. I'm getting ready to do what they call skin-to-skin contact. Why don't you all come down to the nursery?"

"On our way. We've been on the ICU floor, not sure where to go exactly with the situation."

Yeah, this isn't normal circumstances, for sure. "See you soon."

Back in the nursery, the nurse points to an oversized chair and tells me to sit down and take off my shirt. *Well, all right then.* I comply, and she nods her approval. I watch as she unwraps my son then gently places him in my arms.

"Just keep his head supported and hold him close to you," she instructs.

I do as she says, and the little man shudders and exhales a deep breath, almost as though he's relaxing. My heart fucking melts. How can a tiny human bring out such emotion?

"Sorry to interrupt, but there's a family out here looking for a Baby Beckett?" another nurse asks.

"That's me, I mean him." I point my chin down at my son.

"We have him as Baby Knox," she tells me.

"Yeah, that's his mom's name, but my last name is Beckett. We're not married," I explain.

"I see. Well, we'll have to keep our records as Baby Knox until the results are back," she says, frowning.

I'm sure she's afraid that I'm going to freak out on her—and if this were any other situation, I would have. But right now, all that matters is that this little guy is healthy, and getting his momma to open her eyes.

"It's fine," I tell her. "That's my family, so can they come in?"

"No, but you can bring him to the window. You can either carry him and continue how you are, or we can wrap him back up and wheel him over there." She points to the bed on wheels. I notice there's a sign in blue that says 'Baby Knox' so the families can tell them apart. His wristband says the same. I feel a pang of sadness for Melissa that she's missing this. This was her dream to be a mom—*he* is her dream.

"I'll just carry him," I tell her. She nods and steps back, allowing me to stand. I walk ever so slowly, never taking my eyes off him. A tapping sound on the window captures my attention. My family. Mom, Dad, Reagan, and the guys are watching me and my son intently. I smile at them and nod toward the sleeping baby in my arms. Mom and Reagan have tears in their eyes while Dad is grinning from ear to ear. The guys are all wearing looks of disbelief. I know how they feel; this entire night has been surreal to me.

I stand there for I don't even know how long, holding my son against my bare chest, letting my friends and family take him in. He's so fucking tiny.

"Mr. Beckett, why don't I take him so you can go and see your family," the nurse suggests.

I want to argue with her—I'm not ready to put him down yet—but I know my family has questions. Hell, *I* have questions. Sure, her letter answered some of them, but really I just need her to wake up.

I nod and slowly transfer him into the nurse's arms. "We'll be right here. Why don't you go talk to them and then maybe check in on Mom, see how's she doing?" she says.

I grab my shirt and throw it on over my head. On last glance at my son back in his . . . Hell, I don't know what to call it—his bed, maybe? The sign above his head, 'Baby Knox,' lets me know that is indeed him.

My son.

Chapter 7

Ridge

As soon as I walk out of the nursery, Reagan runs to me and throws her arms around my waist. I hug her tight. I try not to let her see how fucking scared and overwhelmed I am, but this is my little sister. She knows me too well.

"You got this, Ridge. Whatever you need," she says softly, for my ears only.

"How you holding up, son?" Dad asks, causing Reagan to release me from her grip.

I look up at my father and see the man who taught me how to throw a football, talked to me about girls, taught me how to build things, which led to my current career and taking over the family business. I vow to myself that I will be that kind of father.

"I-I don't really know. I mean, this is just . . . It's a lot to take in," I say honestly.

He nods. "He looks like you," he tells me.

I smile, because I see it too. "Yeah."

"He's perfect, Ridge," Mom adds.

That's the thing about my family—SO much love and support. They don't question if he's really mine. They go with what I have told them, and they're here for whatever I need.

"He looks tiny when you hold him," Seth says from beside me.

I turn to look at him. "He is that tiny. It's crazy, man. I feel like I'm going to break him or something."

The guys laugh at that. "You need anything from us, brother?" Tyler asks. The others nod, letting me know they're also here for me, for anything I might need.

"Hell if I know. The Allen job?" I ask them.

"All taken care of. We did the final walk-through, cleaned up the site, and have everything ready to go tomorrow with the Williams job," Mark explains.

That's when I notice they're all wearing their work boots and Beckett Construction T-shirts. They must have come straight here from the job site.

"Thanks. I-I guess I need to go check on Melissa. She should be out of recovery now."

"We brought you some food." Mom steps in for a hug.

I wrap my arms around her and fight the emotion threatening to drown me. Once a momma's boy, always a momma's boy. Then I think about my son and Melissa. She has to wake up. He needs her. *I* need her. I can't do this on my own. We might not be together, but who knows what the future holds?

Dad holds up a bag of food. I take it and nod my thanks.

"We're going to stay here for a bit." Mom looks over at my son and smiles.

"We're going to head out and grab a shower, but we'll be back," Kent says, pointing down at his work boots and dirty jeans.

"You guys don't have to come back. There's nothing but waiting right now."

"So we wait." Seth shrugs.

"Walk us out. Some fresh air for a few minutes might do you some good," Tyler chimes in.

I say a quick good-bye to my parents' and sister and follow the guys outside. I take a deep breath, holding it in before slowly releasing it.

"Some crazy-ass shit," Mark says, breaking the silence.

"Don't I know it." It's like one of those movies my mom and sister like to watch on that Lifetime channel.

"You need anything, man, you let us know," Kent offers.

"Just take care of the office. I can't even think about all that right now."

"We got you. I'll bring a deck of cards or something when we come back," Seth says.

"Guys, really, you don't need to sit here. No point in all five of us sitting and staring at her."

"Fine, we'll take shifts. I'll be back later," Tyler states. "You guys—" he points to our other three friends "—can take the next one." Finally, he looks at me. "See you in a bit."

I concede with a nod. Each of them takes a turn giving me a quick hug and slap on the back.

I stand there on the steps, eyes closed, just taking a minute to reflect on everything when I hear my name being called. Slowly, I open my eyes and see Stephanie.

"Are you okay?" she asks.

Three days. It's been three days since I told her I was here. I know we didn't label what was going on with us, but *three days*?

"I'm good." I don't bother further explanation.

She takes me in, seeing that physically I am indeed okay. "You've not returned any of my calls or texts."

"I've been busy."

"What's going on, Ridge? You really believe he's yours?"

I tell her about Melissa, about our night together. I tell her about the night of the gala and end with earlier today when my son was born. I give her the CliffsNotes version, but I don't hold back.

"So, you're falling for this girl's story? Are you sure this kid is even yours? I mean, come on, Ridge. Think about it. How many women try to trap men with 'I'm pregnant'? I thought you were smarter than that."

What. The. Fuck.

"He's mine," I grit out. Sure, we're still waiting on the results of the paternity test, but he looks like me and I just know he's my son.

She stares at me as if trying to see through me. She won't find what she's looking for. He's my son; my gut has never been wrong before.

"So, what, you're just going to play daddy now?"

I take a deep breath, trying to calm my nerves. She's testing me. "There is no fucking playing about it, Stephanie. I'm a father. I have a son."

"I can't believe you're falling for this shit! You really want to be tied down with a kid from a one-night stand?"

"Yes!" I growl. "He's mine. I will be in his life, regardless of my relationship with his mother. His mother who, by the way, is currently lying in a hospital bed, fighting for her fucking life!"

Stephanie shakes her head as if my words are the craziest thing she's ever heard. "Good luck with that. Call me when all this shit blows over and we can get together."

I'm fucking done. "Not gonna happen."

"What, you have a kid so now we can't hook up?"

"My son has nothing to do with it. I don't want you."

She steps forward and runs her finger down my chest. "You sure about that? Why is it that I'm the only one you keep coming back to?"

Fuck this! "You were a bet," I snap. "The guys fucking bet me that I couldn't stay with one person for three months. Sure, we had a good time, but don't mistake that for something more. You were their pick." I shrug, letting her know that she's of no consequence to me.

"A bet?" she asks, appalled.

"Yep. So you can take you're 'better than thou' bitchy self and move on down the road. Even if it *were* more, there is no way I could be with someone who doesn't accept my child."

"You don't even know if he's yours!" she yells.

"Go!" My voice is low and menacing. "I don't want to see you anymore. He is mine, and you are not. Leave now, and lose my number."

I turn and stomp my way up the steps, needing to check on Melissa then go visit my son.

"You'll regret this, Ridge Beckett!" she yells after me. "I won't be waiting for you when this blows up in your face!"

"Good fucking riddance," I mumble under my breath. I don't bother turning around to address her, just keep walking as though I didn't hear her dumb-ass tirade.

I take the elevator up to Melissa's floor. Her room is quiet, nothing but the sounds of the beeping machines. Pulling a chair up next to her bed, I gently hold her hand in mine. She has no one, just me and our son. I think about my family, my friends who were all here for me today, who have been the last three days. There's no one in her corner. How lonely she must be.

"Hey, Melissa," I say, my voice low. "You did good today. He's perfect, and so damn tiny." I chuckle. "When I hold him, he's so small in my arms. I'm almost afraid I'll break him, but the nurses assure me that I won't." I gently run my thumb over her wrist. "You need to wake up now. I need you to fight to come back to him."

That's when it hits me that I need to bring him here. Maybe having him in the same room, or laying him against her chest, might bring her back. Hell, I have no fucking idea what I'm even talking about. I just know they said she could possibly still hear everything. If that's the case, I want her to know he's here. Give her a reason, motivation to open her eyes.

"I'm going to go down to the nursery and get our boy. He needs to see his momma, even if she is Sleeping Beauty. I'll be back." Standing, I kiss her on the forehead before leaving the room.

Once I reach the nursery, I stop at the window and look for him. It doesn't take long to spot the 'Baby Knox' sign, my son sleeping peacefully beneath it. Although it scares the hell out of me, I can't wait to hold him again.

I swipe my bracelet, which gives me access to the nursery waiting room. I inform the girl at the desk that I'm here to take my son to see his mother. She doesn't ask for anything except to see my bracelet. I assume the story of Melissa, her coma, and me not knowing about the baby has rapidly filtered throughout the hospital. Everyone loves a good storyline.

"Hey, Daddy," a nurse I've never seen before greets me, wheeling my son's bed with her. "It's time for this little guy to eat. You can do that here, or I can go with you to Mom's room."

I have a feeling this is not standard protocol; they must be able to see I have no experience with babies or any clue how to take care of one. They're taking pity on me, but I'm grateful.

"Can we do it there? I just want him to be close to her. I thought maybe it could help." I run my fingers through my hair. I know it's a long shot, but I need for her to wake up.

"Absolutely." She gives me a sad smile.

I watch as she signs him out and tells the others where she'll be. As I hold the door open for her, we run into Reagan and Tyler.

"I had to argue with Mom. She wanted to come back first, but Dad helped to convince her that she needs a good night's sleep because when you bring the baby home, you'll need all the help you can get."

Bring him home? I look over at the nurse. "He's doing well. As long as he continues to do so, we can release him as early as tomorrow. However, paternity will need to be proven before you can take him. It might take an additional day or two," she explains.

I nod, hoping those results come back fast.

"Can you keep him here that long? I mean, you won't send him to foster care or anything, right?" Reagan asks.

Her words cut me like a knife. Melissa's letter, her words are flashing through my mind. "No, do what you have to do to speed up the test. I don't care what it costs, but he will not be going into the fucking system," I growl.

Reagan lays a hand on my shoulder. "I'm sorry, I shouldn't have said anything."

"It's fine. Usually, we would involve Child Services and the child would be placed in foster care. However, this is extenuating circumstances. The physician's already ordered for stat results on the paternity, and with Mom being here still, that buys this little guy a few extra days," she assures me.

"See?" Tyler says. "It's all good, my man. Where you headed?"

I know he's trying to get my mind off the fact that my son could go into the system. Even a few days is too damn long when he has family who wants him. Me, his father—I want him.

"Uh . . . We're taking the baby to see Melissa," I tell them.

"She's awake?" Reagan's eyes light up.

"No, but they say that even in a coma they can hear what's going on, so I thought maybe. . . ."

"Good plan. We're coming with. Tyler and I stopped off at the store and bought some outfits, blankets, diaper bag, diapers—things like that." She holds up the bag that's hanging off her shoulder.

"Can we all be in there?" I ask the nurse.

She winks, grinning. "I only see two people, don't you? Two people who are going to be calm and quiet and not disturb the patient. I know nothing."

"You're too kind." Tyler winks back at her. Any other time, I would find this amusing.

The baby starts to fuss. "He needs to eat. Let's get him to Mom, shall we?" the nurse asks politely.

I nod, and the three of us follow her to the elevator.

Chapter 8

Ridge

The nurse sticks around long enough for me to feed him and then leaves us alone. I fight back the panic that threatens to break free. I've never taken care of a baby. My only saving grace is that my sister and Tyler are here with me; Reagan used to babysit for the neighbors' kids all the time.

"Can I hold him now?" she asks me.

I nod, and she jumps from her seat and comes toward me. Like she's done it a million times, she leans down and takes him from my arms. "Watch his head," I remind her.

"Chill, Daddy. I got this."

Daddy.

Tyler chuckles. "That just hit you, didn't it?" he asks.

"I guess so. I mean, it's just weird, I guess. The nurses have called me that, but with Reagan saying it, it's . . . Wow."

"He's so sweet." Reagan brings him to her lips and kisses his little cheek.

I lean over, resting my elbows on my knees, my eyes never leaving my sister and my son.

"Kid's going to be a stud," Tyler jokes. I know he's trying to lighten the mood.

"Care to elaborate?" I ask him.

He shrugs. "You're his dad, and he has four cool-as-hell uncles. How can he not be?"

"Oh, yeah. This little guy is going to have the ladies eating out of the palm of his hand. But he'll be a gentleman; I'll make sure of it. And I'm sure your mommy will too," Reagan coos to him.

"Wh-what ab-bout m-m-mom-my?" a croaked voice asks.

I fly to my feet. "Hey," I say softly, reaching for her hand.

"R-Ridge?" she forces out.

"Shhh, it's okay," I soothe her.

"I'll go get the nurse." Tyler is on his feet and out the door in a flash.

"It's okay. You were in an accident on your way to see me. They found your letter and gave it to me," I tell her.

She nods. Our son makes a grunting noise and her eyes, panicked, search him out.

"He's here, healthy and perfect," I reassure her. "Reagan."

She stands and goes to the other side of the bed. "Hi, Melissa. I'm Reagan, Ridge's sister. I think this little guy would like to meet you." She holds my son out so Melissa can see him. One arm is in a cast while the other has an IV running to it.

Tears fall from Melissa's eyes, and a smile tilts her lips.

"Look at you," a nurse says, entering the room. "Glad to have you with us. I'll need everyone to step out while I examine her."

Melissa looks panicked again.

"It's okay. We're just going to step outside. They need to take a look at you," I murmur.

She closes her eyes, blinking back tears. When she opens them again, she appears to be calmer.

"I promise we'll be right back." I give her hand a gentle squeeze and follow my sister and Tyler out to the waiting room.

"Good news, yeah?" Tyler asks.

"Yeah," I agree, looking down at my son.

"I'm going to call Mom and Dad, tell them she's awake." Reagan skips off down the hallway.

"I already texted the guys, letting them know. You good?" Tyler questions.

"I'm good. Relieved. I don't know how to raise a kid, let alone on my own. She and I have a lot of shit to figure out."

"You can come back in," the nurse informs us.

"Listen, man. I'll give the three of you some time. I'll be in the waiting room if you need me. I'm going to see if Reagan wants to go down to the cafeteria to grab a bite to eat. You want anything?"

"No, I'm good. Thanks, man."

I find Melissa sitting up in bed. "Hey," I say, keeping my voice low.

"Hi," she replies, her voice raspy.

"How you feeling?"

"Like I missed a lot." She eyes our son.

"I think someone wants to meet you." I gently lift him from his bed and carry him to her. Tears are streaming down her face when I place him in her arms. "Here you go, little man. This is your mommy."

A sob escapes her throat. I admit I have to blink hard several times to keep my emotions in check.

"Hi, handsome," she coos. "I love you so much."

He's sleeping, not a care in the world. I can see the love in her eyes, and any anger I had about her not telling me sooner fades away. She was coming to me, and I know without a shadow of a doubt that she is going to be the best mother to our son.

Melissa leans down and kisses his forehead, letting her lips linger. The image is one I know she and my son will cherish forever. I slip my phone out of my pocket and snap a picture, the flash catching her attention. She doesn't chide me about her hair being a mess or that she's not picture-ready. No, Melissa gives me a bright-as-the-sun smile, tears in her eyes.

KAYLEE RYAN

"Can I see?" she asks.

I take my seat beside her bed and show her my phone. "I've taken a few today." I slowly scroll through the pictures so she can see.

"When was he born?"

"Today at 12:01 p.m. He's six pounds, eight ounces, and nineteen inches long. They say he's perfectly healthy."

"He's early."

"Yeah, the doctors gave you something through your IV to make his lungs stronger. His heart rate started to drop, so they delivered him cesarean. You've been here for three days."

"I'm so sorry, Ridge. I was coming to tell you. I wanted you to know, but I was just scared . . . you would reject him, and I didn't want that. I didn't know how you would react."

I take a minute to process what she said. "I'm not mad anymore. How can I be when you gave me him? He's a shock, sure, but he's my flesh and blood. I know we have a lot to figure out, but I want to be in his life." I stop and wait for her reaction. She nods, more tears falling from her eyes. "I want him to have my name," I confess.

"Okay," she agrees, looking down at our son. "He's perfect, Ridge. I've never had family. He's my family." Her voice cracks.

"Hey, how about another picture? This time of the three of us?"

She smiles through her tears, nodding.

I step out of the room and grab a nurse. "Can you take a picture of the three of us?" I ask her.

"Sure."

I hand her my phone and gingerly sit on the side of the bed. Placing my arm around Melissa's shoulders, we smile for the camera.

"Thank you," I tell the nurse, taking my phone back.

"You're welcome," she says, then quietly leaves us once more.

"Did you have any names in mind?" I ask Melissa.

"No, I wanted to meet him first, get to know his personality a little. Any ideas?"

"As long as it ends in Beckett, I'm good with it."

A soft laugh escapes her lips. "Thank you, Ridge. I know you should

70

hate me right now. You could be making this so much more difficult, but you're not."

"No need. He's mine, and I want to be a part of his life. Nothing difficult about it. Do I wish I would have known sooner? Yeah, but at the end of the day, it's the same result. We have a child to raise."

She yawns, and I watch as she battles to keep her eyes open.

"Hey, why don't I take him back to the nursery so you can rest? We don't have to figure anything out today. You need rest to get out of this joint."

"Yeah, I have a little bit of a headache too. Will you stay with him?"

"Nowhere else I'd rather be," I tell her honestly, taking him from her arms and placing him back in his bed. "Get some rest. We'll be here when you wake up." Leaning down, I kiss her forehead.

"Thank you, Ridge. Thank you for our son," she whispers as she closes her eyes.

As quietly as I can, I leave the room and take little man back to the nursery. After I've checked him back in, I decide to head to the cafeteria to join Reagan and Tyler.

"Everything okay?" Reagan asks when I approach their table.

"Yeah, Melissa is resting. I took little man back to the nursery."

"Sit, I'll grab you something to eat." She stands, hugs me, then leaves to do as she said.

"How's she doing?" Tyler asks.

I run my fingers though my hair. "Good. I mean, as far as I can tell, anyway. She was emotional, but happy. She's been through a lot and we have a lot to work out, but nothing has to be decided today."

"True. I told the guys to just stay home. They can come by tomorrow after work."

"Yeah, thanks, man."

"So, did you pick out a name?" Reagan asks, setting a tray with a cheeseburger and French fries in front of me.

"Nope, she said she wanted to get to know him first. I told her I didn't care either way as long as he has my last name."

"What did she say to that?" she asks.

"Nothing, what can she say? He's mine. She seemed fine with it. Almost . . . relieved."

"Good. Now eat up so I can go love on my nephew again before I have to get home. I can't get to him without you."

"Yes, ma'am," I say and do as I'm told.

After I practically inhale my food, we head back up to the nursery. The nurse from earlier, along with another and what looks like Melissa's doctor, is standing outside the waiting room door. When one of the nurses sees us coming, her face pales.

Something's wrong.

My heart begins to beat furiously against my chest. I quicken my stride and stop beside them. "What is it? What's wrong? Is he okay?" I barely register a hand on each of my shoulders; at this point, I'm not sure if they're for support or to hold me back. I look through the nursery window and I don't see him. "Where is my son? Somebody better start talking now," I demand.

"Mr. Beckett, let's step inside." The doctor points to the waiting room.

"Tell me now! Where is my son?"

"Ridge." Reagan grabs my arm. "Let's go in and sit down. I'm sure as soon as we do, this fine doctor here will tell us what's going on."

The doctor nods his agreement.

Once we're in the waiting room, a nurse wheels my son out to us. I don't hesitate this time, lifting him into my arms and holding him close. "Talk! Is he okay? What the hell is going on?"

"Mr. Beckett, I'm sorry to have to tell you this, but Melissa . . . Well, she's gone."

"Gone? What do you mean gone? I was just with her not twenty minutes ago. She's sleeping."

"No, I mean she's passed. We tried everything we could," he tells me.

"Wait, what?"

"Ridge, you need to sit." Tyler lays a heavy hand on my shoulder and pushes me into a chair.

"Explain."

"We think it was a brain aneurysm. When there's trauma to the head, you sometimes don't know until it's too late. I'm so sorry for your loss."

"*My* loss? What about my son? That's his mother."

Reagan tries to take him from me, but I hold tighter. "Ridge, let me hold him, please. You're upset, and he can sense that. I'll be right here, I promise."

"Let her take him," Tyler encourages me.

Reluctantly, I hand over my son. "How is this happening? I was just with her. If I would've stayed, she would still be here."

"No, Mr. Beckett, that's not true. With an aneurysm, it's fast. Those in the brain are more often than not fatal. There's nothing anyone could have done."

I slump forward, my face in my hands. She's gone. My son will never know his mother. He won't get to see that love in her eyes that she had for him. He will never get to see that he is all she ever wanted. He will never get to experience the childhood that I did, with both parents loving and supporting him.

How am I going to do this without her?

What do I know about raising a baby? I was hoping she would guide me. She was awake, and we were going to work it all out. We were going to figure this out. Now she's gone.

"Mr. Beckett, I'm so sorry for your loss," the doctor says again before leaving the room.

I feel a strong hand on my shoulder, Tyler giving his silent support. How did things go from bad to good to terrible in a matter of minutes?

"Ridge," Reagan says hesitantly.

I keep my head buried in my hands until I hear his cry.

My son.

Looking up, I see Reagan trying to soothe him.

"He's crying, and I don't know what's wrong. I don't know how to take care of him. She was supposed to wake up and guide me through this. How am I going to take care of a baby? I don't know what to do."

Reagan bounces him in her arms. "You are going to be the best damn father that any kid has ever had. You are not alone in this, Ridge. You have me, Mom and Dad, the guys. You are not alone. He needs you.

You are his father."

"What if I can't do it?" Fuck, I know I sound like a whiny ass right now, but my fear trumps the fucks I don't have to give at this point. "What happens when I screw it all up?"

"Are you giving up, Beckett?" Tyler asks. "That's not you, man. He's your flesh and blood. He's a part of you. You man the fuck up and be what he needs. Learn along the way. You think you're the first person to do this on their own?"

"You're going to make mistakes, Ridge. That's life. But you will learn from them and move forward. It's going to be hard, but you have a huge support system and we're ready to rally around you and this little guy."

A nurse steps into the room. "It's time for him to eat."

I nod, stand and take him from Reagan before settling back into the chair. The nurse hands me his bottle, and I place it next to his lips. He latches on immediately, gulping it down. No one says a word as we all watch him eat. I see that he's eaten about an ounce, so I pull the bottle from his lips and place him on my shoulder to burp him. He does so quickly, and I repeat the steps.

"You're good with him," Reagan comments.

"They taught me earlier today."

"And look at you now, you're an old pro. It's all going to be a learning curve, Ridge, but you've got this."

I look down at my son who is sucking on his bottle, eyes drifting closed. He has no idea what's going on. That his mother just passed away. I feel an ache deep in my chest, for both of them. I send up a silent prayer that I can be everything he needs. That somehow, I can give him the love of both parents.

"It's just you and me, little man," I whisper in his ear.

"I'm going to go call the guys and your parents." Tyler steps out of the room.

"How's he doing?" the nurse asks.

"Good, he finished the entire thing. You need to write that down or something, right?" I ask.

"I do. You did well, Dad." She makes a note on the tablet in her hands. "Mr. Beckett, I know this is not the appropriate time for this conversation, but I have some paperwork here for you. The little guy is being released tomorrow, and we still need a name."

What? He's being released? "He can't. I thought you said he could stay until we get the results. Who do I have to talk to? I refuse to let my son go into the system."

"Mr. Beckett, the results are in. You are a 99.99% match. He's your son."

My heart stills in my chest.

"Breathe, Ridge." Reagan giggles next to me.

I take in a breath. He's mine. I knew he was—in my heart, in my gut. But now I have confirmation, know he's coming home with me and not going into the foster care system. Melissa would hate that.

"I know this is a rough time for you, but we can't release him until he has a name for the birth certificate."

"Beckett," I say automatically.

Reagan giggles again. "She's got that part, goof. He needs a first name, a middle name. I know you said Melissa didn't have a name in mind. Do you?" she asks gently.

Do I? No, I don't. I've been too busy willing his momma to wake up. I look up and see his bed, the 'Baby Knox' displayed with his birth stats staring back at me.

Knox Beckett. He would always have a piece of his momma—her last name and mine.

"Knox Beckett," I say out loud.

"Oh, Ridge, I love it," Reagan says softly. "What about a middle name?"

I think about that. My middle name is Alexander, as is my dad's. Seems fitting. I hope I'm half the father to Knox that my father was to me. "Knox Alexander Beckett."

"Here is the paperwork you need to complete. Once I have it entered in the system, it will go to the state and they'll issue his birth certificate. You'll get it in the mail in a few weeks."

I hand Knox off to Reagan and complete the stack of forms, pausing when I get to mother's information. I swallow the lump in my throat as I write the word 'deceased.' Too fucking young and full of hope for the life she wanted to give our son. Needing my insurance info, I pull out my cell phone where I have it saved. When I tap the screen, the picture the nurse took of the three of us glares back at me. I feel like an elephant is sitting on my chest. Her smile . . . She was so fucking happy holding our son, and now she's gone. After everything she's been through.

"It's not fair," I blurt out. "Why her? After the life she lived? Why could she not be happy? Raise our son and have a real family, a part of her? It's not fucking f-fair." My voice cracks on the last word.

Tyler walks in just at that moment.

"You're up, Uncle Tyler," Reagan says, handing Knox to him. She doesn't say anything else, just drops to her knees in front of me and wraps her arms around me. That breaks me and I sob into her shoulder, the stress of the last three days—today, especially—overwhelming me. I fall apart; I couldn't stop it even if I tried. I've been fighting back these emotions since I pulled off the road and found her car.

"It's not fair," Reagan agrees. "It fucking sucks donkey dick."

I laugh at that; I can't help it.

"My work here is done," she says through her own tears.

"Uh, guys . . . I think little man here has a present for his Aunt Reagan," Tyler says. He sounds like he's holding his breath.

That just causes me to laugh harder. He may not have his mother, but I will make damn sure he knows how much she loved him. How much she wanted to be a part of his life. He won't have both parents, but he will have me, his aunt, my four best friends—uncles by default—and my parents.'

He will be loved every damn day.

I will make sure of it.

Chapter 9

Ridge

Three days. I've been home with my son for three days. Needless to say, my world has been upturned. Not that I'm complaining. I love cuddling with the little man. My mom and Reagan have both been staying with me, and Dad stayed last night as well, saying he felt like he was missing out. Luckily, I have the space.

Mom and Reagan took care of the basics. They made sure I had a car seat to bring him home in, plus they bought clothes and blankets. When I arrived home, my boys had taken it one step further; not only had they decorated the front porch with blue balloons and 'It's a boy' banners, but they also had the spare room—the one closest to mine—set up and ready to go for my little guy. The once-empty room now sports a baby bed, dresser, and changing table—at least that's what Mom calls it.

I have a hell of a lot to learn.

I don't know what I would do without any of them. They've helped me so much, and I know I can never repay them for all they've done.

Today is Knox's first doctor's appointment. I made him one at the office Reagan and I went to as kids. Our doctor retired, but the office is nice and it's close. I asked Reagan to go with me. Mom offered, but I told her to take a break. She's going to be watching Knox for me during the day—something she has reassured me is an honor and a pleasure. And she might have hinted to Reagan that she needs to give her more grandkids. She and Dad are shopping today; Mom insists Knox have the comforts of home at their house as well.

"All right, little man, I think we're good to go," I tell my son after strapping him into his car seat. He's snoozing away. I double-check the diaper bag: diapers, wipes, clothes, blanket, bottles and toys. Not that he plays with them, but hey, you never know when you might need it. Oh, and the binky. Gotta have the binky.

"Ready?" Reagan asks.

"Yeah, I think I have everything." I grab the envelope from the counter that has all his paperwork already filled out. Gotta love the Internet.

Reagan grabs the diaper bag while I take Knox out to the truck and strap him in. In the past three days, I have never been more relieved that I purchased a crew cab truck. Not having a backseat would mean buying a new car, and that's not something I want to worry about right now. I have enough on my plate as it is.

Reagan hops in the backseat, wearing a mile-wide grin. Knox has been getting lots of attention since he's been home. I read online that if you hold them too much you spoil them, but when I brought this up to Mom and Reagan, they blew me off. I believe Mom's exact words were, "You love them, Ridge. You can't ever give them too much love." I dropped it after that.

The ride to the office is quick. The lady at the desk looks impressed that the forms are filled out and ready to go. I run my own company; you can't be successful half-assing everything.

"Since—" she looks at my forms "—Knox is under three months of age, we'll take you on back to a room. We don't like the smaller babies to be out here with the illnesses."

Good policy. She meets us at the door and takes us to an exam room. "They'll need him undressed down to his diaper," she tells us then shuts the door.

Laying his blanket on the exam table, I lift him from his seat and he stretches. I let him work it out of his system before laying him on the blanket to undress him. This is still something I take my time with, as I don't want to hurt him, even though Mom assures me that as long as I'm gentle and watch his head, I'll be fine. Once he's stripped down to his diaper, I wrap the blanket around him to keep him warm.

"This place hasn't changed a bit," Reagan comments.

I cradle Knox in my arms and survey the room. "Not a bit," I agree.

"Knock, knock," a female voice says before entering the room.

"Kendall?" Reagan greets her. "I didn't know you worked here. I thought you were working over in Mason? How have you been?"

"Yeah, I transferred here about six months ago. It was time for a change, and I was ready to come home. Although, as soon as I did, my parents' packed up and moved to Florida. How are you?"

"Wonderful, just coming to my nephew's first doctor visit." She points to Knox. "You remember Ridge, right?"

"Ridge, it's good to see you. Cute little guy you have there."

"Thanks."

"All right, so let's get him weighed and then the doctor will be in to check him out."

I follow her out of the exam room and down the hall. "All right, Dad, I just need you to lay him on the scales."

I look at the small white scale that is curved on the sides—I assume to keep kids from rolling off. There's a blue padded strip that almost looks like a diaper covering in. "You want me to set him there? Really? What if he falls off?" I question.

"He won't. I'll be right beside him the entire time. We need to get his weight."

Reagan nudges my arm, and begrudgingly, I unwrap him from his blanket and lay him on the scale. I stand right next to it, ready if I'm needed.

Kendall smiles and starts taking off his diaper.

What the hell? "What are you doing?" *Why is she getting my kid naked?*

"We have to get an accurate weight. It's crucial when they are this young to ensure they're gaining weight. He should gain steadily at each visit. We can't have the diaper interfering with that number," Kendall explains.

I nod, biting my lip. I watch as Kendall expertly removes his diaper, gets his weight, and has the diaper back on him. If I had blinked, I would've missed it. Knox's little lip starts to quiver before he lets out a wail.

"Okay, Dad, you can pick him back up."

Not having to be told twice, I take him back in my arms and cover him with his blanket. He calms instantly. I know it's just the warmth, but it's a pretty big ego boost at this point in the game that I can give him what he needs. That being my biggest fear and all.

"All right, guys, the doctor will be right in."

"Ease up, Daddy." Reagan grins.

I scowl at her. "Ease up, my ass. She was getting him naked."

She laughs. "Relax, she's just doing her job. He's not in danger, papa bear."

I can't help but grin. Even though I'm exhausted and it's only been three days, I feel like I'm starting to get the hang of this.

Chapter 10

Kendall

Ridge Beckett. He looks better than he did in high school. The ink that covers his skin, the chiseled abs that his too-tight T-shirt proudly displayed. Time has most definitely been good to him.

The whole lot of them—him, Seth, Mark, Tyler, and Kent—were every teenage girl's dream. The entire school drooled over them. They were the unattainable. Regardless, they were easy on the eyes for sure. Just the chance that you could pass them in the halls was motivation enough to get the girls to come to school. Hell, some of the guys too.

I sit down at the computer and start entering the baby's weight. When I click over to verify the insurance, I see a chart note. Wanting to make sure it doesn't pertain to today's visit, I find myself glued to the computer screen.

Once I'm finished, I just stare at the screen. My heart breaks for Ridge and Baby Knox. Apparently, Mom was in a bad accident and passed away after giving birth. I click over in the chart and verify if Mom has been listed as deceased. *How embarrassing and gut-wrenching would that be for everyone, asking about her?* The chart has not yet been marked, so I flag it and send a 'before visit' message to Dr. Harris, advising him to read the chart note prior entering the exam room. Forcing myself to keep going, I finish my charting and move on to the next patient.

Just as I'm leaving the exam room, Dr. Harris steps out of the room beside me. He was in there with Baby Knox.

"Kendall, can you get the dad in room two the first-year baby guide?"

I nod and head back to the medicine closet where we store samples and information packets. Grabbing the first-year guidebook, I see a small black diaper bag, the ones we get from pharmaceutical reps to give to new parents. The Beckett family situation still on my mind, I grab one. It already has formula, the one they've been using, and I throw in some baby wash samples and a few others before heading back to the exam room.

"All right, here's a bag of goodies. We like to give these to first-time parents. Just a few samples. Dr. Harris has signed his note, so you're good to go. It was nice seeing you both again." I know I'm rambling and rushing them, but my heart is breaking for them and it's hard for me to retain my professional demeanor, especially since I know them. It's been a few years, but that doesn't make my heart hurt any less for them.

Bending down, I gently run my finger over little Knox's foot. "I'll see you next time, handsome," I coo.

"So, what exactly happens next time? He needs shots, right?" Ridge asks.

Taking a deep breath, I stand up and face him. "Yes, he will receive several vaccinations his first year of life. This packet—" I pull it out of the side of the bag I just gave him "—will address each visit. It also goes through milestones that your baby will reach at each month."

Ridge takes a deep breath and slowly exhales. "Great. Thank you, Kendall."

"You're welcome. In that packet, you will also find our after-hours number. Don't hesitate to call if you have questions or concerns. That's what we're here for," I say before stepping out of the room.

I leave them to gather their things and wrap my head around the rest of my day. I try to focus, but I keep thinking about what they must be going through, how that adorable little boy will never know his mother.

The exam door opens and my eyes dart to them.

"Thanks, Kendall," Reagan says with a smile and a wave.

"See you soon," I reply.

"Thank you again," Ridge says in his deep voice.

"Hey, my knight in shining armor," Dawn pipes up.

This causes Ridge and Reagan to stop in their tracks. I whip my head around to my co-worker and best friend. *Has she lost her damn mind?*

She points at herself. "The flat-tire girl. You stopped to help me last week." She grins. "Thank you again."

Ridge visibly stiffens for a second; if my eyes weren't glued to him, I would've missed it. I watch as he quickly paints on a grin. "Anytime. Glad I could help." He doesn't stick around for idle chit-chat; he turns and makes his way down the hall, disappearing behind the waiting room door. Reagan drops the clipboard off at the reception desk with the promise that they'll call to schedule the next appointment.

"What the hell was that?" I hiss at Dawn. I'm mindful of the level of my voice, little ears being everywhere.

"What? He's the guy I was telling you about. The night I had a flat tire on my way home from work, he stopped in the pouring rain to help me. You know him?"

"Yes. I graduated with his sister. He was two years ahead of me in school."

"Damn, they didn't have guys who looked like that at my high school. Please tell me he was a pimply-faced geek back then."

I think back to Ridge and his band of buddies. None of them would even come close to pimply-faced or geeky then—or now, I'm sure. "Sorry, no can do."

"You have all the luck," she whines.

"Listen, he's going through a lot. Their whole family is, so he doesn't need you hitting on him right now. Besides, that's unprofessional," I scold her.

"I wasn't flirting. I was simply showing my appreciation for him stopping to help me."

"Uh-huh." I laugh then mock-glare at her. "Get back to work.

She mumbles something under her breath about being friends with the boss, and I just smile wider.

Dawn and I met in nursing school, and after graduation we got an apartment together in Mason, a few towns over.

That's where I met Cal. He was a third-year resident at the hospital Dawn and I worked at. He was charming, educated, and good-looking. On the outside, we had a ton of things in common. On paper, we were the perfect match. On the inside . . . not so much. I fell fast and hard, thought we were in love, until it was obvious that we weren't. It took me a year to see it, to admit to the signs. By then, it was too late. He lived across the hall, so no matter how many times I tried to break things off with him, he was always there, lurking in the background. When my mom called and said Dr. Harris was looking for a new nursing coordinator, I jumped at the chance to interview. I missed living so close to my parents.'

Dawn began looking too, and I happened to mention that in my interview. To my surprise, Dr. Harris needed a floor nurse as well. The practice has been here since I was a little girl, but the original staff was retiring, including the physicians. It couldn't have happened at a better time. I needed to get away from Cal, and Dawn was more than willing to tag along for the adventure.

After we were both offered positions, we packed slowly, making weekend trips to my parents' to move our things. We both had to give two weeks' notice, and I didn't want to have to deal with the drama that Cal was sure to cause by us moving. Lucky for us, he went away for the weekend with friends and we were gone by the time he came home. No forwarding address. He knows I'm from Jackson, but we're not alone here. Dawn and I have my parents' and grandparents, and that alone helps me sleep at night.

I shake away the memories and try to focus on the task at hand. We've got a full day of patients who need my full attention.

Chapter 11

Ridge

He's growing, gaining weight like he should be, and all looks good according to Dr. Harris. He's only been home a few days, but it's a relief to know I'm doing something right. I'm totally flying by the seat of my pants with this one. I don't know what I would've done without Mom and Reagan. One, if not both of them, has been with me since the moment I brought him home. I appreciate them so much, but at the same time I feel like they're hovering. I have to learn to do this on my own, as a single father. That's not a title I ever imagined being associated with, but life is often unexpected.

"Hey, are you even listening to me?" Reagan asks.

I don't take my eyes off the road—precious cargo and all that. "Sorry, a lot on my mind," I confess.

"What's up?"

I laugh. "Everything."

"Ridge," she says softly.

"I'm good, really. Just thinking about how much you and Mom have helped me with little man." I glance at her in the rearview mirror. "I think I need to try it on my own, you know?"

She's quiet for several minutes. I don't look at her, afraid of what I'll see. Maybe she thinks I'm not capable.

"You're good with him," she finally says. "We just want you to know that you're not alone. We're with you every step of the way."

I take a minute to let her words sink in. "I know, and I love you both for it, but I have to do this. I have to learn to take care of him. You and Mom can't be there every day for the rest of his life. I have to learn to be both Mom and Dad to him."

Silence greets me. I glance in the mirror and see she's wiping a tear from her eyes. *What the fuck? Tears? I hate tears.*

"Reagan?"

"I'm so damn proud of you, big brother. Knox is a lucky little boy to have you for a father. I don't know many men who would be thrown into your position unexpectedly and handle it like you have. Like you are."

I nod, choked up a little at her praise. We drive the rest of the way to my place in silence. It's not until I pull into the drive that I break it.

"I need to run to the store and stop by the office. Do you mind watching him?" I turn to face her. "I'm going back full time on Monday. I just need to stock up on a few things for next week."

"Snuggle time with my adorable nephew? You got it, brother."

"Thanks, sister."

She grins. When we were little, I insisted on calling her 'sister' instead of Reagan. When she was old enough to talk, she called me 'brother.' Over the years, it's just kind of stuck. It's our thing, I guess.

I carry my little man into the house and unstrap him from his seat. Holding him close, I breathe in his baby scent. In just a few short days, I've become addicted to it. Addicted to my son.

I have a son.

That knowledge still rocks me to the core. Melissa and her surprise is not something I would have expected. Losing her after her waking up? Well, my world was rocked once again in just a few short days. I'm pissed. How can someone who had their life's dream in their grasp, someone who lived through so many hardships and obstacles, be taken from this world just when she's getting what she's always dreamed of?

I'm angry, and if I'm being honest, scared out of my fucking mind. Everything he needs falls on me. Those are big shoes to fill.

"All right, little man. I'm going to go run a few errands, but Aunt Reagan is going to keep you company. You're in charge," I tell him.

"Hey!" Reagan says. Her hands rest on her hips as she tries to glare at me, but I can see the amusement in her eyes. "Give me my nephew and be gone. We have cartoons to watch."

I kiss my son on the forehead and hand him over to my sister, doing the same to her once he's settled in her arms. "Thank you. I'll hurry."

"Don't. I have nothing to do today. I go back to work on Monday."

"Thank you, Reagan. For everything."

She smiles and waves me off.

MY FIRST STOP is the shop. Dad has been here every day keeping things going—this *was* his business, after all. I pull into a parking spot and look at the building in front of me.

Beckett Construction.

Last year, Dad decided it was time to retire. Mom has always been a stay-at-home mom, and business has been good over the years. Dad worked his ass off to make it a success while investing in their future. Retiring early and being able to financially do the things they've always wanted to do is the American dream.

As I stare at the building, I wonder if my son will one day want to work for Beckett Construction. Will he want to continue the legacy my father built? I won't be that dad who insists that he does. My parents' let both Reagan and me make our own career choices, and I plan to do the same with my son.

My son.

It's still so new, like I could wake from the dream at any time. Then I remember the heartache, the pain of losing Melissa, the pain that my son will never know his mother. A few quick pictures from my cell phone are all we'll have, other than her last name as his first. It seemed fitting—and let's be honest, Knox is a kickass name for my little man.

Climbing out of the truck, I head inside to find Dad sitting at my desk. His glasses are sitting on the edge of his nose while he reads something on the computer in front of him.

"What's got you so enthralled?"

"Just looking over some invoices. Everything's good to start the Robinson remodel on Monday."

"Good to hear. Thank you, Dad."

He waves his hand in the air. "You forget, I started this business," he reminds me.

"No. I also didn't forget that you retired to spend more time with Mom, yet here you are."

"Son, filling in for a week or two is no hardship to your mother and me. You have our new grandson at home to take care of. Sure, this was all sprung on us, but if you were married and had been expecting, I would've done the same thing, so stop thanking me. Now, how's my grandson? He had an appointment today, right?"

"He's growing. Dr. Harris says all is well. He has to go back in a month."

"Good to hear."

"Yeah, it's a relief."

"You're not alone in this, son. You need to lean on us."

I love this man. "Thanks, Dad. I know that, I just feel like I need to start doing it on my own. I mean, Mom and Reagan have been there each night and I appreciate it, but I have to do this. You know what I mean?"

He nods. "I do. I respect the hell out of you for that, Ridge, and I'm damn proud to be your father. Just remember that you don't *have* to do this on your own. I understand that you need time to settle in and get you and your boy into a routine. I get that. I also understand that it's okay to ask for help. Hell, your mother and I relied on your grandparents, both of them, when you kids were little. Parents need to have a life too. You need to find the balance, and we'll be here to help you do that."

"I know. I just need it to be me and him for a while. It's been a whirlwind and I just want some time with my son, to let it all sink in."

"I'll handle your mother, but Reagan is all yours." He winks.

"She's with him now. I mentioned this earlier, so I think she'll understand."

"Just remember, any time—day or night—we'll be there."

I nod, afraid to speak. Afraid the emotion of the moment will show in my voice. I'm not an overly emotional guy, but anyone who's seen me this past week would never believe that statement.

"Now, the Robinson job." Dad thankfully changes the subject. He knows, but doesn't mention it.

I swallow hard. "Yeah, the remodel."

"Yes. Mr. and Mrs. Robinson are leaving to go house-hunting in Florida in two weeks. Their plan is to sell the house here and buy a condo, so it's less maintenance, and also buy a condo in Florida. I talked to Mr. Robinson this morning, and he assures me that his daughter and son-in-law will be here and can make any necessary decisions."

"Good. Sounds like it's all under control. Do you need anything from me? I'll be back into the swing of things on Monday."

"Nope. Got it covered, son. I'll probably hang out next week and get you caught up on anything I might've forgotten. Your mother will be in Heaven spoiling that son of yours." He grins.

He acts like Mom is the one who will be doing all the spoiling. I'll let him pretend, but we both know the truth. Instead, I just smile back at him and nod in agreement.

After answering a few e-mails, I say good-bye to my dad and head to the store. Mom and Reagan have been cooking and bringing meals, but I still want to stock up on some easy foods. I also want to check out the baby section. My parents' and friends, along with Reagan, picked out everything for Knox's room, and I just want to shop for my son, for once. I have no clue what he needs or what I should even buy, but I just feel this need to get him something. I know clothes are always a good thing, but I don't know what size.

Me: Hey, I'm at the store. What size clothes does he wear?

Pathetic, I know. I have to text my sister to find out what size clothes to buy my son. Newborn, I assume? I don't want to be *that* dad; I want to know how to take care of my son on my own. I still have a hell of a lot to learn though.

Reagan: *0–3 months right now. They're a little big, but he's going to grow. Don't get newborn.*

Well, shit. Good thing I asked her.

Me: Thanks.

Slipping my phone into my pocket, I grab a cart and head toward the hygiene products. I grab body wash, deodorant, razors, shaving cream, and shampoo. From there, I head to the baby section. I can honestly say this is an all-time first for me. Pulling my phone back out of my pocket, I pull up my photo gallery, having snapped a picture of his diapers and formula before leaving today. I grab three packs of diapers, since the little guy seems to go through them like crazy. I also grab a box of wipes, because I don't want that shit on me—literally. Next stop is the formula. I add three cans to my cart and skim over all the other items. Baby food, cereal, teething biscuits. I'm overwhelmed, but I assume he's not old enough for this stuff or Mom and Reagan would've already had a supply ready to go. The next aisle over is toys and pacifiers. My little guy loves his, and it's been a lifesaver at times when I couldn't get his bottle ready fast enough. I throw another pack in the cart; it's the same as he has now, so it should be good to go. On second thought, I grab the package and read the back. Newborn. Perfect. I toss it back into the cart and wheel a little further down the aisle to the toys.

I find a set of plush car keys. The package says they're soft, which I assume is a good thing, so I pick up a few more, plus a couple other toys that the packaging assures me are good for my baby's development. I grab a couple more packs of bottles because those things are a bitch to clean; plus, the more you have the better, right? There's also this basket thing for the dishwasher—that's a must-have. I toss it in the cart as well.

The next aisle is blankets and towels, and I grab a few of each along with a pack of wash cloths, burp cloths, and receiving blankets. Cloth diapers? No, thank you. I roll right on past those.

Onesies? I didn't know that's what they were called, but he wears them. I grab a pack of eight plain white in 0–3 months and toss them into the cart, adding some socks as well. They're so damn tiny.

Turning the corner, I see the clothes. I have no clue as to what I really need, so I'm just tossing random shit into the cart. Sleepers. I know those are easy to dress him in, and who doesn't want to lie around in pajamas all day? I pick out a few and add them to the cart. I come across what looks like the baby version of sweatpants; they are so damn small I can't help the smile that tips up my lips. I grab a couple pairs, thinking he can wear them with those body suit things—onesies, I think it was?

A few more random clothing items and the cart is filling up. I'm now in the furniture, where I see a pen-looking thing that's called a Pack 'n Play. I pull out my phone to do some research. Looks like it's used to travel, with a safe place for him to sleep. Might be useful for the living room, or even the office when I need to get things done. I grab one off the shelf and slide it under the cart.

The next thing that catches my eyes is a bouncing seat. The box says it's soothing, and again I pull out my phone and research. All good reviews. I grab the one that has all the bells and whistles—literally, as it has toys attached. I slide it under the cart next to the pen thing. The next aisle is books, and I grab one about what to expect during the first year of life. Looking down, my cart is loaded with things for my son. A sense of pride fills me that I can afford to do this for him, to give him the things he needs.

With one last quick glance, I leave the baby section behind and head toward the groceries, getting milk, eggs, bread, lunch meat, chips, and frozen pizza. Laundry detergent for me and more for Knox. Mom brought some over, but you never know when you'll need it, and I don't want to run out. Those final additions have my cart overflowing—another first for me.

I head toward the front of the store, needing to get home.

I miss my little man.

Chapter 12

Kendall

Aunt Flow has decided to make her appearance a few days early. I'm cranky and irritable, and the last thing I want to do is brave the grocery store. I don't have a choice, though, since Dawn is working late today. I thought about texting her to bring some supplies home, but I've searched the house high and low and we have nothing. How is it possible that out of the two of us, we have one tampon in this entire house? I strip out of my scrubs, throw on some yoga pants and a Sam Hunt concert T-shirt, and tie my hair in a knot on top of my head.

Good enough.

It's not like I have anyone to impress.

At the store, I don't bother with a cart, just head straight for the feminine hygiene section. I grab two boxes of tampons and two boxes of panty liners and call it good, stopping at the first register to wait in line. I can't help but notice the guy in front of me. He's wearing jeans that mold to his ass, not leaving anything to the imagination, and a black

T-shirt that fits tight around his muscular arms. Tattoos peek through, running down his arm. *Wait, those tattoos look familiar. Tall, dark hair, inked . . . Please don't let it be him. Shit!* I'm not taking the chance of him seeing me like this; I look like hell, and have an entire arsenal of menstrual supplies in my arms.

I turn quickly, as though I forgot something, and bump into the cart behind me. Dammit, why is she standing so close?

"Sorry," the little old lady—who reminds me of my grandma—says.

How can I be mad about that?

"No problem, I just forgot. . . ."

"Kendall?" his deep voice rumbles from behind me.

Shit. Shit. Shit.

The little old lady winks at me. Seriously? I feel my face flush, but know I have to turn around. Sucking in a deep breath, I slowly release it as I turn.

Ridge fucking Beckett, just as I thought. Looking fine as hell and smiling at me.

"Ridge, hi," I squeak out. My hands tug on my T-shirt, wishing it were longer. I feel bloated and nasty, and I just want to wake up from this nightmare. No woman wants to be seen like this by a man who looks like Ridge.

"Hey." His eyes roam over my body from head to toe, eventually landing back on mine. "Early day?" he asks.

"Yeah, just stopping for a few things." I raise my arms and immediately drop them. What the hell am I doing? I'm sure during his appraisal of my body he saw them, but I didn't have to offer up my tampon surplus to him on a silver fucking platter.

"Yeah." He grins. "Me too." He steps to the side so I can see his cart, which is overflowing with baby supplies plus some other items piled on top.

"You do know what 'a few' means, right?" I tease him.

He blushes. Ridge fucking Beckett blushes. *I made him blush!* "Yeah, I just . . . wasn't really sure what he needed and wanted to stock up," he admits.

From the look of his cart, he bought the basics. I would've thought he and the mother had planned for this before now. "Got a little bit of everything, I see. One of the girls at work has that same bouncer; we bought it for her at her shower. She swears by it." Now I'm just rambling. Could this moment be any more embarrassing?

"Yeah, I, uh, read the reviews. They're good. I hope he likes it." A soft smile lights up his already handsome face.

"I'm sure he will." I know it's none of my business, but his situation intrigues me. I would've thought all of this was done, that she would've had a shower.

"Sir?" the cashier says.

"Sorry," Ridge replies before turning to me. "You want to go first?" He eyes the four small boxes in my arms.

"No, you go ahead." *I want to ogle you without you knowing.*

He begins placing his items on the belt, and I watch every move he makes—the flex of the muscles in his arms, the way he stacks each item as if it's his precious baby boy. I watch as he lifts a small blue bear from the cart, tucking it under one arm while he loads everything else on the belt. The bear is the final item, other than the big stuff on the bottom of his cart. It gives me that feeling—you know, the one that makes you feel like your entire body is melting into a pile of goo—seeing this man manhandle a small stuffed bear for his newborn son as if it's the most important thing in the world.

Goo. Big ole pile of mushy feel goodness right here in line at the local Walmart. Not a woman alive could resist the effect the scene before me creates.

Ridge places his bags in his cart and pays. As he's taking his receipt, he turns to me. "Good to see you again, Kendall. I guess me and the little man will be seeing you in about a month."

It takes my brain a minute to catch up; I'm still drooling over him. "Right, his one-month appointment. I'll see you then." I smile politely.

Ridge gives me a small wave and then he's gone. I place my four boxes on the belt and the cashier, a young girl, smirks at me. "He's hot," she says bluntly.

Oh, honey, you have no idea. I don't reply, just smile at her and pull out my debit card. I swipe my card, grab my bag and receipt, and head for the door. I've had enough embarrassment for one day.

At least, that's what I thought. In the parking lot, I find that big black truck I parked beside belongs to him. He's standing at the tailgate with a still-full cart, talking to a guy in another big truck. As I get closer, I see there's a Beckett Construction logo on the side.

"Kendall, hey, you remember Seth, right?" Ridge says as I approach my car.

"Seth, hi. Good to see you," I reply politely, trying like hell to hide my embarrassment.

"Kendall?" Seth asks.

"She was in Reagan's class."

"Yes!" Seth exclaims. "Sorry, darlin,' it's been a few years. Good to see you," he says with a wink.

"You too. Well, I better get going. Ridge, I'll see you soon."

He nods with a wave, and I don't give him time to say anything else as I climb into my car. Lucky for me, the spot in front of me is empty, so I put my car in drive and pull out of the lot, leaving the hotness of Ridge behind me.

Chapter 13

Ridge

Seth and I talk for a few more minutes. I try to concentrate on what he's saying, but the lovely Kendall seems to have taken up residence in my mind. She's gorgeous and sweet as hell. Fuck my life for not being able to pursue her. I love my son, but damn. I shake away thoughts of her and focus on Seth.

He and the guys are going to stop by tonight. I told him that was fine, but they needed to bring food. Apparently, their moms bought some things for Knox. I've never been more thankful for our close knit group. It's nice to know that I have so many people in my corner.

Once home, I unload all the bags, put the food items away, and go in search of my sister and my son. I find them out on the back deck, Knox sleeping soundly in one arm while Reagan holds her Kindle with the other. She's so engrossed in the book she's reading she doesn't even realize I'm watching her.

"You should be more alert when you have my son," I say.

My voice startles her and she jumps, causing Knox to open his eyes before closing them again just as quickly.

Stepping outside, I shut the patio door and walk toward them. Leaning down, I take him from her. She juts her lip out in protest, but I need to hold him.

"You weren't gone long," she comments.

"I was gone for four hours, sister." I laugh.

She grins, holding up her Kindle. "It's really good," she defends.

I just shake my head. She's always loved to read. "I stopped by the office, talked to Dad, answered a few e-mails then went to Walmart."

"How was Dad?"

"Good. He's going to talk to Mom. I just need some time with him, you know?"

"Yeah, we're just a phone call away. You got this, brother."

"Hey, I ran into Kendall."

"Really?"

"Yeah, she was behind me in line. Speaking of, I have a ton of shit—" I look down at my son sleeping in my arms. "I mean *stuff* that I need to unpack for him. You feel like helping?"

"Sure, I love all the little baby stuff. I had a blast when Mom and I went shopping for him," she admits.

I stand and lead the way into the living room, where I left the remaining bags.

"Holy shit, Ridge. Did you buy the entire store?" She laughs.

"No, but he needs stuff, and I'm his dad. It's my job to provide for him. I just got him a little bit of everything—more clothes and blankets and towels and stuff."

"I can see that." She starts unloading bags and comes across the tiny sweatpants, holding them up. "Too damn adorable."

"Tiny," I reply.

"You did good. I'll unpack these clothes and throw them in the washer."

"Thank you. I need to put his pen thing together and the bouncing seat. Can you hang out for a while? I'd like to have that done before I brave my night alone."

"You got it. It's almost time for him to eat anyway."

"I'll do it. Then I'll get started." I need as much practice as I can get; that way, when it's just me and him, I'll feel more comfortable.

I strap Knox into his car seat, not taking any chances, and carry him to the kitchen. I quickly mix up a bottle, something I've mastered in just a few short days. Little man is snoozing away, so I set the bottle next to his seat on the table and make Reagan and me a sandwich. I inhale mine, just shoving in the last bite when he starts to fuss.

Perfect timing. I got this dad thing down.

Knox takes his bottle like a champ. I piss him off when I stop to burp him, but it's for his own good. I hate to hear him cry, but I know this is important or he'll get a bellyache later; the nurses at the hospital stressed it, as has my mom and Reagan. I'm still not sure how Reagan knows so much about kids. I think it's just a woman thing. She played house growing up, feeding and taking care of her dolls while I played cowboys and Indians and pretended to have shoot-outs.

Four ounces, two burps, and a diaper change later, my little man is content and snoozing away. I fold up an old quilt and make a small square on the floor next to me, gently laying him there to nap.

Reagan comes into the room. "Hey, all the clothes and blankets and all that are in the washer. What's next?"

"I'm going to start putting stuff together. You can just relax unless he needs something."

"You don't have to tell me twice." She plops down on the couch and crosses her legs. "Carry on." She waves her hand at me.

I chuckle at her. I love my sister. Surprisingly, the bouncing seat—or bouncer, as Reagan calls it—has very little assembly; I just snap the legs in and the toys bar, and we're good to go. I add the four batteries as needed, and it roars to life. Reagan hops off the couch and picks Knox up from the floor. He stretches his little arms and legs and grunts; he was sleeping well.

"You won't sleep tonight, you little stinker," she tells him as she gently places him in the bouncer and straps him in. She turns it on and he falls right back to sleep. "He likes it." She grins.

He does seem to like it. I open the Pack 'n Play and to my surprise, it's limited assembly as well. It comes in a carrying case for travel—that's a plus. It folds open, and I lock it into place. There's a table-type piece that fits on the top.

"That's so you can change him. Say you're at the office. You don't have to lay him on the floor, or your desk, and you won't have to lean over the side. That would be awkward," Reagan explains.

"That's so handy. At least, I think it will be."

"Yep, it'll be perfect for poker night with the guys. You'll know he has a safe place to play and sleep."

"I doubt there will be many poker nights in my future."

"Why the hell not?"

"I have a baby, Reagan."

"And? You're a dad, Ridge, but you're still you. You need to have a life too."

"He's my life."

"I get that, I do, but you have to live for you too. You have to find the balance. There's nothing wrong with poker night. You just take him with you, and bring this—" she points to the Pack 'n Play "—pack a diaper bag and you're good to go. You know the guys are going to be onboard with it."

"Yeah, it's just going to take some time for me to get a routine. To feel comfortable taking him out like that on my own."

"You have the guys," she fires back.

I stare at her. "Really, Reagan? How many times have you seen them around babies?"

"Kent has a niece, and Mark's sister is pregnant with twins," she reminds me.

"I guess."

"Listen, I know you need time to adjust, but don't lose you in the process."

"It's different now, you know?"

"I get that, brother, I do. You have to find a balance. You can be his father and still have a life. One day, you'll find a woman who will love both of you. How are you going to do that if you stay closed up? You're a kick-ass dad, Ridge. Just look at all this." She waves her hand around the room. "You will stop at nothing to give him what he needs. Just remember you have needs too."

I smirk at her and she tosses a pillow at my head.

"You good here?" she asks.

"Yeah, the guys are stopping by later, bringing dinner. You can stay or come back, whatever."

"I think I'm going to go home and catch up on laundry. Stop by the shop and pay a few bills then curl up with my Kindle and finish my book. You boys have fun."

I stand and give her a hug. "Love you, sister," I say, as I kiss the top of her head.

"Yeah, yeah." She grins. "See you later."

"Later."

The house is quiet except for the soft hum of the bouncer seat that has kept my son in a deep slumber. I grab a few pillows off the couch and lie on the floor beside it. "Sleep when he does" Mom has said more times than I can count. I place my hand on his little leg and allow myself to drift off to sleep.

Chapter 14

Kendall

My phone rings, jolting me awake. Squinting to look at the clock, I see that it's only eight in the morning. It's Saturday, my day off, and I wanted to sleep in.

So much for that plan.

Reaching for the phone, I swipe at the screen and pull it to my ear. "Hello," I mumble.

"Morning, sweetheart," my dad's chipper voice greets me.

"Hey, Dad, everything okay?"

"Yes, why wouldn't it be?" he asks.

"It's early, on Saturday. My day off. I was sleeping," I grumble into the phone.

Dad chuckles. "You're wasting a beautiful day, Kendall. I do have a favor to ask you, though."

"Okay?"

"Well, Grandma and Grandpa are having the house remodeled. They leave for Florida tomorrow house-hunting, and they forgot that your mother and I will be on our cruise to Mexico. Can you check in with the builders? They know what needs to be done, but if they have any questions or run into any snags, can you handle it?"

Me? "Dad, I hate to break it to you, but I know nothing about construction."

He laughs. "I know, sweetheart, and you don't need to. The company is reputable, and they know what's expected. We really just need you to check in with them. If they have questions, you can relay them to Grandpa."

Ugh. "Sure, no problem. How often do I need to check?"

"Every few days. Your mom and I will be gone for two weeks, as you know, so it's just until we get back."

"You're lucky I love you." I can't help but smile.

"I'll make it up to you, I promise."

"I'll be thinking." I already know what that means, though. He takes care of the maintenance on my car—oil change, washing, waxing, and all that jazz. He's a chemical engineer by trade, and he says that tinkering helps him relax. I don't question it, but I do benefit from it. I'm Daddy's little girl, and not one bit ashamed of it.

I admit that the decision to move home wasn't just to get away from Cal—I also missed my parents.' Sure, it was just under a two-hour drive, but you know how it is; life gets busy, and the well-intended trips end up getting put on the back burner. I'm glad to be home. Although I wanted to sleep in, I'm glad that I'm close enough for them to depend on me. I've missed that.

"So, what do you have going on today?"

"Yard work and packing. Are we going to see you before we leave?" he asks.

"Yeah, Mom invited Dawn and me to dinner tomorrow night."

"Good. I'll see you then. Thanks, sweetheart."

"You're welcome. Give Mom a hug for me."

"Will do," he says, and the line goes dead.

I drop my phone and burrow back under the covers, but it's useless; I'm up and can't get back to sleep. I decide to get moving, hoping Dawn might want to go to the mall. This warm May weather has me ready to add to my summer wardrobe. I take my time in the shower before making my way to the kitchen, popping a bagel into the toaster just as Dawn emerges from her room.

"You're up early," she says, noticing I'm ready for the day.

"Yeah. Dad called at eight and woke me up. You got plans today?"

"Nope, you?"

"Thinking about going to the mall."

"Yes! Retail therapy. I need to update my summer wardrobe."

This is why we're best friends. We share a brain sometimes—at least, it seems that way.

"Sounds like a plan. They don't open until ten though, so we have some time."

Dawn pops her own bagel in the toaster. "We need to eat lunch at the Cheesecake Factory. That place is soooo good."

"Deal." I dive into my bagel and mentally go over my finances, working out a budget for today's shopping adventure.

Five hours later, both Dawn and I are exhausted from a full day of shopping. The pre-Memorial Day sales were in full swing, and we got some great deals.

"Feed me, woman," Dawn says dramatically.

"I'm starving too. That bagel lost its effect hours ago," I admit.

We drag our bags out to my car then head back in to the Cheesecake Factory. We're standing in line waiting for a table when I hear my name.

"Kendall."

I turn and see Reagan standing there with her mom. "Hey, stranger," I greet her. "Dawn, this is Reagan, a friend from high school, Reagan, this is my best friend and roommate, Dawn," I introduce them.

"Flat-tire girl." Reagan smirks.

Dawn laughs. "Yep, that's me. He really did save me," she insists.

"Mom, this is the girl Ridge stopped to help that night. The night of the accident." She says the last bit softly.

Her mother's eyes show recognition. "It's nice to meet you, ladies."

"Hi, how many?" the hostess asks.

"You guys want to join us?" I offer. This place is crazy packed, so it could be a while otherwise.

"We don't want to intrude," her mom replies.

"Actually, I have a table for four now. Don't know how long until another opens," the hostess offers.

"Well, if you don't mind," Reagan says.

"Not at all," Dawn assures them. "Besides, Kendall tells me that your brother has some good-looking friends, so we need to chat." She links her arm through Reagan's and we follow the hostess to our table.

I look over at her mom. "Sorry about that. She really has no filter."

"No need. You've met my children, right? Not to mention that she's right—or you are, rather. Those boys, all five of them, are more handsome than should be allowed. All good boys too," she adds.

"I have to show you this outfit," Reagan says once we're seated. She reaches down and digs through her bags. "Look at this." She holds up the smallest pair of Levi's jeans I have ever seen. With it is a short-sleeve plaid shirt. "Isn't it adorable?"

"It really is. Those jeans are too cute," I agree.

"They had shorts too." She holds up a tiny pair of blue jean shorts. "This having a nephew business is going to cause me to go bankrupt. I'm going to have to increase my schedule at the shop," she comments.

"What do you do?" Dawn asks her.

"I own my own salon on Main Street, called Reagan's." She grins.

"I am long overdue," I tell her. "I don't think I've had my hair done since moving back six months ago. It's on the to-do list."

"Six months? I can't tell; your hair is beautiful as ever. I've always wanted your hair."

"It's the curls. She can hide it. Now me, on the other hand, not so much. I went to Macy's salon, but I wasn't impressed with how she cut it. I can't get it to lay right. You up for the challenge?" Dawn asks her.

"You know it. Call me next week, and I'll work you both in. Better yet, what are you all doing tonight? We can meet at the shop later."

"You don't have to do that," I tell her.

She waves off my concern. "No problem. I've been off several days helping Ridge get settled, so it'll be good for me to get back in the swing of things before Monday."

"I'm in," Dawn announces.

Well, okay then. "All right, if you're sure?" I say.

"Positive. What's the fun of owning your own shop if you can't use it whenever you want? Meet me there at six? Give me your number, and I'll text you the address."

I rattle off my number and not a minute later my phone pings with her text. We spend the rest of our lunch catching up, she and her mom showing us the deals they got for Baby Knox. He's spoiled already. Splitting the tip, we part ways with the promise to meet Reagan at the shop at six. It gives us just enough time to run home, unload our loot from today, and change before heading back out.

WE FIND REAGAN'S shop without any trouble. I've driven past it several times and never put together who owned it. Small world.

She greets us at the door, her phone to her ear and a concerned expression on her face. "Come on in," she says, holding the door open for us. "Dammit." She hits end on the call and then calls again.

Dawn and I stand just inside the door, watching her. Whoever she's trying to call still doesn't answer.

"Sorry, guys. I've been trying to call Ridge for the last hour. He's on this 'I need to learn to do this on my own' kick, but when your sister calls you need to answer the damn phone," she rants.

"I'm sure everything is fine," I try to calm her down.

"But what if it's not? He's a new dad, new at all of this!" She dials again, placing it on speaker phone.

The loud ring echoes throughout the shop. This time, she hits ends and runs her fingers through her hair.

"Why don't we just drive over there? How far is it?" Dawn asks.

"Like fifteen minutes, at the most. You guys don't mind?"

"Not at all. I'm sure it's fine, and seeing for yourself will put you at ease," I say.

"I'll drive," Reagan states, reaching for her purse and keys from the nearby counter.

Dawn and I follow her out and wait for her to lock the shop. Within minutes, we're on our way to check on Ridge. He's probably going to wish he'd answered his phone once he sees the three of us on his doorstep.

Reagan pulls up to a sprawling brick rancher. It's well landscaped and looks every bit the family home.

"Come on," she says, climbing out of the car.

Neither Dawn nor I argue, just follow her up on the porch. She doesn't knock. Instead, she tries the door and it's unlocked, so she walks in and motions for us to do the same.

"Why are you not answering your phone?" she hisses in a low voice.

"It's on vibrate. He's been fussy, and I finally got him to sleep." Ridge's deep voice is low as he hisses back his reply.

"We dropped what we were doing to come and check on you. I was worried," Reagan whispers.

"We?"

It's then that Reagan steps out of the way and reveals Dawn and me standing behind her.

In no way am I prepared for what I see. My mouth waters and I know I'm staring, but at this moment in time, I have no fucks to give. Ridge is sitting on the couch, shirtless and sporting worn jeans with holes in them, looking sexy as hell with bare feet and his tattoos on full display. I want nothing more than to trace them with my tongue. This alone is not what's causing my girly bits to take notice though. What has my body screaming his name is his baby boy, cradled in his arms. This man—tall, dark, handsome, looking like sex personified—is holding his baby boy close to his chest.

Ovary explosion!

"Hey," he says softly, his eyes capturing mine. "Good to see you again." He chances a quick glance at Dawn, but then his eyes are right back to mine.

Is it legal for him to be this sexy?

Chapter 15

Ridge

Reagan brought the cavalry—a beautiful one, at that. I'm trying hard not to be pissed at her. I know she's worried about me and it comes from a good place, but does she think I can't take care of my son?

"What are you doing?" she asks.

I pull my eyes from the lovely Kendall and address my sister. "I told you, he was fussy. At the hospital, they said skin-to-skin contact, so I tried it and it worked."

"Why didn't you answer your phone?" I can hear the hurt in her voice. My anger instantly fades.

"I read that babies can feel tension, so I shut it off, shut out the world. My son needed me," I explain. I just about said 'Knox comes first, always,' but I don't want to hurt her any more than she already is. I love my sister, but this little guy, he's a part of me. Whatever he needs, no matter what.

"I get that, but holy fucking shit, Ridge. I was scared something happened."

"We're fine, Reagan. What are the three of you up to?" I ask, keeping my voice low.

"I ran into Kendall and Dawn at the mall today. I was meeting them at the shop to do their hair, and they got there just as I reached my manic freak-out mode. I'd been calling you for over an hour."

"I see. Well, you all might as well make yourself comfortable. The guys will be here in about an hour. There's gonna be beer, pizza, movies—you know, just a regular Saturday night with a single dad and his buddies."

Dawn laughs. Kendall has a beautiful smile that graces those pouty lips of hers.

"What do you think, ladies? Kendall? You up for seeing some of the guys?" Reagan asks her.

"She's in," Dawn speaks up.

"I'll run out and pick us up some more snacks and drinks." Reagan looks at Dawn and Kendall. "Any special requests?"

"I'll go with you, if you don't mind? Ridge, do you care if I use your kitchen? I have a craving for buffalo chicken dip," Dawn says.

"Sure, have at it."

"Great, we'll be right back." Reagan winks at me, grabs Dawn by the arm and pulls her behind her.

"I guess I'm staying here," Kendall says as the girls rush out and slam the door.

Knox stirs in my arms, and I make a mental note to smack my sister.

"He's not been sleeping?" Kendall asks, keeping her voice soft and low.

"No, he has, but not today. He's been fussy all day."

"Gassy, probably. It's common in babies. I'd be happy to take him, if you have things you need to do," she offers.

"Actually, I would love to take a shower. Are you sure you don't mind? I know you didn't sign up for babysitting."

"Please, it's no hardship to hang out with this little guy. I get my baby fix and you get to no longer smell like ass. It's a win-win." She winks at me.

She's fucking adorable.

I stand from the couch and make my way to where she's standing in the doorway. Carefully, trying not to wake him, I transfer my son from my arms to hers. Her scent invades me—sweet, just like her. "Shhh," I say softly as Knox stirs. Poor guy. He's had a rough day, for sure.

"It's okay, sweetheart, I've got you," Kendall coos to him.

Leaning down, I kiss the top of his head, his baby smell mixed with her sweet scent. I lean in to them, placing my lips next to her ear. "Thank you, sweet girl," I whisper. Standing to my full height, I hightail it out of there and to my room, needing a cold fucking shower all of a sudden. I have no business hitting on the beautiful Kendall; my life is ten shades of fucking crazy right now. I need to learn how to be a dad, take care of my son, run my business, and do it all well. I don't have time for distractions.

Must stay clear. That's my mantra.

I take my time in the shower, trying to tamp down my desire for Kendall. She's beautiful, and today when she walked in . . . There's just something about her, something I would have explored two weeks ago. Today though, I have more than just me to think of. Life is funny like that; it has a way of changing on you when you least expect it. I need to learn how to live in this new reality. I know that's what I need to do, but the beautiful woman who is downstairs taking care of my son, she's suddenly front and center in my mind. I know that I need to keep myself in check, but I can't seem to stop thinking about her all of a sudden. Figures that I would find someone who interests me at the time in my life when distractions just are not possible. I quickly finish getting dressed so I can get back to them, both of them. I may not be able to touch her, but I'm dying to get my eyes back on her.

I hear voices in the living room. When I reach the end of the hall, I see Kendall feeding Knox, looking like she's done it a million times, and Tyler is sitting close to her on the couch—too close. His arm is resting on the back of the couch behind her as he leans over and watches my son eat. It pisses me off.

"Tyler," I growl. What the fuck is wrong with me?

"Hey, man, he's got a good appetite." He motions his head toward Knox. "Of course, if I had a beautiful woman holding and feeding me I'd eat like a champ too." He winks at Kendall.

Rage. Toward one of my best friends, I feel rage. "Ty, you want to give them some space?" I'm being a dick, but fuck if I care right now.

Tyler's head snaps toward me and he furrows his brow. I raise mine to him. He knows what I'm trying to say. *Are you going to move, fucker?* I can tell by the look on his face that he's confused. *Join the club, my man.* I don't know what's come over me, but I do know that I don't want him that close to her, or flirting with her. Hell, let's just go with I don't want him near her. Period. End of.

"You getting enough rest, man?" he asks. He still hasn't moved away from her.

"Plenty," I snap, and then try another tactic. He's obviously not getting the hint. "Can you help me in the kitchen?"

"Sure, man. Kendall, you need anything?"

Fuck me! She doesn't need him to take care of her.

"I'm good, Tyler. But thank you," she says in her sweet-as-sin voice.

I watch as he removes his arm from the back of the couch, pats her knee, then finally stands to follow me into the kitchen. I turn and stalk away from him.

"What's up?" he says, taking a seat at the island.

"Not her," I say flatly.

"Come again?"

"Not her. You can't have her."

The fucker grins. "She yours?"

Yes. "No."

"One of the guys, then?"

"No," I say through clenched teeth.

He shrugs. "Fair game then, brother."

Un-fucking-believable!

"Not her, Ty." My voice is tight as I grip the counter.

"What's wrong?" he asks, looking down at my hands and then back up to meet my gaze.

I close my eyes and take a deep breath. "What's wrong?" I laugh humorlessly. "What's wrong is I'm losing my motherfucking mind. That's what's wrong."

"I'm going to need more than that," he pries.

"Drop it."

"Nope. Spill it," he bites back, an amused smirk on his face.

"Fuck off."

"Really? That's how it's going to be?"

I glare at him.

"I got nothing but time." He leans against the back of the chair and crosses his arms.

The sound of the front door opening pulls my attention. I relax when I hear Reagan's voice.

"Hey, you two." Reagan kisses Tyler on the cheek and places two shopping bags on the counter. Dawn follows suit, setting two more right beside it.

"Hi, I'm Tyler." He holds his hand out for Dawn.

"Dawn. Nice to meet you." She grins up at him.

I take a deep breath and release my grip on the counter. Maybe he'll leave Kendall alone now.

"Knock, knock." Seth's voice, although he's attempting to be quiet, carries throughout the house.

"Well, hello, beautiful," I hear him say.

"Motherfucker!" I stomp off to the living room. Are all four of my fucking horn-dog friends going to hit on her?

"You've been holding out on us," Kent says, his eyes glued to Kendall.

"Kitchen. Now," I demand.

Five sets of eyes—four large one small—stare back at me. I give my friends the look, the one that says 'do that shit now.' Once they've left the living room, I walk over to Kendall, sitting on the end of the couch.

"How you two doing?" I ask her. "You want me to take him?"

"No. I mean, not unless you have to. I love holding him. I don't usually get to snuggle them at work, and this little guy is great at snuggling." She lifts him so her lips meet his little cheek.

I should be thinking about germs, about how this girl who I've seen less than a handful of times since high school is loving on my son.

Instead, I'm thinking about how lucky my little man is to get to feel her soft lips against his skin.

I'm truly fucked! I need sleep or a night out or something. This is not me. I've lost my damn mind!

"No, you're good. I just don't want to take advantage. You're my guest, after all." I reach out and tuck a loose curl behind her ear. *Her hair feels like silk.*

"No, you're not, I like holding him, if that's okay."

"Yeah, sweet girl. That's more than okay."

"So, what are we watching?" Tyler asks.

He's leading the pack into the living room. *Fuck, I forgot that I need to warn them all away from Kendall.*

I toss the remote to Tyler and settle in next to Kendall. I can use the excuse that she has Knox. At least that's what I'm telling myself—and them—if they ask.

"I think the ladies should pick," Reagan chimes in.

"I agree," Dawn adds.

Tyler smirks. "What about you, Kendall?"

She looks up at him then down to Knox. "I'm good with whatever."

"You're hogging my nephew's cuddles." Reagan mock-glares at her.

"Hey, you left me here, that's your own fault. I'm not giving him up until Daddy says it's bedtime."

"He's hard to resist," Reagan says. "Come on, ladies first and all that," she says to Tyler.

He takes the seat next to her on the loveseat and pats her head, handing her the remote.

Seth and Kent sit on the floor, kicked back against the chair they both insisted Dawn sit in. That leaves Mark to take the seat beside me. I visibly relax knowing they won't be next to Kendall. Irrational, I know, but fuck if I can make it stop.

Chapter 16

Kendall

Baby Knox is sleeping soundly in my arms. Every once in a while, his little lip sticks out, and it's the most adorable thing ever. I try to keep my attention on him and the movie, but I'm not really sure what's going on. I may be looking at the screen, but really I'm just thinking about Ridge. About how close he's sitting to me. How his thigh rubs against mine. How incredible he smells. How, for the first time in months, my body is reacting to a man. I thought Cal had ruined me, broke my desire to ever want to go down the path of dating ever again.

"You're good with him," Ridge says, just low enough so only I can hear.

I'm lusting after him, and I'm hit with a feeling of guilt. He just lost his . . . Girlfriend? Wife? Fiancée? And here I am thinking inappropriate thoughts about how it feels to sit close to him. He's feeling out how to live without her, how to raise his son without her.

There is something seriously wrong with me.

"He's such a good baby."

"That's what they tell me, but I have nothing to gauge it on." He chuckles. "To me, he is. He hardly ever cries. He was fussy today, but it was like he just wasn't feeling it, you know?"

I nod. We all have those days, even babies.

"I'm proud of you, brother," Reagan says.

Apparently, we weren't talking as softly as we thought.

"You know him so well already. You're a good dad, Ridge," she says, a sad smile on her lips.

"You going to hog him all night? Can I take a turn?" Mark asks me. I look to Ridge for permission. Not that he would care that his friends are holding his kid, but it's not my place. Besides, I did vow to not give him up until bedtime. I was just messing with Reagan, but I wouldn't complain.

He nods. "Don't corrupt my son, Marcus." He grins.

Slowly, I slide to the edge of the couch and stand. I feel Ridge's hand on the small of my back, helping steady me. I don't look at him, afraid he'll see that as each second ticks by, I grow more attracted to him. Instead, I stop in front of Mark, lean down, and transfer Knox into his arms. I return to my seat next to Ridge, my body even more aware of him now that I don't have a baby to cuddle, to distract me.

I focus on the movie and try like hell to block out the feeling of his thigh against mine.

The night carries on, and we eat, watch movies, and even play Battle of the Sexes. The guys all take their turns holding Knox, and let me tell you, it's a sight. There is nothing like the image of a man loving on a tiny baby. It makes you have all kinds of thoughts. From all the warm tingling to 'I want to have your babies, let's start practicing.' From what I could tell, Dawn and Reagan were just as affected as I was. Although, Reagan seems to keep her attention on Tyler most of the time. I need to ask her about that later.

Ridge yawns, and I immediately feel guilty. He's been through so much in the last couple of weeks, and here we are invading his space. He should be resting while Knox is.

"We should get going," Reagan says. She must have noticed as well.

I stand. "Thank you for having us," I say to Ridge.

He stands, as well as the others, everyone stretching from sitting through the movie. "It was nice to hang out and have adult conversation."

That causes all of us to laugh.

"I'll walk you guys out." I watch as he lowers Knox into his Pack 'n Play and follows us to the front door. "Drive safe," he yells out to the guys, who are already loading up in what appears to be Kent's Jeep. All of them except Tyler.

"Kendall, a pleasure," Tyler says with a wink.

"Always." I chuckle.

"Ladies, sorry about the change of plans. Call me this week and we can set up something," Reagan says.

"Definitely, not that this change was a bad thing." Dawn fans herself with her hands. She has a flare for the dramatic at times.

"Brother, see you later." Reagan stands on her tiptoes and kisses his cheek before she and Dawn head to the car.

I step off the porch to follow them when Ridge grabs my hand. I stop and look over my shoulder at him.

"Thank you, Kendall, for tonight . . . I mean, for your help with Knox," he rambles.

I smile. "I didn't do anything but snuggle the little guy. It wasn't a hardship, trust me. Thanks for letting us invade your space."

He nods, but doesn't let go of my hand. I turn my body to face sideways and look down where his large fingers are wrapped around my wrist. My pulse is pounding from his touch. I wonder if he can feel it racing. With a gentle squeeze, he releases me, and I don't stick around. As soon as he lets go, I race down the steps and climb into the backseat of the car. Luckily for me, Tyler has been talking to the girls by his truck, and they didn't even notice that I wasn't behind them.

As I try to slow my thundering heart, I realize how wrong these feelings are. He's mourning. I'm going to Hell for the thoughts in my head about Ridge Beckett.

⁂

THE BLARE OF my alarm clock wakes me up way too early. I didn't sleep well last night, thoughts of Ridge keeping me up. One minute, I'm feeling guilty for lusting after him, considering his situation and the next, I'm imagining what those big hands would feel like running over my body.

I have to stop by my grandparents' place before heading to work, hence the reason I'm up at the ass crack of dawn. They left yesterday for Florida, and the remodel of their house starts today. What my dad thinks I can do about anything the construction company may need is beyond me, but he thinks it's necessary, so I'll be there.

Yesterday, Dawn and I spent the majority of the day at my parents.' We grilled out and just caught up. Dawn isn't close to her family, so anytime mine invite us over, she's always willing. I'm glad they all get along so well.

Just as I'm getting ready to walk out the door, she emerges from her room. My best friend is not a morning person.

"Have a good day, dear," I say over my shoulder. I don't stick around long enough for her to throw anything at my head.

It's a warm morning for May, so I open my sunroof, put on my shades, and crank up the radio. I arrive about twenty minutes earlier than Dad said I needed to and make myself at home, diving into my muffin I brought from the house. It's so calm and peaceful here. I hate that they're selling it, but I understand; they need something low maintenance like a condo that will allow them to travel back and forth with limited worry.

At seven thirty on the dot, I hear the sound of a diesel engine. *Right on time.*

I step out onto the front porch to greet them and stop in my tracks. In the driveway sits two trucks adorned with the Beckett Construction logo on each side.

Ridge.

The man of my dreams—literally—climbs out of the driver's seat, clipboard in hand. Tyler, following behind him, glances up and notices me.

"Kendall!" he yells out my name.

This causes Ridge to stop walking and look up. Tyler steps around him and continues toward me. "You live here?" Tyler asks, leaning down to kiss my cheek.

"Uh . . . no. My . . . my grandparents live here."

"Kendall," Ridge's deep voice greets me.

Looking up, I see those dark eyes of his trained on me. Tyler throws his arm over my shoulders.

"This is her grandparents' place. Small world, huh?" he says to Ridge.

"Tyler," Ridge growls. He doesn't seem too happy with him at the moment.

Tyler just chuckles and drops his arm.

"Morning." I wave awkwardly at Ridge, and a small smile tips his lips. It really is too early to be subjected to this man and that dimple. The rest of the guys are now gathered around, so I smile and wave to them as well. "So, my grandparents are out of town, as are my parents.' My dad sent me—not that I can be of much help," I explain quickly.

"No problem, we know what he wants done. Your grandfather, I mean. We do need a set of keys though," Ridge says.

"Right. Sorry, I have them. Come on in." I open the door and go inside. Grabbing the envelope on the table with the keys, I hand it to Ridge, who's now standing right next to me. "Here you go."

"Thank you. So, if something does come up, should we call you?" he asks.

"Yeah, for the next couple weeks anyway. My grandparents will be gone longer, but my dad will be back in town after that."

Ridge pulls out his phone. "Number?" he asks.

He's not asking because he's interested in you, it's for work purposes. I rattle off my number and he types it in his phone.

"Thanks, beautiful," Tyler says, shoving his phone into his pocket.

I just smile and laugh at his antics. Ridge, however, closes his eyes and takes a deep breath. "I'm not paying you to stand around," he says, irritation lacing his voice.

Tyler smacks him on the shoulder, laughing as he and the rest of the guys—who were oddly silent—head back outside.

Chapter 17

Ridge

I spent the remainder of my weekend trying to work out my reaction to Kendall in my head. Why all of a sudden do I feel this pull to her? She's beautiful, with long dark hair, and big blue eyes. There's something about her, something I can't quite figure out, but whatever it is, it pulls me to her.

Now here she is.

"Small world," I say once the guys are out of earshot.

"Yeah." She tucks a curl behind her ear. "How's Knox?"

I can feel the smile as my lips tip up. "He's good. He's with my mom. She's going to be watching him for me." I'm rambling now.

"You're lucky he's with family. Most are not that fortunate."

"Yeah, I feel bad, though. Dad's only been retired a couple of years, and I feel like I'm tying them down again."

"Doubtful. First of all, he's adorable, and from how your mom was talking this weekend, she's flying high being Grandma. Seems like your dad is as well."

"You talked to my mom?" *When was that? How did I not know this?*

"Yeah, Dawn and I had lunch with her and Reagan at the mall. I thought we told you that."

Well, shit. Reagan said she ran into them, but she didn't mention Mom being with her. Why do I hate the fact that she got to see Mom, but I wasn't there? It's not like Mom never met her—she and Reagan graduated together, and this is a small town—but still, I feel like I should have been there with her, like I should have been the one introducing her, not Reagan.

"Yeah, that's what they tell me."

"Well, if you ask my parents,' that's the point of retirement. However, I seem to be throwing a wrench into their plans." She grins.

"Not ready to settle down?" I ask. *What the hell? Why am I prying into her life?* It's none of my damn business, but I want the answer.

"That's not it. Just keep hitting roadblocks."

Her eyes seem to lose some of their sparkle. Now I want to know what—or who—the roadblock is. Or has been, anyway. Is she seeing someone? Why does the thought of her being someone else's bother me?

"Roadblocks?"

She chuckles. "Yeah, you know, dating one loser after another. Falling for the lines, finally seeing the smoke through the mirrors."

"Boyfriend?" I have to know.

"Nope."

"He's an idiot." I blurt the words out without thinking. No truer words have been said, but I still should've kept my mouth shut.

She blushes.

Sweet girl.

"I would have to agree, although I'm sure it's for different reasons."

"Regardless, he's an idiot," I say again.

"Yo, Ridge, we doing this?" Kent yells through the front door.

"I should get started. We're good here, but I'll call you if something comes up."

"Sounds good." She looks down at her watch. "Shit, I need to get to work. Have a good day, Ridge."

I watch her grab her purse and rush out of the house, and then I stare at the door for several minutes, transfixed by her. It's not until Seth comes into my line of sight that I snap out of my Kendall trance.

"You good?" he asks.

"Yep. You all got everything unloaded?"

He nods. "She's cute." He motions his head toward the door.

"She is," I agree. She's more than cute—she's fucking gorgeous, and sweet as hell.

"You think you can give me her number?"

What. The. Fuck.

"No," I growl.

"Dude, come on. It won't interfere with the job, promise."

"What's taking you two so long?" Mark asks.

"I'm just trying to get Ridge to give me Kendall's number," Seth tells him.

"Hell yes." Kent holds his fist out to Seth and they bump.

"Not fucking happening," I say, my voice low and stern.

"Come on, man. Why are you being stingy?" Tyler asks.

I glare at him.

"Unless . . ." Mark taps his finger against his chin. "You want her for yourself."

Yes. "She's a client's granddaughter," I say instead.

"I call bullshit," Seth fires back, the peanut gallery voicing their agreement.

"What the fuck business do I have getting into a relationship right now? My son needs me. I have to be both Mom and Dad, and it's a fucking daily struggle. I don't have room for anything else right now."

Kent crosses his arms over his chest. "Who said anything about a relationship?"

Fuck!

"That's not your MO, man," Mark points out.

123

"Like I said, I'm calling bullshit." Seth smirks.

"We're wasting time," I say, trying to get them off the subject of Kendall. Of me and Kendall.

"You didn't seem to mind so much when you and the sexy Kendall were chatting it up," Kent accuses.

"We have a schedule to keep," I say, ignoring his jab.

"Ridge and Kendall sitting in a tree, K-I-S-S—" Tyler sings.

I punch his shoulder, effectively cutting him off from finishing his little song. "Work," I grit out. I don't stick around for more of their ribbing, stomping out of the house to my truck. I grab the folder that holds the details of the renovations and try like hell to wrap my mind around what needs to be done. The here and now—that's what I need to concentrate on. Kendall is beautiful, but I was serious when I said I need to learn how to take care of my son. Sure, I've been doing okay up to this point, but it's been a week. One whole week, and only three of those days did I have him on my own. It's tiring and scary as hell. I'm man enough to admit that.

I need to learn how to take care of him, make sure he has what he needs. Maybe then I can live a little for me. Right now, though, I live for him—my little man.

Chapter 18

Kendall

I've managed to avoid my grandparents' house all week. After Monday and seeing Ridge, I decided to let them do their thing. Dad wanted me to check on them, but I trust Ridge and his crew. In my defense, on Wednesday I had all intentions of going over there, but Reagan called and mentioned she was going to Ridge's later that night to see Knox. I asked her to ask him if he needed anything. She texted me a couple hours later; he, of course, said no. And just like that, I had successfully filled my obligation to my dad, without having to actually see Ridge. Score!

Today, however, I have to go. Grandpa called me first thing this morning and asked to send him pictures. I'm sure it's just demolition, but he still wants to see them. Mom got him and Grandma a smartphone for Christmas, and believe it or not, they're doing better with it than I ever thought they would.

I'm off work today, since I work Saturday this week, which means I don't have work as an excuse. I stay in my room until I hear Dawn leave for the day. Once the door clicks shut, I climb my procrastinating ass out of bed and head to the shower. I take my time, enjoying the hot spray, not getting out until I feel the water turn cold. Dressing in a pair of jean capris and an old Def Leppard concert T-shirt, I blow-dry my hair and pull it into a topknot. I don't want to appear to try too hard. Although, with all my curls, the style is cute, but I would never admit that.

After a quick breakfast that consists of a bagel and cream cheese, I slide into my flip-flops, grab my purse, keys, phone and hit the road. On the drive over, I mentally prepare myself to see Ridge. I have to keep reminding myself that he's mourning and his life is chaos right now; I should be offering my support, not thinking of ways to get him in my bed. Not to mention that those thoughts aren't me—well, not usually. For Ridge Beckett, I can make an exception.

Pulling into my grandparents' driveway, I see both Beckett Construction trucks. I don't see any of the guys, but the sound of power tools lets me know they are indeed inside the house. I'm excited to see what they've done. Grandma insisted the house be 'modernized' before they put it on the market. My parents' agreed that if it were 'move-in ready,' they would get a much better price for it.

Making my way inside, I follow the noise to the kitchen and see Kent, Mark and Tyler. The three of them have their shirts off as they work together to install the new hardwood floor. The kitchen is gutted of all cabinets and flooring, but the image of the three hot guys bending over distracts me from the sadness that my grandparents are doing this to sell and move to another state.

I stand just inside the doorway and openly stare at them. The music is loud so they don't know I'm here, and I'm taking full advantage of the view. I walk further into the room, getting ready to alert them to my presence, when Kent stands and grabs another piece of flooring. He holds it on his shoulders, swinging around. I feel two large hands grab my hips and pull me out of the way. I land with a humph against a firm chest.

"Careful, sweet girl," a deep voice whispers in my ear.

I shiver, though I'm not cold—no, his hard body pressed against me ensures that. It's all Ridge causing my body to react this way.

"Ridge." His name falls from my lips in what sounds like a breathy moan. So much for the pep talk on the drive over.

His grip on my hips tightens. "You need to be careful around here. I don't need you getting hurt."

I swallow hard, trying to control my body's reaction to him. "You all have been busy," I say, my voice barely above a whisper.

"We have." His lips are still next to my ear, his hands still on my hips.

"Well, look who it is. Hey, Kendall," Seth says from beside me.

I turn my head to look at him, which places Ridge's lips next to my cheek. "S-Seth," I manage to greet him.

He smirks then reaches out and grabs my hand, giving a gentle tug. Ridge is two steps ahead of him, his firm grip preventing my body from moving. Seth throws his head back in laughter.

"What the . . . ? Oh, hey, Kendall," Mark says.

This causes Kent and Tyler to turn, and my face heats when their eyes roam over me in Ridge's possessive hold. I move to step away, and he holds me still.

"No," his gruff voice whispers.

"What brings you by? You missing me?" Tyler asks, walking toward us.

"I . . . um . . . My, uh, grandpa wanted to see some pictures of the remodel. He asked me to stop by." I hold up my phone to prove that's my true motivation for being there.

"Here, let me." Tyler reaches for the phone and grabs it from my hands.

I watch as he swipes the screen, and I regret not having a password. I stand frozen with the sexy Ridge Beckett holding me against him, while one of his hot best friends and employees makes himself comfortable as he sifts through my cell phone. A slow grin tips his lips, and then I hear his phone beep in his pocket. Tyler looks up. "You never know when I might need some company for dinner. I hate eating alone." He bites his lip to keep from grinning.

He texted himself so he would have my number. Tyler is hot, but he doesn't make me shiver in eighty-degree temperatures. He doesn't have my knees locking and refusing to move from his grip of my hips. Sure, Ridge's hold is tight, but I didn't exactly put up much effort to escape.

It was all for show. I'll stand here as long as he does, soaking up his heat, the feel of his hands on my waist. The way his fingers slip just under my T-shirt, his thumb lightly caressing my bare skin. Yep, I'm good right here.

"What the fuck?" Ridge growls. "Did you just send yourself a text from her phone?"

Tyler's grin grows wider. "Good, right?" he asks.

"Motherfucker," Ridge swears under his breath.

I can feel the tension rolling off him in waves. This time, when I try to step away, he releases a heavy sigh and lets me. "I can take the pictures," I tell Tyler, holding my hand out for my phone. He winks and hands it back to me.

I quickly grab it and pull up the camera app. I step further away from Ridge, and it's as though my body can feel the separation. I ache to be back in his arms. Saving me from being hit in the head, holding me for real—at this point, I'll take whatever I can get.

"Watch your step," Ridge tells me.

Looking down, I see the uneven terrain of the flooring. It's an inch at the most. I look back up and find his eyes locked on me. His stare is intense and a little intimidating. Not intimidating like Cal, no. Ridge's intense is . . . sexy and all-consuming. In the best of ways.

Chapter 19

Ridge

What is it about Kendall that makes me forget everything else but her? When she's near me, the chaos that runs through my head on a daily basis quiets down. The stress of raising Knox on my own, the worry of being able to give him what he needs, the love of both parents—that all fades into the background to simmer while in the presence of Kendall Dawson. It's not just that; I also seem to forget how to act when she's around. Although I don't know any man who, given the opportunity to have his hands on her curves, to be able to trace her bare skin, wouldn't have reacted the same way. I didn't want to let go. Leave it to my band of brothers from different mothers to bring me back to reality.

"Time for a break," I tell them, not tearing my eyes away from Kendall. I can't. I hear them snicker while their heavy-booted feet carry them out the door. I don't think either of us takes a breath, waiting for them to leave.

"How was your week?" she asks, breaking eye contact and looking down at the phone in her hands.

I thought about you all week. "Good. Busy. Just taking it one day at a time." I don't know if she meant here at her grandparents' place or at home with Knox, but I gave her both. I'm exhausted from middle-of-the-night feedings, and work is stressful when it lies on your shoulders and those shoulders are exhausted from the weight of the world. "How about yours? I thought I would've seen you around here before now." Hoped is more like it. I was disappointed when Reagan said she talked to Kendall earlier on Wednesday and she asked her to check in with me about the job. I wanted to call her, text her and demand she ask me myself, telling myself it's not because I wanted to hear her voice or read her words.

"Same old."

"You have plans tonight?" *What the fuck am I doing?*

"No, I work tomorrow. It'll be a quiet night in for me."

I chuckle. "Me too. Little man isn't much for conversation these days."

She grins. "He's adorable. Don't worry, he'll be chatting your head off soon enough."

"That's what I hear. To hear my parents' tell it, if I blink I'll miss him growing up."

"I've heard that." She looks around the demolished kitchen. "So, things good here? Do you need me for anything?"

Nope, just you. "We're good. It looks rough now, but I promise when we're through it will be magazine-worthy."

A sad smile crosses her face. "I love this house. The big backyard. I have so many memories of my childhood here. Mom and Dad worked a lot, so I stayed with my grandparents a lot. I'm sad that they're selling."

"Great view," I say, commenting on the backyard that has her rapt attention through the kitchen window.

"I'll get out of your hair. I have a few errands to run today, and then I'm parking it on the couch with a book."

She heads toward the door, and I want to reach out for her as she passes and demand she stay here and talk to me. I grip my fists tightly to keep from doing just that. I turn and follow her like a puppy out of the house, not bothering to look at the guys as we head to her car. Instead, I keep my eyes trained on her ass, those long, tanned legs and the gentle sway of her hips.

I should have been paying attention to where I was walking, because she stops suddenly and I barrel into her. My hands land on her hips, keeping her from falling. Keeping her close. She smells incredible, sweet like honey. I rest my chin on the top of her head and soak up the feel of her in my arms. I'm sure any minute now she's going to pull away from me.

"Ridge," she whispers.

Instantly, my cock is hard. Her fine ass pressed against me, my name falling from her lips—how the fuck am I supposed to resist that? "Kendall," I growl, turned the fuck on.

"I-I should go."

Fuck. I know she's right; plus, I have work to do. I'm not getting paid to try and fuck the granddaughter of the home owner, but I want to. Oh, how I want to, though. Instead, I bring my mouth next to her ear. "Drive safe, sweet girl." My lips land on her cheek and then I step away. I have to make myself release her. She doesn't bolt like I expect her to, just stands stock still, the only movement the rapid rise and fall of her chest. She's just as affected; her body confirmed it.

I watch as she takes a deep breath and slowly releases it. Turning to look over her shoulder, those baby blues lock on me. "Good-bye, Ridge," she murmurs.

I don't get time to reply as she quickly turns around and takes the final few steps to her car. I stand there like a lovesick fool and watch her drive away.

"Break's over," one of the guys' yells—I think it's Mark.

I'm not ready for their mocking. They're going to give me shit about this for the rest of the day. I knew that, but it didn't stop me. There's just something about her that reels me in. I slowly turn and walk back toward the house, not that getting there any slower is going to prevent what my friends have in store for me.

"You good, man? You need a tissue or something?" Kent asks. He's trying to keep a straight face.

"Trouble in paradise?" Seth chimes in.

"I bet I can get her to say yes to a date before you can," Tyler says, pulling his phone out of his pocket.

"Don't even fucking think about it," I warn him.

"She's fair game, brother. Unless you're calling dibs," he fires back.

Yes, I'm fucking calling dibs! "Can we just agree that she's not available?"

"Fuck, man. Have you seen her? Why the hell would we let her get away? One of us—" Mark points around the group "—needs to hit that."

"Not fucking happening." My voice is low and stern. Not that my friends are the least bit affected. No, the assholes laugh at me.

"One of us has to call dibs for the rest to back off," Kent states, reminding us of the pact we made years ago.

Mark opens his mouth, "I—"

"Mine," I spit out, interrupting him. No way will I let them have her; she's too sweet for any of them. Too sweet for me. They've forced my hand, but that doesn't mean I have to act on it. I called dibs, which means they leave her be.

"Remember, you can't be messing with anyone else after calling dibs. That happens, she's up for grabs. And she's not an ex, so . . ." Seth trails off, but I know what comes next.

Son of a bitch! I forgot that small aspect to the pact. Fuck. Taking a deep breath, I close my eyes and try to think this through. It's not like I'm out in the dating pool at the moment, and it won't be hard to stay away from women in general. I have a newborn son to raise. I'm in so fucking far over my head it's not even funny. I have too much to learn to let a woman distract me. He's depending on me.

"Noted," I finally say. The four of them are wearing matching smirks. Fuckers, they knew what they were doing. "Get your lazy asses back to work."

They do as I say, but not without riding my ass about my girlfriend.

What the hell did I get myself into?

Chapter 20

Kendall

What the hell was that? I can still feel his body next to mine, the feel of his lips against my skin. The touch was feather-light, but the impact it had on my body was apparently a lasting impression. I've just finished my final errand, having already gone to the bank, the post office, and the grocery store. It's mid-afternoon and my body is still calling for his. How is that even possible? And that voice, the deep timbre next to me ear. The way he calls me 'sweet girl.' Apparently, my body is telling me that taking a hiatus from men is not what it wants. I've got to get this attraction for him under control.

Grabbing a bag of chips and a bottle of water, I settle on the couch with the remote. I was going to read, but I think it's wise to watch some TV instead; those book boyfriends of mine remind me too much of Ridge. I need to learn to deal with this . . . whatever it is before I go adding any more fantasies in my head. Then again, who needs the fantasy when I still remember the feel of his chin resting on my head, his hands on my hips . . . Yeah, TV is a much better option.

I settle for getting caught up on episodes of *Lip Sync Battle* on my DVR. No romance there, just laugh-out-loud ridiculousness. I love it.

Hours later, my stomach growls. My DVR selection served its purpose to distract me from Ridge; I feel like I have a better handle on this than before. He's hot as hell and a nice guy, but I swore off men for a while, and I need to stick to that. After my disastrous relationship with Cal, I need the break. Ridge needs one as well.

I'm in the kitchen making a turkey sandwich when my cell rings. I run into the living room to get it. "Hey, I'm not coming straight home," Dawn's voice greets me. "Some of the girls and I are going to grab something to eat. Want to meet us?"

"No, I'm good. I'm actually making a sandwich now."

"You sure?"

"Positive. I think I'm going to turn in early tonight anyway. I'm having a lazy day."

"Okay. Well, if you change your mind, we're going to the Mexican place just down the street from the office."

"I'm good."

"All right, see you later."

I go back to my food, adding lettuce and tomato. My mouth waters and my stomach growls yet again, reminding me I've had nothing but junk today. I grab my plate, another bottle of water, and some more chips and head back to the living room. Just as I get settled on the couch, my phone rings again, and I curse the fact that I left it in the kitchen. Setting my plate on the table, I run back to the kitchen and swipe the screen without even looking.

"Hello," I say breathlessly.

"Kendall?" Reagan's voice comes over the line. She sounds confused.

"Yeah, sorry. I had to run to get to my phone. What's up?"

She laughs. "Been there. So, the reason I'm calling—No, wait, I'm on the phone," she says to someone else. "Sorry about that. Ridge is here to pick Knox up. Anyway, I wanted to invite you and Dawn to the Memorial Day get-together my parents' have every year. It's a good time. Dad usually sets off fireworks, because he loves them." She laughs.

"Anyway, there are always a ton of people here, and it would give us the chance to hang out again."

Ridge will be there. Count me in! "Sure, that sounds fun. I'll run it past Dawn, but as far as I know we didn't have anything going on. Thanks for the invite. What should we bring?"

"Nothing. Mom goes overboard every year, so there's always way too much food left over. Just bring your swimsuits for the pool or hot tub. Other than that, unless you have a specific drink you want, just bring you."

"Sounds good, thanks."

"No problem. Okay, I better get off here. Ridge is already taking Knox out to the truck, and I forgot to tell him that his bottles were in the dishwasher. Talk to you soon." With that, she hangs up.

I shouldn't be this happy or excited that an old friend from high school invited me to a holiday cookout. I've got two weeks to learn how to deal with my body's reaction to Ridge. Now to just figure out how to do that.

I take my seat on the couch and dive into my dinner. The TV is on, but I have no clue what I'm watching, my mind wandering to earlier today. Maybe it's not Ridge that's causing my body to betray me. Maybe I just need to put myself back out there, go on a date.

I finish my sandwich and fight to keep my focus on a Lifetime movie, but I give up after an hour and decide to go to bed. As soon as I slide under the covers, my cell alerts me to a text message. I assume it's Dawn, letting me know she's on her way home.

It's not. It's Ridge.

I stare at his name on the screen until it goes dark, then hit the Home button again, just so I can make sure my mind isn't playing tricks on me.

One photo attachment.

What the hell?

I slide my finger across the screen to open his message. It's a picture of the kitchen. The floor is completely finished, and it looks really good. I save the picture and make a mental note to send it to my grandparents in the morning.

Ping. Another message.

Ridge: Thought you might want to send them an update.

Me: *I do. It looks great.*

Ridge: Thanks.

Me: *Thanks for the picture. They're going to love it.*

Ridge: You're welcome.

Me: *Good night, Ridge.*

Ridge: Good night, sweet girl.

The smile on my face is huge. Who wouldn't be smiling getting a text from the hotness that is Ridge Beckett? I place my phone on the nightstand and drift off to sleep with thoughts of him and his hands all over me.

⁂

I'M AT THE office an hour early. With being off yesterday, I wanted to be able to check my e-mails and go through the pile that's always waiting for me on my desk after a day off. I get lost in the daily grind getting caught up. It's not until I hear voices down the hall that I realize that it's time to start the day for real. I'm covering today for one of the girls. She works every Saturday, but this week, her son had something going on, so I told her I would cover for her. It gave me yesterday off, which was nice.

The schedule is filling quickly as I work on keeping the patients roomed. This keeps the doctors happy, which makes everyone else happy. There is a small break in the schedule. This gives me time to scope out the rest of the day. Scrolling through the patient list, I stop when I see his name.

Knox Beckett.

I open his chart to view the chief complaint. It looks like he's been fussy for a few days. Poor guy. Last weekend, Ridge had said he'd been off all day. He's my last patient before lunch, so that will give me the opportunity to take my time. Pathetic right? Excited to delay their visit just to be with him, both of them really. That baby boy is too precious for words.

The rest of my morning seems to drag on. I keep watching the clock wishing for time to move faster.

Finally, the little green bubble beside his name, letting me know that they've checked in appears. I waste no time.

"Knox," I say to the waiting room.

Ridge stands. His inked arms grip the baby carrier as he walks toward me. "Kendall," he says. It's almost like I hear relief in his voice.

"Hey." My voice is all breathy, and I can feel my face flush with embarrassment. *Get it together, Dawson!* "We're going to be in room four," I say, walking along behind them. Once in the room, I shut the door for patient confidentiality and pull up Knox's chart on the computer. "So, what's going on with the little guy?" I ask, trying like hell to remain professional.

Ridge runs one hand through his hair, while the other rests on Knox's seat that is on the exam table. "He's been fussy. I thought maybe it was just me and that he could tell I was nervous, you know? But then Mom said he's been that way for her too."

"Any changes in the household? Wet diapers? Bowel movements?" I fire off a round of questions. Ridge answers them all and just as we finish, Knox starts to fuss. I watch as Ridge carefully lifts him from his seat and lays him against his chest. He's patting his back and bouncing him a little in his arms to try to soothe him. His efforts are wasted as Knox starts to cry. I can see that Ridge is exhausted, so I step in. "Can I hold him? You look like you could use a break."

He gives me a small smile. "Is that in your job description?"

Shit. "I—"

Ridge chuckles softly. "I'm kidding, Kendall. Are you sure you won't get in trouble?"

"Never, gimme." I hold my arms out. He transfers him to me, not before his hand rubs across my boob. I don't dare look up, just keep my eyes trained on Knox. "Hey, handsome." I keep my voice low and even. "I'm sorry you're not feeling well." Knox whimpers but his cries have quieted down.

"He hates me," Ridge says, his voice defeated.

"He doesn't hate you. Babies can sense your emotions. He knows that you're exhausted. He doesn't know how to handle that. It makes him irritable. Besides, you said that he was fussy with your mom as well," I point out.

He doesn't say anything, so neither do I, at least not to him. I speak softly to Knox, letting my voice help soothe him.

"You're good with him," Ridge finally says.

"So are you. Don't forget I've seen you in full force dad mode. We all have good days and bad days, Ridge. Especially since this little guy can't tell you what's wrong."

"Yeah," he agrees.

"Knock, Knock," Dr. Harris says, entering the room. He eyes me holding Knox.

"Sorry, I'll just—"

"No, stay." Ridge's request leaves no room for negotiation.

"You two know each other?" Dr. Harris asks.

"Yes. I graduated with his sister, Reagan."

He nods. "All right, well what seems to be going on with Mr. Knox these days?" he asks, washing his hands.

Ridge tells him how Knox has been fussy, and basically every detail of the last week. And he thinks he's bad at this dad gig. I tune them out as I hum softly to Knox, rubbing his back.

"Kendall," Dr. Harris says.

I turn to face him. He's wearing an odd expression, but Ridge is wearing a smile. He's so damn sexy. *Focus, Kendall.* "Yeah," I answer him.

"Can I examine my patient now?" Dr. Harris smirks.

Shit. I nod and hand Knox over to him. I decide that I should leave them to it and reach for the door handle. Ridge, who is sitting in the chair next to the door, reaches out and grabs my arm. He doesn't say a word, but the look in his eyes is pleading. He's been telling his mom and Reagan that he can do this on his own and he can, but I can see it plain as day that he doesn't want to be alone. I smile, letting him know we are on the same page. Instead of taking the seat next to him, I lean against the counter and watch as Dr. Harris examines Knox and asks Ridge a few more questions.

"So, I think we should switch his formula. I hear some bubbles in there." He gently pats Knox's belly. "It's common in infants. Let's try this sensitive formula." He pulls a pad of paper out of his pocket. "Here's the name. All major retailers should carry it. Kendall, why don't you check the supply closet to see if we have a sample we can give him until he can get to the store."

I nod my agreement and quietly leave the room. I hear Ridge ask, "So he's okay?" just as I close the door. He's a good man. A man who is dealing with being a father for the first time all on his own, and he loves his son. If I wasn't already over-the-top attracted to him, that would have sent me over the edge.

I meet Dr. Harris coming out of the room. "He's all set once you give him the sample. I'm off to lunch with Helen. See you in an hour."

I knock lightly and then push open the door. "Here you go. I brought two cans. We have a ton of it back there. That will also give you some time to see if this helps his issue before you invest a lot of money into buying formula that doesn't quite work with his system. If this one doesn't work, don't get discouraged. There are many more we can try."

"Thank you." He finishes strapping Knox into his seat before looking up at me. "Lunch time?" he asks.

I look at my watch. Why, I have no clue. Of course I know it's lunch time. "Yeah, days almost over."

He picks Knox's seat up from the exam table. "Can you join us?" he asks, motioning with his head down to his slumbering son.

Do I? Is spending more time with him a good idea? I already think about him way more than I should. "Yes," falls from my lips before I can contemplate it even further. I guess that settles that. "How about a drive-thru? I've got a few things I'll need to finish up before we start with afternoon patients. I have about thirty minutes." *I spent my morning thinking about the two of you and got behind.*

"Anything you want. We can take my truck since I have the car seat."

"Okay. Just let me grab my purse."

"You don't need it."

"Uh, yeah I do." I laugh. "I mean, unless you've changed your mind."

"No. I didn't and you won't. I asked you to lunch. It's on me. So unless there is something else in your purse that you have to have in the next thirty minutes, we're good to go." With one arm bent to carry Knox, the other presses on the small of my back. "Time's wasting, sweet girl," he says next to my ear.

I fight back the bolt of electricity from the heat of his touch and let him guide us out of the building and to his truck.

"Where to?"

"I'm thinking . . . Taco Bell," I suggest.

"Sounds good to me. So how has your day been?"

"So far so good. Although, I will admit that once I saw that Knox was on the schedule, it began to drag." Why I just told him that I don't know. It's like my nerves are causing me to spill my guts.

"How so?"

Great. Now I have to explain it. "Just excited to see you guys," I say honestly.

He doesn't say anything, just reaches over and rests his hand on my thigh. My scrubs are thin and the heat from his touch is searing. He leaves his hand there while he orders, only removing it to pay, then quickly places it in the exact same spot.

He drives us next door to a church parking lot where we take off our seat belts and devour our lunch. "So, any big plans for the weekend?" he asks.

"Nope. Dawn and I are going to stay in and have a movie night. You?"

"Nah, with the little man being so fussy, we really just need the sleep."

"Why don't you see if your mom or Reagan will watch him for a few hours while you get a nap."

"I can't do it," he says firmly.

Reaching out, I place my hand on his arm. I wait for him to look at me before speaking. "Of course you can. You're an amazing dad, Ridge. No one would fault you for needing a little help now and then. I could even. . . ."

"Thank you, but we got this," he responds, looking into the back seat where Knox is now sleeping peacefully.

"So, how is the house coming?" I change the subject, not wanting to get him upset with me or just agitated in general. He seems calm and both he and Knox need that right now. We chat for another ten minutes about random things. It's nothing and it's everything.

"I guess I need to get you back."

"Yeah." I sigh. "Duty calls and all that." He chuckles. I gather our trash and put it all in one bag, so I can throw it away at the office. Ridge starts the truck, pulls out of the lot and his hand, as soon as he has the truck in gear, rests on my thigh. It's confusing and stressful, and I never want to leave this truck.

"Thank you for lunch," I say, climbing out.

"Always, sweet girl." He winks.

I give him a bright smile. "Give him a kiss from me," I say and quietly shut the door. I turn and walk away before I won't allow myself to. Ridge Beckett the man is tempting as hell. Ridge Beckett single daddy is almost impossible to resist.

❊❊❊

THE REST OF my weekend flows by. Dawn and I just hung out Saturday night at the house. We had our wild days in college; now it's Netflix and Ben and Jerry's—at least that's how it's been since we moved here. We often go to my parents' for Sunday dinner, but they're still out of town until Friday. I haven't talked to them, but Mom sent me an e-mail with a few pictures. They look like they are having a great time.

Today starts the work week. I've gone back and forth a thousand times on whether or not I'm going to stop by my grandparents' on the way to work. Considering I was just there on Friday, and I spent time with him on Saturday, I'm going to wait until tomorrow. I'll drop in on Tuesday and Thursday. Dad will be back on Friday, and then I'm off the hook. I have to admit that makes me a little sad.

"We riding together today?" I ask Dawn.

"Works for me. We are on the same shift right? Hell, I can never remember." She walks to the fridge and checks the staff schedule we keep there. "Yep, we're both eight to five today."

"Even better. You about ready to go?"

"Yeah, just let me get my watch and shoes and I'm good," she says, rinsing out her juice glass.

Work is uneventful, just the daily grind. That is until my phone alerts me to a text message while I'm sitting at my desk, working on the staff schedule for next month. Pulling my phone out of my purse, I see it's from Ridge.

Ridge: Delivery.

Attached is a picture of several boxes stacked up in the living room.

Ridge: Cabinets, sweet girl.

Me: Right. I should've known that. Looks like a busy day.

Ridge: Busy is good. Keeps the mind busy.

Me: My mind is plenty busy. Staff schedule.

I'm not sure why I tell him what I'm doing. It's not like he cares about my staffing schedule.

Ridge: Ahh. Good luck.

Me: Thanks.

I slide my phone back into my purse and try to focus on the schedule. *Distracting sexy man.*

Chapter 21

Ridge

I jolt at the sound of my son crying. Looking over at the alarm clock, I see that he slept for six straight hours. My alarm is supposed to go off in ten minutes. Reaching over, I turn it off. I feel like a new man. Climbing out of bed, I pad to Knox's room in nothing but my boxer briefs. As I get closer, his cries grow louder; when I open the door, they're deafening.

I reach into his crib and pick him up. "Hey, little man. You're belly feeling better? You hungry?" He continues to cry, which is not his usual MO; usually he quiets down when I pick him up. I lay him on the changing table, and as soon as I pull off his sleeper I can smell why. At least I think that's why. I'm still learning all his cries. It's so fucking hard when he can't tell me what he needs. I have to guess and—let's be straight here—I'm clueless.

I strip him out of his sleeper and see his diaper has indeed leaked. He has shit all over his legs.

Awesome.

"No wonder you're so pissed, bud. Let's get you cleaned up." I take off his diaper and he kicks his little legs, covering them in shit as well. All right then, looks like a bath is in order. I remove the shitty diaper and toss it into the . . . bucket . . . thing Reagan said I had to have to help with the smell. Not sure it's going to be able to do much for the bomb I just gave it, though. Since the sheet on the changing table is shit-splattered already, I pull it off the rest of the way, wrap it around him and head toward the bathroom.

Although not as loud, the little guy is still pissed off. Can't say I blame him; I'd be pissed too if I had shit all over me. Once in the bathroom, I turn on the water to let it warm, then grab his baby tub and the little yellow duck that tells me the water is the right temperature. Reaching down, I run my hand under the water to see if it's close. It's still a little cool.

"Shhh, it's okay. Daddy's got you. We're going to get you all cleaned up, and then get your belly full, I promise," I try to console him. I'm gently bouncing him in my arms when I feel warmth and wetness on my chest. "What the . . . ?" Pulling him away from my body, I see he's pissed all over me, all over both of us. Looking down at my son, mad-as-hell face scrunched up, red and wrinkled as he wails, I want to cry with him. Instead, I take a deep breath and slowly release it. "I got you, bud. Shhhh, I got you."

I pull his baby tub out of the bathtub and set it on the bath mat. Checking the temperature with the little duck, I see the water is ready. I lay Knox down in his tub, which pisses him off even more. Quickly, I remove my boxer briefs, strip him out of his sheet, hold him against my chest, lift the lever to turn the shower on and climb in under the spray.

Holding Knox in one arm, I use the other to bring the detachable shower head down. I turn it to the gentlest stream option, using my leg as leverage. Once I have it where I want it, I slowly rinse us both off. Once we're both free of the shit and piss we were coated in, I reach for the baby wash. "Looks like Daddy will be smelling powder fresh today," I tell him.

His little lip quivers, and I'm not sure if he's cold or if it's the result of the cry-fest he just had. Either way, I work fast, lathering us both up as good as I can with one hand. I even manage to use it on my hair one-handed. Once we're both soaped up, I rinse us off quickly and step out of the shower.

The lip quiver gets worse, so I wrap him in a towel and take off for his room. I'm dripping wet, but I didn't bring a diaper and the little guy is cold. I have him dried and in a diaper in no time with no further mishaps. Dressing him in another sleeper because they're easy, I use his towel to dry my hair and body.

"All right, little man. Daddy needs some underwear, and then we'll get you fed." In my room, I lay him in the center of my bed, making quick work of slipping into a pair of boxer briefs and tossing the towel in the hamper. "Let's get some breakfast," I tell him when I pick him up. I can still see the slight quiver of his little lip so I hold him closer, still not sure if it's cold or sadness.

I've gotten pretty good at one-handed bottle-making, so I don't even attempt to lay him down; I hate it when he cries, and right now he's content. I hear the coffeemaker turn on just as I pull his bottle out to check the temperature. Perfect. My brew will be done just as he finishes his. I settle into the couch and the little guy begins to gulp. "Slow down, bud. You don't want a bellyache. Take it from me, that shit is not fun."

If Mom or Reagan were here, they would give me hell for cussing in front of him, but come on, he can't repeat it. I look down at him while he eats. I've never known this feeling in my heart, the way it swells every time I look at him. To love your child is a feeling that unless you experience it for yourself, you will never understand the meaning. It's moments like these, like this morning, where he and I get through it together, which make me think that although unexpected, my little man and I will learn to live with our new reality.

By the time he finishes his bottle, he's sound asleep. I take him to his room and place him back in his bed so I can get us both ready to head out today. In my room, I grab the baby monitor and carry it with me as I get dressed, then head to the kitchen to get his bottles ready for Mom's. Once that's done, I go back to his room and as quiet as I can, pack his bag. Diapers, wipes, toys—not that he plays with them—clothes, and just for good measure I throw in extra of all of it. You never can be too careful. I throw his bag over my shoulder and gently lift him from his crib. Downstairs, I strap him into his car seat then gather the diaper and bottle bags. I tap my back pocket to make sure I have my wallet, then the front to check for my phone and keys.

I stop and take a deep breath, and that's when the smell of coffee hits me. I dig through the cabinet, find the biggest travel mug I can, and fill it up. Not willing to leave him in the house alone, I throw both bags over my shoulder, picking up his carrier with the same arm. Taking my keys out of my pocket, I grab my large steaming mug of coffee. It's a little challenging to get the door shut, so I end up setting Knox's carrier on the front porch so I can pull it closed. Placing my coffee on the bed of the truck, I open the door, click the baby seat into place, and throw the bags on the floor. Checking the seat just to make sure it's secure, I grab my coffee and we're on the way to Grandma's.

✻✻✻

I ARRIVE TO the job site fifteen minutes late. Normally, this isn't a big issue, but today it is. It's a big fucking issue. When I pull in, I park behind Kendall. *She's here with them. Are they hitting on her? Did they see through my bullshit of saying I was staking my claim? Fuck!* I throw the truck in park, pull the keys from the ignition, and stalk to the house.

What I find has me clenching my fists at my sides. I have to remind myself that these guys are my best friends, and she's not mine. Kendall has her head thrown back laughing, my four best friends laughing and watching her like she's the star of every fucking wet dream they've ever had. She has her hand on Tyler's shoulder as if she needs him to hold her up. Fuck that, I should be the one holding her up if she needs it.

I stalk into the room and stand behind her. "Morning," I say. My voice is terser than I want it to be, but it is what it is. She stops laughing and turns her head at the sound of my voice.

"Ridge." She breathes my name like a fucking caress.

"Didn't know you were stopping by today." Although I'd hoped she would.

"Yeah, just wanted to check in."

"Dude, you fucking smell like little man." Kent leans over and sniffs me.

"Yeah, we had a diaper malfunction so a bath was required, then he pissed on both of us so I just got in the shower with him. I used his bath stuff too, since I couldn't use mine on him." I shrug.

"I love the baby smell." Kendall blushes.

"Fuck, that shit is a chic magnet. We need to get some," Seth says.

"Good luck with that," I say under my breath. Kendall hears me, though, because her eyes sparkle with laughter. Those blue eyes of hers

146

light up the room. She's fucking gorgeous.

"We should totally bring him out with us one night. The smell might work, but having the real thing with us? Guaranteed pussy, my man," Mark suggests.

I reach over and smack him on the back at the head at the same time Kendall gasps.

"You can't do that." She turns to look at me. "You ever need a sitter, you call me before taking him with you." Her hand is on her hip and she looks so damn sexy when she's fired up. "I mean it. You cannot let them use him to get women in their beds." As soon as the words are out of her mouth, she blushes a deep red. "I–I mean, if you want to use your son for that, I can't stop you, but I would be happy to keep him . . ." She looks at the ground.

She's embarrassed. By this time, I'm standing beside her so I turn to face her, her eyes still on the floor. With my index finger, I lift her chin so she's looking at me. Only at me. "I would never do that." I keep my eyes locked on those baby blues, willing her to believe me. She gives a subtle nod, and I run my thumb over her bottom lip. I would give anything to kiss her right now.

"Right, we're going to unload the trucks," I hear Kent say.

I don't acknowledge them, just the fact that I hear their heavy footsteps leaving us alone. My eyes stay on her. I can feel her heavy breath against my hand. Those full lips of hers dying for me to kiss her. "I want to taste these lips, sweet girl," I whisper.

A sound almost like a moan escapes her. "Ridge," she murmurs.

I take a step closer.

"I don't know if this is a good idea. You're mourning, and I can't . . ."

Fuck! She doesn't know about Melissa. To her, it looks like I'm some douche who just lost the love of his life and is already hitting on someone else. I hear the guys outside, so instead of kissing her like I want to, I run my thumb over her bottom lip one last time before releasing her and stepping away.

"It's not like that, Kendall. Now is not the time to get into it, but I want to. I want to tell you all about Knox's mom," I tell her honestly. There's something about Kendall that draws me in. She's got me wanting to tell her my entire life's story, if it gets my lips over hers.

"Yeah." She clears her throat. "I'm always here to listen anytime you need."

The guys make a lot of noise, alerting us to their presence before the door slowly opens and they file back in the house. Reaching out, I grab her hand and give it a quick gentle squeeze before releasing her. "Soon."

"Delivery just pulled in," Tyler says, watching me closely.

"I better go. You have my number if anything comes up. Dad is back in town Friday." She waves to each of us before rushing out the door.

Chapter 22

Kendall

What the hell just happened? I almost kissed him. I *wanted* to kiss him. I can still feel the rough pad of his thumb as it traced my bottom lip. He's mourning and lonely, and I almost took advantage of that. Even knowing he's hurting, I still want it. I still want to kiss him.

I'm going to Hell.

I arrive at work right at eight and it's crazy already. The first hour of appointments all got here at the same time. It's a relief really; being on the floor keeps my mind focused . . . Well, more so than it would be if I was just sitting in my office. The morning flies by, which I'm thankful for.

"Hey, you bring lunch?" Dawn asks.

"No, I left in a rush to check on the house."

She laughs. "I can tell from that blush on your cheeks that you got to see the guys. One in particular?"

"They were all there," I tell her.

"And?"

"And what?"

"And you would not be blushing just from seeing them. Grab your purse, we're going out to lunch," she demands.

I do as she says, hoping some fresh air will do me some good. We walk to the diner down the street. The place is packed, but we're able to find a small table near the door. As soon as the waitress takes our order, Dawn's on me.

"Spill." She crosses her arms over her chest and sits back against the chair.

"They were all there. The house looks good, it's coming along."

"Kendall," she says in warning.

I huff out a breath. "Fine! I almost kissed him," I hiss.

A smile brightens her face. "You almost kissed him?"

"Yes, no, I mean I don't know. We almost kissed. He's mourning and lonely and raising this baby on his own and vulnerable, and I took advantage of that!" I whisper-yell at her.

"Okay, first of all, he's a grown man. Yes, he's now a single father, but do you know the full story? How do you know if he's mourning? He doesn't look like he just lost the love of his life to me."

"He has to stay strong for his son," I say, exasperated.

She looks over my shoulder then leans in. "You wanted to kiss him." It's not a question, more of a statement.

"Yes! Yes, I wanted to kiss him," I say, louder than intended.

It's then that I feel strong hands on my shoulders and hot breath next to my ear. "I wanted it too, sweet girl."

Ridge.

I look across the table at Dawn, and she's got a smug look on her face. Bitch! She knew he was back there.

Ridge gently massages my shoulders as he and the guys say hello to Dawn.

"You guys want to join us?" Dawn asks.

I close my eyes and pray they say no. Not to mention that we only have a small four-person booth. There are seven of us now, and these guys are huge—no way they would fit.

"No room, sweetheart," Mark replies.

"We can—" I kick her under the table. "Ouch!" She glares at me, all the guys laughing.

I can feel the burn of the flush of my cheeks for the second time today in their presence.

"I think we'll just grab a seat at the counter," Ridge says.

Dawn and the guys say "good-bye" and "nice to see you" and all that. Ridge still has his hands on my shoulders. I shiver when I feel his hot breath next to my ear. "We'll get there, you and me. It's going to happen, Kendall." He kisses my cheek and then he's gone. The warmth of his hands, the feel of his hot breath, the deep timbre of his voice, the woodsy scent of his cologne—gone.

Unable to stop myself, I watch him saunter off toward the counter. I don't turn away until he's seated. When I do finally pull my eyes from him, Dawn is smirking as she hands me a napkin. I raise my eyebrows in question.

"You got a little something, right here." She points to her chin.

"We are no longer friends," I pout.

She throws her head back and laughs.

"Eat," I mumble as I pick up my cheeseburger and take a huge bite. I've lost my appetite but if we're both eating, I hope we can avoid any more talk about Ridge and any further embarrassment for me. I've reached my limit for the day.

Our waitress appears about ten minutes later, asking if we need anything.

"Just the check," I tell her.

She grins. "Those gentlemen at the counter took care of that." She points over her shoulder.

"Thank you."

Dawn and I both lay tips on the table and stand. "We have to say thank you," she tells me.

I nod, knowing we do. It would be rude not to, and it was nice of them. We walk to where they're sitting and Dawn hops on the stool next to Mark on one end. Ridge is sitting on the other. I step behind him and admire the way his Beckett Construction T-shirt forms to his muscles. Without thinking, I reach out and place my hand just below his shoulder blades. He turns his head at the contact.

At first, he looks annoyed until he works out that it's me. I step closer. He doesn't move his body, but turns his head to face me. I take another step closer, my hand still resting on his back. We're close. It's . . . intimate.

"Hey, sweet girl," he says softly.

"Thank you, for lunch. You didn't have to do that." The words tumble out of me.

"You're welcome."

Neither one of us moves. His eyes are so dark, a deep chocolate color. I find it easy to get lost in them, in him. I slide my hand up his back to where it's resting on his shoulder. He surprises me when he tilts his head and kisses my fingers.

"Ready to go?" Dawn's chipper voice asks from behind me.

No. I don't want to leave. I want to stay in this moment. Just need another minute. One more minute to be lost in him. "Yeah," I say instead. As I go to pull away, Ridge places his hand over mine.

"I'll see you soon." His voice is low, just for me.

I don't respond, just pull my hand from his shoulder, wave to the guys who are watching us closely, then turn and walk as quickly as I can out of the diner.

Dawn throws her arm over my shoulders. "That was hot as hell."

I look at her like she's lost her damn mind.

"Sexual tension at its finest. I think you're wrong, by the way."

"How so?"

"About the 'mourning rebound' thing. You need to talk to him. Be straight up, get it from the horse's mouth and all that."

I think about that the rest of the short walk back to the office, and surprise surprise, the rest of the afternoon as well.

Dawn has an appointment at Reagan's shop to get a manicure. "You sure you don't want to come with me?"

"Yeah, it's been a long day. I just want to chill. Tell Reagan I said hello."

"All right then, see you later."

I breathe a sigh of relief as soon as the door closes behind her. All day, I've tried to put up a front that today has not been the hardest in history to keep focused. Now that it's just me, I can let my mind replay it all, in slow motion. Every touch, every word, every breath between us. I think about what Dawn said, and he doesn't seem like a man in mourning. But then what does that say about him? Ridge is a good guy, and that seems out of character for him. Dawn's words filter through my mind. *You don't know the full story.* But I want to. I want to know what happened, know how he's handling all of this. I want to be there for him for reasons both selfish and unselfish. I'm such a hypocrite. I want to be someone he can lean on because he needs it. I also want to be that person just to be next to him.

Ping. I jump from the couch and run to get my phone from the kitchen, all the while praying it's him.

> **Ridge:** How was your day?

I'm sure my smile is blinding, just from a simple text message.

> **Me:** *Uneventful.*

Work was smooth today. Thank goodness. We had a full schedule, but nothing out of the ordinary.

> **Me:** *Yours?*
> **Ridge:** Great, actually.
> **Me:** *Good deal.*

Lame, I know. What else do I say? 'Tell me, I want to hear about every second'?

> **Ridge:** It is. Want to hear about it?

Do I? Hell yes, I do. I type a response but wait to send it, slowly counting to sixty first. I don't want to sound desperate—when, in reality, that's exactly what I am. Desperate for any little piece of interaction with this man.

Me: *Yes.*

I clutch my phone in my hands, waiting for his next message. Time seems to creep as I wait, staring at the screen. When it rings, I jump and my phone goes flying. When I finally have it back in my hands, I see the screen.

'Ridge calling.'

Chapter 23

Ridge

I wait forever for her reply and when it finally comes, I smile. Three little letters—YES. Knox is asleep in my arms; he's got a full belly and couldn't resist the pull. I know I should put him down, he's going to want to be held all the time—at least that's what Mom tells me—but he's peaceful, and to be honest, I just like to snuggle the little guy. It's a shock to me, but he's mine, a part of me. That makes a difference.

I've been using text-to-speech; it's much faster than texting with one hand. Just as I'm about to reply, I decide that I need to hear her voice. I bring up her name and hit send. It rings more times than I would like, and just as I'm about to hang up and text her to ask why she won't talk to me, she answers.

"Hello," her soft voice comes over the line.

I close my eyes and let the sound fill me, relaxing into the couch. "Hi, sweet girl," I reply just as softly.

Knox is sleeping. That's my excuse and I'm sticking to it.

"So, tell me about your day," she says, keeping her voice soft.

"Yeah?" I ask.

"Mmmhmm."

"It was pretty great," I tell her. "You see, this girl, she's kind of barreled into my life, and I got to see her today—twice, in fact."

"I see," she replies. Something in her voice tells me that she doesn't realize it's her.

Could she be jealous? "Yep, she's gorgeous and sweet as hell," I say, hoping she gets the hint.

"That's nice."

"I almost kissed her. I had my hands on her, and I almost kissed her."

She's quiet.

"I think I scared her though, because she backed away."

"You wanted to kiss her?" she asks.

Finally, she gets it. "More than anything."

She's quiet, but I can hear her breathing softly. "I don't want to be your rebound, Ridge."

Just like that, she's stopped this game we're playing and brought us both back to reality.

"I know you're hurting and lonely, but I can't be that person for you. I don't have it in me. I've spent too much time in my life being with men who just want me around when it's convenient for them. I can't do that anymore. I won't."

"Kendall, you are not a rebound," I say emphatically.

"You've been through so much. You may not think so now, but that's what this would be and I want it. I want to kiss you. I wanted to, I mean."

Fuck me! "What do I need to do? How can I prove to you that this isn't what you've made up in that beautiful head of yours?"

"I don't know."

Knox stirs in my arms and starts to fuss. "He must need a diaper change. He's only ever fussy when he's hungry or needs changed. He's got a full belly." I don't know why I tell her that.

"How is the little guy?" she asks, and I can tell she genuinely wants to know.

"Good. We're taking it one day at a time. I need to change him, I just . . . don't want to hang up." I'm a fucking wreck with this girl. Never in my life have those words fallen from my lips. She's got me waxing poetic and shit.

"He needs his daddy," she says. I can hear the smile in her voice.

"Yeah."

"I'll be home all night . . . I mean, if you want to talk some more."

Yes! "Yeah, let me get him changed and settled. I have to get his bag ready for tomorrow, but I'd like that. To call later."

"Give him a kiss goodnight from me."

"Will do. Talk to you soon." I hang up. "Little man, let's get you changed," I tell my son.

By the time I give Knox a bath, pack his bag for tomorrow, throw in a load of laundry, load the dishwasher, and pick up the living room, it's time for another bottle and to get the little guy to bed. It's after ten by the time he falls asleep. I kiss his little cheek. "That's one from Kendall," I kiss his other cheek. "That's one from Daddy. Love you, little man." I get him settled, turn on the monitor, and slowly creep out of his room before rushing down the hall to mine, ripping off my clothes and hop into the shower. After the quickest shower in the history of showers, I'm crawling into bed and reaching for my phone that's been charging on the nightstand. It's ten fifteen. I hesitate, not wanting to wake her, but I told her I would call.

The thought of her sleepy voice answering has me tapping her name and placing the phone next to me ear.

"Hey," her groggy voice greets me.

Just as I imagined it would sound. "Sorry, I didn't mean to wake you."

"You didn't, but another ten minutes and you might have." She laughs. "Everything okay?"

She's so damn sweet. Not just the taste of her skin—the little I've had the pleasure of sampling, anyway—but her heart. She truly cares. She's so different from the girls I've dated in the past.

She's the first I've pursued like this. Yes, I'm pursuing her. I can admit that much. I want what I told the guys to be true. I want her to be mine.

"Yeah, just a lot to do. Bath time, packing for tomorrow, laundry, dishwasher, bedtime bottle." I ramble on about what all I've done since I last talked to her.

"Babies are a lot of work."

"Yeah, they are. So, how was the rest of your night?" I change the subject, not wanting to be that guy, the one who whines and gets the girl. I want to know about her—everything there is to know.

"Good. I just chilled, read a book."

"You read too? Reagan seems to always have a book in her hand."

"I do. I love it."

"What else do you do? How do you spend your free time?"

"You don't really want to hear how boring my life is."

"I do. I want to know everything about you." Shit! My mouth just keeps spewing words at her. She's going to think I'm a stalker.

"Dawn and I are roommates. We work together, so we do a lot together. Shopping mostly, plus she reads too, so we talk about our book boyfriends."

Fictional, but I don't like it. "What else?"

"We spend a lot of time at my parents' place. I moved back six months ago, and Dawn came with me. I've been gone since I left for college, so it's nice to be able to spend time with them. I guess I'm trying to catch up on all the time we lost."

"Sounds like you're close to them?"

"Yeah, I missed them when I was gone. It made the decision to move back home even easier."

"What are you leaving out?"

"Nothing really, I was just ready for a change."

I won't push her to tell me. Not yet. I need to learn more about her, let her see that I'm not rebounding. I'm devastated that Melissa lost her life, and heartbroken that my son will never know his mother, but I'm not rebounding from her.

"So, other than these book boyfriends you speak of, do I have any other competition?" Might as well let her know where I want this to go. I don't like to play games. My thoughts travel to Stephanie. That entire clusterfuck was a game, one I hated and vow to never play again. I don't care what the dare is; if those are the stakes, I'm out. Never again.

"Not anymore."

Good. Not that it would matter, since he would have to prove to me that he was the better man before I backed away from her. She consumes me. "Care to share?"

She hesitates.

Come on, sweetheart, open up to me.

"Cal and I dated for about two years. He was great at first, nice, sweet, and attentive. You know, everything a girl wants." She laughs humorlessly. "Until he wasn't."

My heart stops a few beats at her words. If he laid his hands on her, I'll kill him. "Elaborate," I urge, trying to keep myself calm, my tone controlled.

"He got into the wrong crowd. He started a new job in a factory, and the guys he hung out with were into drugs pretty heavily. Looking back, I don't know how they all kept their jobs. Anyway, he changed. The drugs changed him. I didn't know that's what it was at first, but when I found out, I ended it. Well, I tried to, anyway. He was mean and angry that I left him. To make matters worse, he lived in the apartment across the hall. It was like I couldn't get away from him and his anger."

I clench my jaw. "Did he put his hands on you?"

"No, not really. I mean, he pushed me a few times, but it was nothing. He never hit me, really." She stops and sighs heavily into the phone. "You don't want to hear all this. I can't believe I'm even telling you."

"Keep talking," I blurt out.

"Excuse me?"

"I need to know, Kendall. So help me, if you don't finish telling me, my ass will be on your doorstep in however the hell long it takes me to get to you and you will tell me."

"Ridge." She sounds shocked.

"Kendall," I give it right back to her.

"I don't see how this is any of your business. I should go."

"Let me tell you something—*you* are my business. I want you, Kendall. There is something between us, and I want to be able to see

159

what it means. Anytime you're near me, I gravitate toward you." I take a deep breath and soften my tone. "I won't be able to sleep until I know."

"Once. He hit me once. That was the last time. He left that next weekend to go out of town, and Dawn and I packed up and moved here. He's called a few times, but I've avoided him. It was more of a slap, but that was the last straw for me. I knew I needed to get away before things got worse. Dawn's not close with her family and she said she had nothing holding her there, so she moved with me. We stayed with my parents' for a few weeks until we found a house to rent. We were lucky enough to both find jobs at the same place. We've just been settling in ever since."

He fucking hit her! I focus on my breathing to keep myself calm. Red-hot rage roars through me like I've never felt before. "If he comes around, if he bothers you, you tell me. No exceptions, no excuses—you come to me. Got it?"

"Ridge, that's crazy, you can't—"

I interrupt her. "I can and I will. I need to hear you promise me, Kendall. He shows up, you come to me. You call me, fucking send a carrier pigeon, but you come to me."

"Okay," she says, so quiet I almost miss it. Then she yawns.

"I meant what I said, Kendall. I want to see where this goes."

'Ridge, I—"

"I know we need to talk. I need to tell you about Knox's mom and I will, soon, but I want

to do it in person, not over the phone. I want to know that you can see me, see that my words are true."

"Okay," she says again.

"Night, sweet girl."

She hesitates. "Sweet dreams," she says, and then the line goes dead.

Sweet fucking dreams indeed.

Chapter 24

Kendall

I didn't see Ridge yesterday, but we texted off and on all day. He sent me a picture of Knox sleeping on his chest last night. He claimed to be exhausted as well, having not slept well the night before. I know the feeling. I kept running our conversation over in my head. I can't believe I just spilled my guts to him about Cal, that I admitted he hit me. Dawn is the only person I've told. I never wanted to tell anyone else, but Ridge has such a commanding way about him that he had me singing like a damn canary.

Mom and Dad are due home tomorrow, and my original plan was to stop by the house this morning on my way to work. I'm hesitant; I want to see him, but will it be different? He said he wanted me, but what does that mean exactly? That question alone has kept me awake for the second night in a row. I climb out of bed and shower, even though I still have two hours left to sleep. It's just not happening.

After my shower, I dress for work and make my way to the kitchen, deciding to make some homemade cinnamon rolls. I'm just finished with my third cup of coffee and cleaning up when Dawn strolls into the kitchen.

"How long until they're done?" she asks.

I laugh. I knew as soon as the smell hit her room, she would be awake; my homemade cinnamon rolls are her weakness. It's actually my dad's recipe. We would make them every year for Mother's Day and Mom's birthday. "About five more minutes," I say, sliding a cup of coffee across the counter to her.

"Bless you." She moans as she takes her first sip. "Why are you up so early?"

"One guess," I tell her.

"Ridge fucking Beckett." She giggles. "Even his name is hot as hell."

I nod, because she's right.

"Have you heard from him?"

"We texted last night. He sent me the cutest picture of Knox." I grab my phone and pull up the message to show her the picture.

"So, yeah, the baby is adorable, but look at his dad."

I blush, because yeah, I did that too. Knox is in nothing but a diaper, curled up in a ball, his little hands under his chin as he sleeps on Ridge's bare chest. His hard arms, his ink, the tiny baby, that he has his large hand on his back, holding him close. . . .

"Ovary fucking explosion," Dawn says.

"Right?"

"So, you going over there today?"

"That was the plan, but I don't know. I didn't tell him I was."

"Do it. See how he acts. I mean, damn, Kendall. He told you he wanted you—not that it was a surprise to anyone. Hell, even Reagan said she thinks he's interested."

"Wait, she did? When? How did you not tell me this?"

She laughs. "The same night as your epic phone call. She did my manicure, which I wasn't expecting, and we talked."

"What did she say, exactly?"

"Just that she thinks her brother is into you. She wanted to see if you were seeing anyone and if I thought you were interested."

"And you told her what?" It's like pulling teeth to get her to talk.

"That you were available and you were interested as well."

"Dawn! Shit! Do you think that's what the phone call was about?"

"No, definitely not. She and I went to dinner after and we closed the place down. It was after eleven by the time we left the restaurant parking lot. You said you talked to him until a little before eleven, right?"

"Yeah."

"See, that was all him. No outside influence, but honestly, I want to see you happy, so I hope she tells him."

"Gah!"

"Relax. You're interested, right?"

Hell yes! "Yeah," I say instead. "But I can't be a rebound. I won't be."

"Talk to him. He said he wanted to tell you about Knox's mom, right? Don't assume, Kendall."

I study her. "What do you know?"

She shrugs. "I'm willing to plant the seed, but I'm not about pulling the damn weeds. You have to talk to him. Open up, tell him about Cal."

"I already did," I say, shocking her.

Her mouth drops open, but she quickly recovers. "Good. Now, you need to let him tell his story. After you're both informed of the other's past, you can decide together what the future holds, if anything. Just don't push him away until you know the facts."

I don't reply, because there really is nothing to say. That's exactly what I was trying to do. She knows me all too well.

"What are you going to do with all of these? If I eat them all, I'll have to live in the gym for the next month."

I look over at the double batch of cinnamon rolls. "I guess I'm going to see if the boys of Beckett Construction are hungry."

"Boys?" She scoffs. "There isn't anything boyish about any of them. Those five are all men." She winks. "I'll help you wrap them up so you can go get yours."

"He's not mine."

"Not yet." She smirks.

Twenty minutes later, I'm pulling into my grandparents' driveway. The guys aren't here yet. I grab the cinnamon rolls and the gallon of milk and paper cups I picked up on the way here. It's a nice morning, so I set it all up on the back deck. Once it's ready, I sit in the lounger and scroll through the texts between Ridge and me. I save the picture of him and Knox and add it to his image in my contacts. That's what I'll see anytime he calls or sends a message, which makes me smile.

"That smile is something to start the day with," Ridge's deep voice startles me.

"Hey," I say, jumping from my seat.

He surprises me by stepping toward me and wrapping an arm around my waist, hugging me to him. This is how the rest of the guys find us.

"About fucking time, brother. I was worried you'd lost it," Tyler says with a smile.

I expect Ridge to retaliate, but he doesn't. Instead, he leans down and kisses my temple. If his arm weren't holding me up, I would've melted into a puddle of goo right here on the back deck.

"What's all this?" Seth asks.

"I, um . . . I couldn't sleep, so I made cinnamon rolls. This is more than Dawn and I could eat, so I thought you all might enjoy them."

"You good?" Kent asks Ridge, who just looks at him in question. "Because if you're not, I'm fucking calling dibs, my man."

Ridge's grip on my waist tightens. "Mine" is all he says, but the guys seem to understand what that means. Mark, Tyler and Seth are grinning, while Kent looks a little amused and possibly disappointed.

"Thank you," Ridge says, his lips next to my ear.

He holds on to me as long as he can, but I'm set on putting distance between us, eventually stepping out of arm's reach.

Mine. I assume he means me, but we're not really to that point . . . are we? I mean, we just started talking, and I really need to know about Knox's mom before I let myself get any further invested. I need to know that what he says is true, that I'm not just a rebound.

I really hope I'm not.

Chapter 25

Ridge

When we pulled in and I saw her car parked in the driveway, I knew. I knew in the moment that she was with me in this. When I spotted her on the back deck, I just had to touch her. It's a new need for me. Yes, *need*. Yes, I wanted to touch her, but the need to do so was what pushed me to wrap my arms around her, witnesses be damned.

I watch her as she talks to the guys. Kent made me show my hand, but that's fine; I was going to anyway. The more I talk to her, touch her, spend time with her, the more the need grows. I don't understand it; it's fast, and it's . . . not normal. I've had so many changes in the last month, that I'm just rolling with this. Dad always said, "Trust your gut, son. When you find her, it will let you know. Don't fight it; it'll just make you both miserable." That was part of his speech on my sixteenth birthday. That, along with wrapping it up no matter what. My son is proof that even when you do, things can happen.

"I should get going or I'm going to be late for work."

I watch as she starts to clean up after us. "We'll get that, Kendall,"

Seth tells her. "That's the least we can do."

"I'll walk you out," I say, holding my hand out for hers. She only hesitates for a few seconds before linking her fingers through mine. She waves over her shoulder at the guys as I lead her back into the house then out to her car.

"Thank you for that."

"Like I said, I couldn't sleep, and Dawn was cussing about having to spend the next month in the gym." She laughs.

She stops and leans against the side of her car. I stand in front of her, moving closer, removing the distance between us. I cup her face in my hand and run my thumb over her bottom lip, just like before. "I'm glad I got to see you."

"Me too." She blushes.

This girl. Sweet as hell. "When do you think I might get to do that again?"

She shrugs. "Not sure. I have plans with my parents' this weekend. They've been gone for two weeks."

"Can I call you, at least?"

"I'd like that." She smiles up at me. I know she has to get to work, but I need just one more second with her. Every second counts—at least with her. I drop my hand and pull her into a hug, breathing her in. She melts into my hold. Perfect.

Reluctantly, I pull away, even though I could stand here all day. I'll analyze that thought later. Instead, I block the feelings she evokes in me and kiss her forehead. "Have a great day, sweet girl."

She surprises me when she stands on tiptoes and kisses my cheek. "You too," she says softly. I step back, reaching around to open the door for her. I wait until she's strapped in before shutting the door, watching her pull out of the drive until I can no longer see her. It's my ringing cell phone that finally breaks my trance.

Tyler.

"Yeah," I say, turning to go into the house.

"Just want to make sure you weren't running off into the sunset," he jokes.

"Not yet, man, not yet."

"Wow, okay. Not the answer I expected." I can hear the others in the background wanting to know what I said.

"Get to work." I laugh. How can I not? Life has a way of shaking things up until you feel like you can't breathe, but then it settles into a calm where it feels like all that pain brought you to this point. Maybe it's Melissa—hell, I don't know if I even believe in all of that—but I know this is coming fast and hard, and for some reason, I don't want to stop it. I want it, all of it . . . all of her. I want to see where this unexpected reality leads me this time. I've lived it the last month. It gave me my son, and I wouldn't change that for anything. Maybe, just maybe, it will give me Kendall as well.

A man can only hope.

The guys are already working on the trim around the cabinets by the time I make it inside.

"No shit?" Mark asks.

Tyler must have filled him in. I shrug in response. What can I say? I want her. I can't explain it, and honestly, I don't want to.

"What's the plan for this weekend?" Kent asks.

"There's a fight on Saturday night," Seth suggests.

"Sounds good to me. My place. I don't want to have Knox out that late."

They all nod their agreement. "I'll call Reagan, we'll need food," Tyler says. It's on the tip of my tongue to tell him to have her invite Kendall and Dawn, but I don't. I keep my mouth shut. We'll get there; with everything in me, I feel it.

"You all will have to keep it down, or I'm kicking your asses out. Can't have you waking my boy," I warn them. It's still strange to me, but then again it's not. We seem to be settling in okay. I guess like Mom always says, "God will not give you more than you can handle." I think I've had my fill for a while, unless it's Kendall. He can give me Kendall.

I push thoughts of Kendall and my son out of my mind and dive into work. It's not until the guys start complaining that they're starving that I realize how much time has passed. I suggest we go to the diner, hoping to run into her again. Overnight, I've become the guy who chooses a restaurant just for the chance to get a glimpse of the girl. I let that sink in, and surprise even myself when I realize I really am good with it.

"You just want to see your girl," Seth teases.

"Yep." No point in denying it. Not to them.

"Holy shit," Kent says.

"You're sunk, brother." Tyler laughs.

I nod. "Yeah, I think you might be right."

"Fucking crazy shit, Beckett," Mark chimes in.

"It is," I agree. This is not me—hell, any of us really. We've been good flying solo with the occasional hookup, settling down not on our radar.

Wait, settling down? Is that what I want?

"I bet—" Kent barely gets the words out before I cut him off.

"No," I grit out. "No more bets. Stephanie was a huge mistake, and just . . . No. I won't make any bets that have anything to do with Kendall. I want no part of that shit."

He holds his hands up, palms out. "Got it."

"Lunch," Mark grumbles.

I couldn't agree more. I can only hope we run into my girl.

❄❄❄

WE ALL ARRIVE at the diner at the same time, and I quickly scan the room. They're not here. I tamp down my disappointment then pull out my phone and text her.

> **Me:** At the diner. Was hoping to see my girl.
>
> *Kendall: Your girl?*
>
> **Me:** Yeah. She's gorgeous. Her name's Kendall, you know her?
>
> *Kendall: You seem sure of yourself.*
>
> **Me:** I am.

"Dude, you gonna order?" Seth asks.

I get a burger and fries with a sweet tea and go back to Kendall.

> *Kendall: I packed today.*
>
> **Me:** How's your day going?

Kendall: *So far so good.*

Me: Knox will be in to see you next week.

Kendall: *I'll have to check the schedule and make sure I stop in and say hello to him.*

Me: Just to him?

Kendall: *Well . . .*

I'm smiling like a lovesick fool. I can feel it. I can also feel the stares of my friends, but I have zero fucks to give at the moment.

Me: I'll call you later.

Kendall: *Enjoy your lunch.*

Me: You too, babe.

"They coming?" Mark asks.

"Nah, they're eating at the office today."

"Were you sexting?" Tyler smirks.

I turn to look at him where he sits beside me. "What?"

He points at my face. "That grin of yours—you sexting or what?"

"No." I don't elaborate.

"Pussy whipped," Mark coughs into his hand, just as the waitress is dropping off our food.

I wait until she's gone to reply. "I'd need to have had it to be whipped by it."

"Burn!" Kent says.

"Nope. Just the thought of it has you tied in knots," Mark defends his statement.

"It is what it is," I say, not giving one single fuck that they're going to razz me about this for eternity.

"Damn, he's too far gone. We've lost him," Kent says in all seriousness.

"Har har. Eat your damn food so we can get back to work."

We spend the rest of the lunch hour talking about the fight this weekend and who we think is going to take the win. The afternoon flies by and I'm glad; I'm anxious to get home and see my boy. Mom said he's been great today, not fussy at all.

Then, after some male bonding, I'm going to call Kendall, if for no other reason than to just hear her voice.

＊＊＊

I GET TO Mom and Dad's about five thirty. The saint that she is, Mom has dinner ready and insists I stay and eat. I don't fight her on it, as it'll give me more time at home tonight. Not to mention frozen pizza can only take a man so far.

I'm sitting at the table with Knox on my lap; I haven't put him down since I walked through the door. I miss the little guy during the day.

"How's work?" Dad asks as we sit down to eat.

"Good. The remodel is going well. We should be done with the kitchen tomorrow and then we'll move on to the bathrooms."

"Need anything?" he asks.

"Nah, I'm good." I take a bite of my pot roast.

"He was an angel today, like always," Mom chimes in.

I laugh. "When he's two, running around and terrorizing the place, you'll still say he's an angel."

Dad chuckles. "That's our right, son."

I'm fortunate that they want to watch him every day. Sure, there are daycares, but I like the fact that he's with family. I know he's safe and his needs are met. I'm not used to having to worry about that, but now it's at the top of the list.

"How's he been sleeping?" Mom asks.

"The last few nights he's slept six hours straight. I've felt like I won the lottery."

"I remember those days," Dad says.

"He's a good baby," Mom tells us.

We finish dinner and I offer to help clean up, but they both push me out the door, telling me to get home and get settled. Mom has Knox's bags already packed, so I load him in the truck and we head home.

We run through what's starting to be our routine. Knox gets his bath, which he seems to enjoy—well, at least he's not crying. He hangs out in the swing while I clean up the house and pack his bag for the next day. I make his nighttime bottle and settle in on the couch. He's sleeping soundly, so I don't wake him up to eat. Instead, I pick up my phone and call Kendall.

"Hey," she says brightly.

"Hi. How was the rest of your day?"

"Same old. How about you?"

"We'll be done with the kitchen tomorrow, and then we can start on the bathrooms. The guys and I are hanging out here Saturday night to watch the fight."

"That's great. You guys are making good time. Do you need a sitter?" she asks.

"What?"

"For Saturday, do you need a sitter?"

"Uh, no. I mean, we're going to be here, so it's fine."

"I just thought I would ask. I know you're doing this on your own, and it helps to get a break every now and then."

She's just. . . . "Thank you, sweet girl, but I'm good. I feel like I spend a lot of time away from him as it is."

"You have to have a life too, Ridge. There's nothing wrong with leaving him to go out with friends."

Honestly, since the day I found out I was a father, the thought hasn't even crossed my mind. My biggest worry was childcare while at work, but before I could even voice that, my parents' were asking if they could watch him.

"Yeah, I just . . . We're still learning. He and I are starting to get into a routine," I tell her. I look down at him, grinning a toothless grin in his sleep. "He's smiling," I tell Kendall.

"Aww, I want to see," she says.

"I read that he shouldn't do this for a couple more weeks. My boy's a genius."

She laughs. "He'll be four weeks on Sunday, right?"

"Yeah."

"He's on the timeline," she tells me. "You have to snap a picture so

I can see him."

"Let me call you back and we can video chat," I suggest.

"Good idea." The phone goes dead.

"She's excited to see you, bud. Keep those smiles coming, yeah?" He's snoozing away with a little grin tipping his lips while I video call Kendall back.

"Lemme see." She's smiling.

I turn the phone so she can see little man sleeping in my arms. "Look at him! He's getting so big."

"He's tiny," I argue with her.

"Yes, he is, but he's growing. I can tell."

"He's a good eater, that's for sure. It's actually time for his bottle, but the books say not to wake them to eat."

"Yeah, stretch it out as long as you can. That will help him go longer and sleep longer at night."

We talk about anything and everything for another fifteen minutes or so before Knox starts to stir. "Looks like someone's hungry." I point the phone back to him so she can see him. His little lip, which was just tilted in a smile, is now jutted out. He's getting ready to cry. "I better change him and get him fed."

"Give him a hug from me."

"Will do. Talk to you soon. Hey, uh . . . the guys are coming over Saturday night to watch the fight. Reagan will be here. You and Dawn are welcome to come."

"I have plans with my parents' this weekend."

"Right, of course. Well, if you change your mind, you know where we'll be."

"Okay," she says softly.

"Goodnight, sweet girl."

I slide my phone in my pocket then walk through the house, turning off all the lights and locking the door. Upstairs, I change his diaper and settle into the rocker to give him his bottle. He takes it like a champ as always, and then he's right back to sleep. After placing him in bed, I make sure the monitor is turned on and quietly close his door.

I take a long, hot shower and feel exhaustion setting in. Slipping into some boxer briefs, I climb into bed. As soon as my eyes close, I hear the vibration of my phone on the nightstand. I debate on letting it go until morning but decide against it. I reach for it and see a new text message.

Kendall: *Good night.*

Me: Good night, sweet girl.

I drift off to sleep with a smile on my face and thoughts of the beautiful Kendall.

Chapter 26

Kendall

Today has flown by. I had a text when I woke up from Ridge—just a "good morning, have a good day," but really it was more than that. It's the fact that I was on his mind when he woke up. He's on mine too, been there for days. Mom called about two hours ago and said they were on their way home from the airport. They invited Dawn and me to dinner this evening, but I suggested we bring dinner to them. They've been traveling, and I'm sure going out to dinner is the last thing they want to do. Mom happily agreed, so I told her we'd be over around seven.

"You sure you're good with hanging out with my parents' tonight?" I ask Dawn.

"Seriously, Kendall? I can't wait to hear about their trip."

"Okay, just thought I'd check."

"I'm ready to go, you?" she asks.

"Yeah, I just need to grab my phone from my room." I grab it, throw it in my purse, and we're off to pick up the pizza.

My parents' are on the front porch when we pull in. Their arms are around each other, and they're both wearing relaxed smiles.

"You two look great," I say in greeting.

"That's what two weeks of pampering will do for you," Mom replies.

"We need to take a cruise, Kendall," Dawn says.

"I agree. We should look into that, for sure."

"Come on in, girls, and fill us in on what we missed," Dad says, holding open the door.

"We want to hear about the trip," I tell him.

"Your mother took a ton of pictures." He laughs.

We devour the pizza and listen to them tell us all about their vacation. "Tell us about you two. What have we missed?" Mom asks.

"Kendall has a boyfriend," Dawn sing-songs.

I smack her arm. "What the hell?"

Mom and Dad laugh. "Oh, really? And who is this guy? Is he worthy of my little girl?" Dad asks, amused.

"He's not my boyfriend."

"He wants to be." Dawn laughs.

"What do *you* want?" Mom asks.

Have I mentioned that my parents' are amazing? Not one day growing up did I not ever feel loved and wanted. I owe them everything.

"I-I don't know."

"Liar," Dawn taunts.

I seriously need to look for a new best friend.

"Fine, I . . . like him. Okay, there, I like him."

"And . . . ?" Dad urges with a smile.

"And, he says he likes me. He's a single father."

"What's wrong with that?" Mom asks.

I sigh. "Nothing. His baby is adorable, but his mother, she didn't make it. He's only a month old and I just . . . I don't think he's ready, and I don't want to be the rebound girl."

"How do you know you will be?" Dad asks.

I just stare at him, waiting for him to say more.

"How do you know what the relationship was? I can tell you that if he loved her, he wouldn't be ready to move on, telling you that he likes you," he says.

"Thank you!" Dawn exclaims. "That's what I've been trying to tell her for days now. She needs to get his story."

"We've talked about it, but he said he wants it to be face to face. We just haven't had the time. We both work, and he has his baby to take care of."

"Bring the baby to us, and you two can have a night out," Mom suggests. "It's been years seen I've had a little one to cuddle."

"Speak of the devil, that's his sister calling now," Dawn says, holding up her phone.

"Do we know them?" Dad asks.

"Do you remember Reagan Beckett? I graduated with her?"

"Yeah. Nice girl, that one," he says.

"It's her older brother, Ridge."

"Beckett Construction?" Dad laughs. "I take it having you check in on him worked out for both of you?"

"It didn't hurt." I cross my arms over my chest. I really want to laugh too, but I'm biting my tongue.

"Sure, thanks for the invite. I'll talk to Kendall and one of us will get back with you," Dawn says, ending the call. "Reagan invited us over to Ridge's house tomorrow night."

"Yeah, they're all watching the fight."

"Did he invite you?" she asks.

I nod. "He invited both of us, but I told him I wanted to catch up with Mom and Dad."

"Nope, not happening, sweetheart. Do not hide behind your mother and me," Dad mock-scolds me.

"I already turned him down," I whine.

"Yeah, but you didn't turn Reagan down." Dawn smirks.

"That will make me look desperate."

"No, it will make you look interested, which you are," my mother corrects me.

"What is this, 'gang up on Kendall' day?"

"No, it's helping Kendall see what's right under her nose. Help her see that risking getting her heart broken is worth it. It's trying to get you to see that there is that one person out there who will love you like your father loves me," Mom says defiantly.

"Hey, Reagan, it's Dawn. Hey, listen. I talked to Kendall, and we're in. We're with her parents now, so we are suddenly free tomorrow night." I hold my breath, waiting for what she'll say next. "Okay, great, see you then." She ends the call. "We're supposed to meet Reagan at her place at seven. I guess the preliminary fights start at eight."

Taking a deep breath, I slowly release it. "What do we need to bring?"

The three of them cheer at my acceptance of the situation.

I love my crazy family.

❄❄❄

THE NEXT DAY, Dawn and I tag-team cleaning the house then just kick back and relax in the afternoon. She keeps grinning at me, more excited about this than I am. That's when it hits me—there must be more.

"What are you so happy about?"

"I want you happy," she says.

I watch her as she bites her bottom lip before quickly releasing it. If I didn't know her so well, I wouldn't know it's a tell.

"Which one?" I ask her.

"What do you mean?"

"Which one of the guys do you have your eye on?"

She blushes, which is not something that I see my best friend do often. Hell, ever.

"Mark."

"Nice." I grin at her. "You didn't have to drag me along just to hang out with them. You and Reagan have hung out a few times."

"Yeah, I know, but it'll be easier if you're there. Besides, you need to stop hiding and jump in the deep end. Let life take you on the journey, Kendall."

I think about what she's saying and realize I kind of have, in a way. At least I thought I had. I haven't heard from Ridge since early yesterday. I started to text him goodnight last night, but I don't want to be that girl, the clingy 'have to see you and talk to you all the time' kind. Not to mention that we aren't in a relationship. He told me he wants me, but that doesn't mean that whatever this is will be going anywhere.

"Yeah," I finally answer her. "We'll see how tonight goes."

A few hours later, we're pulling into Reagan's driveway. For some reason, I'm nervous knowing she and Dawn talked about me and Ridge.

"Hey hey," she says, greeting us on the front porch. "I'm all set." She's carrying a huge Crock-Pot.

"What you got there?" Dawn asks.

"Meatballs. Tyler loves them and begged me to make them for tonight."

"Tyler, huh?" Dawn grins.

"Wait a minute. What did I miss?" I question.

"I kind of sort of have a thing for one of my brother's best friends."

"Nice."

"Oh, hush, you. You want my brother."

Dawn laughs, and we both turn to face her.

"And you, you have your eyes on Mark," Reagan points out.

Complete silence, until the three of us break out in laughter at the same time. After we compose ourselves and keep the meatballs from eminent disaster, we load up and head to Ridge's place.

"So, I have a confession," Reagan starts. "I didn't tell him you were coming." She looks at me briefly in the rearview mirror.

"Is that going to be an issue? I don't have to go."

"No, he wants you there. He said he was going to invite you, but you already had plans. I decided to intervene."

"Great," I mumble.

"Trust me on this, Kendall. He's not going to be anything but thrilled to see you walk through his front door."

"So, Tyler?" I ask, changing the subject, and we spend the rest of the drive listening to Reagan tell us how she's crushed on him for years. We both encourage her to tell him how she feels, but she's still resistant.

Maybe I need to intervene as well.

Chapter 27

Ridge

Last night and today have been . . . an adventure. Knox was up and down all night, and he's been fussy all day. I'm struggling right now and scared as hell. I should have called Mom, but she has him every day. Reagan was working at the shop, and the guys . . . Well, they're like me and know nothing about babies. I started to call Kendall, but I don't want her to think I only want her because she's willing to help me with my kid.

So here I am, a half hour before everyone is supposed to show up, and the house is a wreck. Knox and I are both tired and cranky, and I don't know how I'm going to get through the night. The guys don't want to hang out with me being in a pissy mood, with a baby who's unhappy as well. Not exactly what they would call fun times.

I'm just about to call and cancel when I hear a car pull up in the drive. Of course, today of all days someone would be early. Knox cries, and I gently bounce him and pat his little butt. "Shhh, Daddy's got you, bud. I don't know what's wrong. I'm sorry. I wish you could tell me what you needed. I'm failing you, and I'm so fucking sorry." Instead of soothing

181

him, he cries harder. I begin pacing the floor again, surprised I have carpet left as many trips as we've made today.

"Anyone home?" Reagan calls out.

"Hey, bud. Aunt Reagan's here. You want to say hi?"

He continues to cry.

"Hey," she says, coming to stand next to me. She places her hand on his little back. "What's up, sweet boy?" she coos, and he quiets a little. She looks up at me. "How long has he been like this?"

"He barely slept last night, and he's been fussy all day. I was just getting ready to call and cancel."

"Why the hell didn't you call me or Mom? You know we would have come over to give you a hand."

"Because he's mine!" I yell at her, which causes Knox to cry harder. "Shhh, Daddy's sorry, bud. Shhh," I try to soothe him. "He's my responsibility. I have to learn how to do this, Reagan. What will I do if you or Mom isn't there to bail my ass out, huh? Then what do I do? This is my fucking life now. I have to learn how to do this, to deal with my son when he's fussy."

"Let me have him." She holds her hands out.

I would love the break, just a minute to rest my arms, but I'm stubborn as hell. "No, I got this."

"Ridge, let me have him." She's pissed off now.

"No, I got him. Just call the guys and tell them tonight is off." I turn away from her and that's when I see them. Kendall and Dawn are standing in the doorway, watching me unravel.

Perfect.

Knox is still crying. I bounce him, pat his butt, but it's not helping. Kendall hands the bag she's holding to Dawn and addresses Reagan. "Hey, can you two give us a minute?"

"Good fucking luck." She stomps over to pick up a Crock-Pot, Dawn hot on her heels as they take everything to the kitchen.

"Hey," Kendall says softly, her eyes on me. "Rough day, I see."

"Yeah, you could say that."

She pulls my hand from his back and replaces it with her own.

Moving in close, she begins to run slow circles on his back. "He can tell you're tense. He can feel it. Babies are smart, and he's upset because you are," she says in a low, soothing voice.

"I don't know. He's been fussy all day, and even last night. He didn't sleep well."

"Yeah," she coos, and I feel myself relax just at the sound of her voice. "You're exhausted, and he senses that." She steps closer and places her other hand on my back, begins to gently rub there as well.

I can literally feel the tension melt away at her gentle touch. "I've missed you," I whisper in her ear.

She laughs softly. "I was wondering why I didn't hear from you, thought maybe you changed your mind."

"Never. I just need to learn how to do this."

"I agree," she says, surprising me. "However, you need to remember that even two parents in one household need help and a break every now and then. You don't have to do this alone, Ridge. You could have called Reagan, your mom . . . Hell, you could have called me."

"I almost did," I confess. "I just didn't want you to think that's what this was. That I was only pursuing something with you so you could help me with my son. I'm doing it because I want you."

"I know that. Can I hold him?" she asks.

I nod and slowly transfer him to her arms.

"Shhh, little man, it's okay. Daddy's just really tired. He needs some sleep, and I think you do too," she coos to him.

Instantly, he starts to calm. *She's bewitched me too, son.*

"My own kid hates me."

"Hey," she scolds me with a whispered voice. If I weren't so tired, I'd tell her how fucking cute she is right now. "You've both had a rough twenty-four hours. How long since he ate?"

"He's due anytime." I should have tried to get him to eat. Maybe that was the issue, but I tried that several times today. Nothing worked for long, until she took over. Can't say I blame him.

"Good. You need to go upstairs and take a shower. Take as much time as you need. I got this little guy."

"Kendall, I can't ask you to do that."

"You didn't ask me, Ridge. I want to. You need help, and that's okay. Please, for me. Just trust me, okay?"

I lean in and press my lips to hers. I have to; there's no other way to explain it. It's quick, but the meaning behind it is no less than what it is. A 'thank you,' plus an 'I don't know what I would do without you in this moment' kiss. Sure, my sister offered to do the same thing, but we butt heads; my sweet girl moved right in before I knew what hit me. That's what she's done since the day I met her.

"Thank you," I murmur next to her ear before dashing upstairs. I rush through a shower; even though I would love to stand under the hot spray, the need to be near her trumps that. The fact that she's downstairs, in my house, taking care of my son . . . Yeah, I take the quickest shower known to man. Regardless of how fast it is, I still feel revived, but then again, that's probably just Kendall.

I'm just hitting the bottom step when I hear Reagan. "How'd you do it?" she asks Kendall. I stop and listen.

"He's stressed, Reagan. He just needed someone to help him feel like it was okay to ask for help, and it is. He needs to lean on us."

'Us.' Not 'you,' not 'your parents,' but 'us.' My sweet girl.

"That's what I was trying to do," Reagan says, exasperated.

Kendall laughs softly. "Maybe, but you also got pissed off when he didn't do what you expected."

"He just wants in your pants," Dawn teases.

"Maybe, but he also needs support."

I've heard enough. Taking the final step, I walk the short distance down the hall and into the living room. "Hey," I say, but only to Kendall. She's all I see, holding my son, who is now blissfully sleeping in her arms.

"Hey, that was the quickest shower ever." She smiles up at me.

I take the spot next to her on the love seat and lean in to her, my lips close to her ear. "Yeah, didn't want to miss this," I tell her honestly.

She runs her thumb over Knox's hand, which is gripping her finger tightly. "Miss what?" she asks, watching my son sleep in her arms.

I don't hesitate when I say, just for her, "You, sweet girl. I didn't want to miss you, here in my house, where I can be close to you. You make it all better."

She sucks in a breath. I've managed to shock her. Good, that's what I've felt since the moment I met her—like I've been shocked, and the only balm is to be near her, talk to her. Hell, a simple text from her changes the outcome of my day.

"Ridge," Reagan says softly, and I can hear the apology in her voice.

"I'm sorry, sister."

"What can I do?" she asks.

"I have nothing ready. There are drinks in the garage refrigerator, but that's about it."

"We got this." Dawn stands and heads toward the kitchen. Reagan smiles in our direction and follows her.

"The guys will be here soon," I tell Kendall.

"Hey," Reagan calls from the kitchen. "I told the guys to hold off until eight thirty. I recorded the prelims, since we always bitch about the commercials anyway," she informs me.

Kendall smiles. "Go take a nap, Daddy. I got this little guy."

Come with me. "I can't—"

"Ridge, you can and you will. I'll be right here. I promise, if I need you I'll wake you up. Go get some rest. You'll need it to take care of him when we're not here."

Reaching out, I gently smooth the hair out of her eyes. I could stare into them for hours, get lost in their blue depths. But I don't have hours—not today anyway. Instead, I lean in and press my lips to hers. "Thank you."

Pulling back, I watch as she licks her lips. "Go rest, Mr. Beckett." She points to the ceiling.

I chuckle. "I'm going." I lean in and give her one more quick, chaste kiss and slowly stand. She doesn't push me away, and I'm going to keep stealing kisses until she does. Three times. Three times I've had her soft lips next to mine, and I'm already addicted.

I wake to laughter and sit up, startled. Then I remember—I've got company. Peering over at the alarm clock, I see it's two minutes to nine. I rub my hands over my face before climbing out of bed. I hate to admit it, but I needed that. Hell, I could go back to sleep and not wake up until the morning, but I can't. I have a son to take care of, and then there's Kendall.

She's here.

I'll sleep later.

"Hey, princess," Seth greets me as I enter the living room. I flip him off with a grin, which causes everyone to laugh.

"Sleeping beauty," Tyler chimes in.

"Feel better?" Kendall asks.

"Yeah." I walk toward her, stopping beside her chair. "You had him the whole time?"

"Pretty much," Reagan pouts, and I turn to look at her. She's sitting on the love seat with Tyler, while Dawn, Mark and Kent are on the couch. Seth is in one chair, Kendall in the other.

"Hey!" Kendall pretends to be offended, but I can tell by the look on her face she's not in the slightest.

"She's got the touch," Mark says, patting Reagan's knee as if consoling her.

"The touch?" I ask, confused.

"Yeah. I held him but he started to fuss, so I passed him off to Reagan," Dawn explains.

"Except that's not what he wanted at all," Tyler adds. "The little guy continued to fuss, until Kendall convinced Reagan to let her try to get him calmed down."

"Dude, as soon as she had him, he stopped. Just absolutely stopped, like he wanted her all along. Like he was trying to tell us the whole time," Seth adds.

"It really was weird, so we had them try it again. He cried with both of them, but stopped when Kendall had him," Kent finishes.

I look down at Kendall. "Really?"

She shrugs. "Babies can sense tension," she says, as a way of explaining why my son's latched onto her.

Bending over, I whisper in her ear, "Can you stand a minute?" She looks confused but does as I ask, my son still in her arms. Once she's on her feet, I settle into the chair.

"Hey . . ." Reagan starts to defend her when I pull Kendall gently into my lap, who stiffens at the contact.

"I got you, sweet girl. Both of you," I say, rubbing my fingers on my son's head while my other hand massages circles on Kendall's back. Within minutes, she's relaxing into me and I can't keep the smile from tipping my lips.

"This is . . . new," Reagan says with a grin. "Is it serious?" she asks, like the protective little sister. I know damn well she's just calling me out.

"Yes." I see all six of them with varied versions of shock on their faces.

"Ridge," Kendall turns and whispers.

"Yes," I say to her. No room for negotiation. I don't understand it, the pull she has over me, but I'm not fighting that shit. "You find her, and you hold on" That's what Dad always said.

I've found her, and I'm not letting go.

Chapter 28

Kendall

I should climb off his lap and tell him to go to Hell. I should tell him that he can't make decisions for me—or for 'us,' as it seems—without consulting me first. I *should* do that, but I don't. Instead, I just sit here on his lap and melt against him. I told myself that I wanted to see where this went, but to say it's serious?

I think about how I feel when I'm with him. How I feel in this moment with him openly claiming me.

Yeah, it's serious. At least my reaction to him is, anyway.

His friends as well as Reagan and Dawn seem to accept his one-word reply of "Yes" and move on. The guys are talking about the upcoming fight, Ridge included. Dawn and Reagan are talking about going to the local amusement park tomorrow.

"Kendall?" Dawn laughs. She knows better.

"Nope. No desire."

"Come on, Kendall, it's going to be a blast," Reagan begs.

"Not for me. I'm scared to death of heights."

"What about you?" Reagan asks Tyler.

He shrugs. "Sure, I'm in. Fellas?"

"I told Dad I'd help him finish their deck tomorrow," Seth declines.

"Kent?" Tyler asks.

"I'm out, man. I plan to sleep all fucking day."

"Mark?" Dawn asks. I can see how badly she wants him to say yes. I'm sure the others are oblivious, but I know my best friend.

"Yeah, sounds like a plan."

"Ridge?" Reagan asks.

"We have plans," he says, pulling me to relax further against him. This has me sitting almost beside him, my legs lying across his lap, Knox still sleeping in my arms.

"We do?" I whisper.

He tucks my hair behind my ear. "Yeah, I want to spend the day with you." He gives me a shy smile. "I'll have Knox, though. I can't have Mom watch him when she already does all week." He sounds apologetic.

Placing my hand on his cheek, I have his full attention. "He's a part of you, Ridge. This is a package deal, and I'm good with that."

He closes his eyes and his lips find my forehead, placing a tender kiss there. I drop my hand and lean against him, and we sit like that for the next hour. His hands tenderly rub circles on my legs, draped across his lap.

"Is the food ready?" Tyler asks.

"Yeah, I'll go set everything out." Reagan stands and heads to the kitchen.

"I'll help." Dawn follows her.

I stand as well, and without thinking, kiss Knox on his little cheek. "Here, Daddy, I'm going to help too." I gently place Knox in Ridge's arms. His hands slide around the back of my neck, pulling me closer. His lips touch mine, all too briefly, and then he's releasing me.

I can feel the guys staring as I walk to the kitchen, and I wonder what they think of all this. Of Ridge and me, the way he acts with me? I don't get to dwell on it long because as soon as I clear the kitchen door, Dawn and Reagan are all over the topic.

"Holy shit, my brother just claimed you." Reagan claps her hands loudly.

"What? No, he . . ." Well, shit. He did, and I have not rebuttal.

"That was so hot," Dawn adds.

"I mean, he's my brother, so there is some ick factor there, but damn, if that were Tyler . . ." She lowers her voice. "Hot hell." She fans her face with her hands.

"When did this happen? How could you not tell me?" Dawn asks.

"It just did."

"What?" she asks, confused.

"You saw it happen." I can't help but grin when I see understanding cross her face. "We've been talking, and he's told me he's interested, but this . . . Tonight was it. He made it official." I shrug.

"Is that what you want?" Reagan asks me.

"Yes. He's all I've been able to think about. I look forward to his phone calls, his messages. I think it's worth seeing if there's something there. I just. . . ."

"You just what?" she repeats when I don't say anything.

"I don't want to be his rebound," I confess.

"What are you talking about?" Her expression shows that she's truly confused.

"He just lost her, Knox's mom, and now . . . It's too soon."

"Shit. I thought you two had been talking?"

"Pretty much every day, either by text or phone."

"Have you asked him about all of this?"

"Yeah, but he said he wanted to do it in person, and we've just not had the opportunity."

"You let him claim that this was serious before you knew," Dawn points out.

"Yeah, I just . . . I really want to see where this goes. I guess I'm willing to get my heart broken to find out."

"That won't happen," his deep voice says from behind me.

Shit.

Slowly, I turn to face him. He stalks forward and wraps his arms around me, his large arms engulfing me in the best hug I've ever received. His chin rests on top of my head.

"Give us a minute," he tells Dawn and his sister.

I don't try to pull away to see if they granted his request. Instead, I grip the back of his shirt and enjoy the fact that I'm in his arms. It's almost as if both of us are afraid the other will disappear.

"We need to have that talk," he finally says.

This time, I do pull back. "Where's Knox?" I ask.

He chuckles. "Tyler has him, although I would bet one of the girls has stolen him by now. I need you to take a walk with me. Will you do that?"

"Ridge, you have people here," I try to protest. I don't expect him to leave his home when he has company just to pacify my worries.

"Don't care. They know where everything is."

"We can talk tomorrow."

"No, now. I don't want another second to go by with you thinking you're not what I want or that I'm not ready to give you all of me."

"Where are we going?" I concede.

"Just for a walk. I have a small pond out back with a gazebo. We can go there."

"Okay."

He kisses the top of my head, laces his fingers through mine, and leads us back out to the living room. We're both surprised when we see Tyler still has Knox. Reagan whispers something about baby whisperers, and I giggle. I just can't help it.

"Hey, can you all keep an eye on him for a little while? We're going to take a walk."

Reagan and Dawn must have clued the guys in, because they didn't bat an eye when all six of them assured Ridge that little man was in good hands. He nods his thanks, grabs a throw blanket from the back of the couch, and leads me through the dining room to the patio door.

"Watch your step," he warns as we make our way down the deck steps.

"Steep," I say, holding onto his hand for dear life. The dew has set in, making them slippery.

"Yeah, something I'll need to change for the little guy. Probably add another level to the deck or something."

"You have time for those things later." He worries so much.

"Yeah," he agrees, pulling me into his chest and wrapping his arm around me.

"Wow, this is really nice."

"Thanks. It's part of why I bought the place. I wanted some acreage, and the guys and I like to fish and have a few beers. Makes it a hell of a lot easier when you can walk home after."

"I bet."

The silence of the night takes over, but it's not uncomfortable. It's actually nice, enjoyable even. When we finally reach the pond, Ridge leads me down the dock until we reach the gazebo that sits at the end.

He takes a seat on the built-in bench and pulls me onto his lap. Grabbing the blanket, he wraps it around me. "Better?" he asks.

"Yes."

He buries his face in my neck and just holds me tight. I don't speak, not sure what I'm about to hear.

"I've not exactly been excited to share this with you. Not that I'm ashamed, but I didn't want you to think differently of me."

I don't say anything, just lean my head against his shoulder and wait for him to continue.

"Little under a year ago, the guys and I had a job out of town. It was a good gig; we would stay there through the week and drive home on the weekends. We started to frequent this local bar. It was basically a hole in the wall." He laughs. "Anyway, it was the perfect place to grab some dinner and a cold beer after a long day."

I'm hanging on to every word, waiting for the part that he wasn't thrilled about telling me to fall from his lips.

"Anyway, our last night in town, we settled in for a few beers. That's where I met her—Melissa, Knox's mom."

He pauses, collecting his thoughts. I remain still.

"She was beautiful and drinking alone. She seemed sad, so when I went to the bar and got us all another round, I invited her to sit with us." He clears his throat. "She was easy to be around. One thing led to another, and she invited me back to her room."

I feel him stiffen at his own words. Lifting my head, I place a tender kiss against his neck then snuggle back into my spot, resting against his shoulder once more.

He tightens his hold on me. "We used protection, of that I'm sure. Melissa even confirmed it in her letter."

"Letter?" I finally break my silence.

"Yeah. See, she slipped out of her own room in the middle of the night. When I woke up the next day, she was gone."

My mind races with where I think this is going, and my heart aches for him.

Chapter 29

Ridge

Fuck! I hate telling this story, but she needs to hear it. I need her to understand that I'm not some insensitive asshole who's moving on like nothing happened to the love of his life. I just hate to think of how she'll see me after this. When she knows that my one-night stand resulted in my son.

"Yeah, so the night I stopped to help Dawn with her flat tire, I also drove up on an accident. A car had slid over the embankment. The driver was trapped, so I called for help and stayed with her until they arrived. Once they had her freed from the car, something in my gut told me I needed her to be okay. I followed the ambulance to the hospital. Of course, they couldn't and wouldn't tell me anything—hell, I didn't even know her name. That is until my cell phone rang."

"Who was it?" she asks in a quiet voice.

"The hospital." I close my eyes and remember that day, just a month ago. The call that rocked me to my core and changed my life forever.

"The hospital?" she asks, confused.

"Yeah, they were calling me to let me know that I was listed as the next of kin to a Melissa Knox, and that she was in the hospital."

"Knox," she whispers.

"I wracked my brain for a Melissa Knox, but the only Melissa I could come up with was the one from that bar several months before. I was already in the emergency room, so I told them I would be right there. I had them take me to see her and it was her, the girl from the accident."

"Oh, Ridge."

I hold onto her. It was just last month, but it feels as though a lifetime has passed since then.

"They found a letter with my name on it in her belongings. It basically said that I was the father and that she was on her way to see me. That if she chickened out, she would mail the letter because she thought I deserved to know that I was going to be a father."

"I'm so sorry," she says, grabbing my hand and holding it to her chest.

"They had to deliver him while she was still in a coma. A paternity test was done so I could be listed on the birth certificate."

"Did she . . . Was it the delivery?" she asks, her voice fill of emotion.

"No. She actually woke up, got to hold him. I even took a few pictures. She was really tired, so I told her to get some rest, that I would take Knox back to the nursery."

"I'm sorry," she says again. This time, I feel her silent tears seep into my shirt.

"I took Knox, who they referred to as 'Baby Knox,' because we hadn't named him yet. I tried to get them to change it to Baby Beckett, but the results weren't back yet, so I had to wait. Anyway, I went to the cafeteria to eat, since I had been burning the candle at both ends. When I made it back to the nursery to check on Knox, the doctors and nurses were standing around, and I could tell something was wrong. I flipped, thinking it was him because he was early. They'd said he was fine, but my emotions got the best of me. Only it wasn't Knox, it was Melissa."

"Oh, no," she murmurs, her voice barely audible. I can feel the rumble against my neck where she's burrowed close to me.

"Aneurysm."

Kendall sits up and I grip her tight, not wanting to let her go. "I'm not leaving," she assures me. Instead, she straddles my lap. I grab the blanket and wrap it around her shoulders, and she surprises me when she hugs me.

My arms circle around her and I hold on tight, crushing her to me. I'm overwhelmed with emotions—sadness for Knox, for Melissa, for the fact they'll never know each other. Fear, for me and for Knox, that I can't be both father and mother and give him what he needs. And something else, something I'm not willing to name, which is all wrapped up sitting on my lap. Everything I feel for her is . . . unexpected, but it's real. I'm certain about that. It's not a feeling I've ever had, and that's also scary as hell.

She finally pulls away, her blue eyes watching me. There is something hauntingly familiar about them, but I know it's just her. Just Kendall. It's the pull she has on me.

"So you see, sweet girl, you're not a rebound. You're so much more. It's new to me, but I'm not running from it. I want you to be in my life, but like you said earlier, it's a package deal and I have to think of my son. I can't let him grow attached to you—although, he may already be." I chuckle nervously. "I need to know that you're in this with me. It's fast and it doesn't make any sense, but I've learned that life is too short and you need to learn to roll with the changes it throws at you."

She's quiet for a while, just staring over my shoulder at the pond. "I don't know how to give less than everything, Ridge. That's what happened with my ex. I put everything I am into our relationship, and he broke me. Not just from the drugs and the anger, but my heart. He crushed it, crushed me. I vowed that I would never again put myself in the situation to get hurt like that again."

"Kendall, I—"

She places her fingers over my lips, stopping me.

"I was with him for a year before things started to get bad, and two years altogether. Even when times were good with us, I never felt for him what I do for you in just this short period of time. I know I won't be able to come back from you, Ridge Beckett."

Well, fuck me. Kendall Dawson, my sweet girl. She unmans me.

"Jump, baby. Jump and let me catch you. I can't explain it. There are no words to explain this, or how I feel. I just know that I would never,

ever hurt you. I know I want to hear your voice every day. I know a simple text from you changes the outcome of my day. I know I've tasted your sweet lips four times, and that's not nearly enough." Leaning in, I kiss her.

This time, I trace her lips with my tongue, coaxing her to open for me, and she does. I don't waste time, sliding my tongue past her lips to truly taste her for the first time.

Fucking addictive.

I have her face cradled in my hands, hers resting atop mine as we get lost in each other. It starts slow and easy, but suddenly that's not enough. My tongue battles with hers, and I fight to taste more of her. She moans deep in her throat, and it fuels me. I nip at her bottom lip and soothe it with my tongue before plunging back inside. Her hands drop from mine to grip my shoulders, pulling me toward her as if she can't seem to get close enough.

I know the feeling.

She rocks her hips against me, and that simple act alone lights a fire inside me. My hands fall to her waist, my grip tight as I help her find a rhythm that's driving us both crazy with need.

"Ridge," she pleads.

"I got you, sweet girl." My hands slide down to her ass, cupping each cheek, not breaking the rhythm we've created. My lips trail across her neck, nipping, sucking, and licking, driving her crazy.

Who am I kidding? I'm driving myself crazy.

She's so damn responsive.

"Please don't," she gasps.

"I won't, babe. I'm not stopping until I see you come undone," I say, reading her mind.

"Please."

"Open your eyes, Kendall. Let me see those baby blues."

Her eyes pop open and lock on mine.

"I want you to come for me, sweet girl. I want to look into your eyes and watch you fall apart." Her head falls back, breaking eye contact, but the moan that falls from her lips tells me she's losing control. For me— because of me—this beautiful creature is losing her inhibitions.

"Ridge!" she cries out into the night air.

Wrapping my hand around the back of her neck, I pull her to me and crash my lips to hers. She pulls away long before I'm ready to stop and buries her face in my neck.

"I can't believe I just did that."

I raise my hips so my rock-hard erection shows her exactly what I think about what we just did. Not her—*we.*

She reaches for the waistband of my jeans, but I place my hand over hers to stop her. She sits back, settling her fine ass against my cock. "I want to. It's not fair to you."

I chuckle. "I got what I wanted, what I needed. I got to make you lose control."

"Ridge," she says hesitantly.

"We better head back. They're going to think we ran off."

"Not without Knox," she says, and my heart soars at her admission. He's a part of me, and she accepts that.

I kiss her again quickly before helping her off my lap. She wraps her arm around my waist and settles into my side as we walk back to the house.

Inside, the guys have the TV sound low. Dawn is sleeping, her head on Mark's shoulder. Seth and Kent have their eyes glued to the fight, while Reagan and Tyler are talking to what sounds like a soon-to-be-upset Knox.

"He's hungry," I announce, alerting them that we're back.

"I was just getting ready to make him a bottle," Reagan says.

"I got it." I kiss Kendall on the temple then take my son from my sister. "Hey, bud, you hungry?" He quiets at the sound of my voice. "Let's go make you some dinner." I carry him into the kitchen with me, making his bottle one-handed like I've learned to do over the past few weeks.

He whimpers pitifully.

"I know, little man. It's almost ready."

Once the bottle's ready, I head back to the living room. "I'm just going to take him upstairs and feed him. I'll be back when I get him down."

"You need help?" Kendall asks.

"No, babe. I got it. You didn't get to eat. Help yourself, and I'll be down in a bit." I wink at her and head upstairs to settle my boy in for the night.

Chapter 30

Kendall

I relax in the chair Ridge and I shared earlier and stare at the screen. I'm not the least bit interested in what's going on; instead, my mind wanders to what just happened. How I let myself go with him.

"Kendall," Reagan says, grabbing my attention. "You not going to eat?"

"Yeah, I'll just wait for Ridge."

My answer causes her to grin, and I feel my face blush. I wonder if she can tell her brother just rocked my world in his backyard. Just as my mind starts to drift again, we hear the crackle of the baby monitor as Ridge enters Knox's room. Looking around the living room, I see the receiving end sitting on a small table next to the TV.

"You doing better, little guy? You seem to be in a better mood," Ridge says to Knox.

Reagan chuckles, as do the rest of us. He's so good with him. I don't think he even realizes it.

"Daddy's doing better too, but you already know that, don't you? I think Kendall has worked her charms on you just like she has your old man."

I stare wide-eyed at the monitor. I should stand to turn it off—this is his private moment with his son—but I can't move. Instead, I tune everything out except the sound of his voice.

"We're lucky, Knox. She wants both of us. Oh, you like that idea, do you? I see your smile." Knox coos at him. "You're probably too young for this conversation, but my dad once told me to trust your gut and when you find the one to not let her go. In this case, she's not just mine—she's ours. We've found our one."

We're all listening to him, so I stand to turn it off. Just as I reach the monitor, he says something that has tears welling in my eyes.

"I think your mommy would approve. She just wanted the best for you, for you to feel loved and know you're wanted. I love you, little man, and Kendall . . . Well, she's important to me, and I hope that whatever this is grows. I think that would make your mom happy. I know it would me. What about you, huh?" Knox coos. "Good, glad we're on the same page. Good talk." He chuckles and I reach for the receiver, turning it off.

Taking a deep breath, I slowly release it before turning to face the room. I don't make eye contact as I walk straight to the chair Ridge and I were sitting in and focus my gaze on the television.

"Kendall," Dawn tries to get my attention. Of course, she would wake up to hear what happened.

I don't look at her, just keep staring at the TV as if I didn't hear her.

"He's different with you," Tyler says. His deep voice makes it impossible to ignore him.

I'm trying to work this out in my head—how I respond to him, how to act after what I just heard. My heart feels like it could beat out of my chest, and there are millions of butterflies in my stomach.

"Hey, did you eat?" Ridge asks, sitting on the arm of the chair.

I'm so zoned out I didn't even know he was back. "No, I, uh . . . I waited for you."

He grins a boyish grin. Standing, he holds his hand out for me and I take it, allowing him to lead me to the kitchen. Ridge grabs my hips and lifts me up to sit on the counter, settling between my legs.

"You okay?" He cups my face with one hand, keeping a tight grip on my hip with the other.

"Yeah, I uh . . . I heard you. We all did." I can't lie to him. I don't want to start out that way.

"Heard me?" he asks, confused.

"The baby monitor. It was on, and we all heard you."

He grins. "Good, now those fuckers who I call friends will keep their eyes off you."

Wait, what? "You're not mad? And what do you mean 'keep their eyes off me'?"

"No, babe, I'm not mad. I meant every word. I have nothing to hide. And those four knuckle heads in there, they watch you."

I push on his shoulder, but he doesn't budge. "Get real."

"They do. They even forced my hand at calling dibs." He kisses my neck.

"Dibs?"

"Yeah, we have this rule that if one of us calls dibs the rest back off regardless. They could tell I was interested, but hesitant with being a single dad and all that. One of them—and no, I won't tell you who—said he was going to call you. I saw red and told them you were mine." He shrugs.

"When?"

"Weeks ago, before I had even worked it out in my head that this is what I wanted. I knew I didn't want anyone else to have you, it just took me time to realize I could be a dad and whatever it is you need, too."

Butterflies—millions, trillions of butterflies take flight in my belly. Grabbing his shirt, I pull him to me and kiss him.

Someone clears their throat behind me.

Ridge pulls away and rests his forehead on my shoulder. "I need to get the monitor."

"This one?" Reagan holds it up as she enters the kitchen. "Your girl turned it off, but since you're back down here with us I thought it was safe to turn it back on." She smirks.

He takes it from her and sets in on the counter beside me. "My girl didn't have to do that," he says, leaning in to me, facing them. He crosses his arms over his chest.

"You told him?" Mark asks.

"Yeah, I mean, I couldn't lie about it."

"Dude, you fuck up and I'm stepping in." He punches Ridge in the arm.

"Not a fucking chance in Hell," Ridge fires back.

Everyone laughs, and that sets the tone of the rest of the night. We laugh, talk, eat and then when the fights are finally over, Ridge walks me to Reagan's car.

"So tomorrow, you're not going to stand us up, are you?" he asks.

"No, what time?"

"Now. Just stay with me. We can stop by your place tomorrow for you to change and get ready."

"Not tonight, but you name the time and I'll be here."

"Seven."

"Seven, okay. Dinner, then?"

"In the morning, sweet girl. I want all day with you."

"Are you being serious?"

"This is you we're talking about, so hell yes, I'm being serious. How about as soon as you wake up you get ready and come to me. I want the day with you."

"Okay," I concede.

"Text me when you get home, so I know you're safe."

"Ridge, I'll be fine. Go inside and go to sleep. Knox will be up soon."

"Not until I know you made it home." He looks through the window of the car to Dawn. "Make her call or text when you get home, so I don't worry."

"Gotcha." Dawn grins like the cat that ate the canary. She's loving this.

He leans down and kisses me on the lips; it's quick, but the meaning is still there. "Be safe. I'll see you in a few hours," he whispers.

I nod and climb into the back of Reagan's car.

"He's got it baaaddd," she sings once we're on the road.

"He's not the only one," Dawn adds.

Thankfully, they change the subject to their plans for the next day while I get lost in thoughts about mine. We're spending the day together. I'm trying hard to tamp down my excitement. It took everything I had not to take him up on his offer and just stay the night. I'm sure his seven a.m. request will be fulfilled; I can't see myself getting much sleep.

The drive from Reagan's house to ours is filled with Dawn's excited chatter about her day tomorrow with Mark. I'm happy for her. She's not having the best of luck with guys, and he seems like one of the good ones.

As soon as I walk through the door, I text Ridge. He needs to get to bed.

> **Me:** *Just walked through the door.*
>
> **Ridge:** Make sure you lock it. See you soon.
>
> **Me:** *Already done. Night.*
>
> **Ridge:** Sweet dreams.

Chapter 31

Ridge

Maybe two hours. That's the amount of sleep I got last night. It took me a while to finally close my eyes and when I did, it was the early morning hours. Two hours later, my little man decided it was time to eat. I'm not going to complain, because he slept for eight hours. That's a record, and amazing, and I can only hope he continues to do so. He was up at five and after he got his belly full, he was ready to play—well, as much as a one-month-old can. He was talking up a storm, making all kinds of cute baby babble sounds. I admit I'm that dad, the one who records multiple videos of their kid. And I've taken hundreds of pictures. I need to invest in a good camera, not just my cell phone. Maybe that's something we can do today.

I'm lying on the floor with Knox when my phone alerts me to a new message. Stretching, I reach up and snag it from the coffee table.

Kendall: *I'm here.*

Giddy. Those two fucking words make me giddy like a teenage boy.

It's seven o'clock on the dot and she's here. "We have company, buddy. Kendall's going to spend the day with us, and Daddy is really excited about that."

Me: Be right there.

I gather Knox into my arms and—I will deny this—we run to the front door. Twisting the lock, I take a deep breath to calm my racing heart. Pulling the door open, she's standing there in simple gym shorts and a hoodie, her hair is piled on top of her head and she's a fucking beautiful sight for my tired eyes.

"Missed you, sweet girl," I say, clamping my free hand around her waist and pulling her to me. I kiss her temple.

"I missed you guys too." She grabs Knox's little hand. "Morning, cutie. You feeling better today?"

He smiles at her because—like father like son—he's enamored with her.

"Have you had breakfast?" I ask her.

"Actually . . ." She holds up a bag of takeout. "I swung through the drive-thru and picked us up a variety of breakfast sandwiches. I'm exhausted," she admits.

"Me too. It took me a while to fall asleep and then this guy decided he was ready to jam this morning, so we've been up for a few hours," I say, covering a yawn.

Reluctantly, I release my hold on her and allow her to step inside. I close the door and flip the lock back, my way of locking out the outside world—today is just our time. Something I've been craving with her for weeks. I find her in the kitchen unloading the bags.

"There's milk and juice, I think, in the fridge. There's also bottled water and a fresh pot of coffee. It's what keeps me going these days."

"Water's fine with me. What about you?"

"Milk, but I can get it." I walk toward the fridge.

"Ridge, sit down and let me do this."

I don't argue with her because I don't want to ruin today. I don't want her to leave when she just got here.

"Eat," she says as she sets a tall glass of milk in front of me. She does the same, unwrapping a sandwich. "Looks like someone's losing steam."

Sure enough, I look down at Knox and his eyes start to fall shut, then pop back open. He's fighting it, but he's not fussing. Whatever was bothering him must have subsided. I hate that he can't tell me what he needs.

She finishes her sandwich and holds her hands out for Knox. "You finish, I'll take him."

"You don't—" I stop myself when she gives me a 'don't argue with me' look. Instead, I transfer him from my arms to hers, steal a quick, chaste kiss, and tear into one of the other sandwich.

"What do you want to do today?" I ask between bites.

"I'm up for anything."

I watch as she gently sways back and forth, patting his little bottom. His eyes finally fall shut and stay that way. "You are the baby whisperer."

"Nah, just love kids."

I quietly crumple up my wrapper, drain the last of my milk, and stand. "I'll go lay him down."

"I can do it."

I nod, knowing the less we transfer him back and forth the more likely he is to stay asleep. "His Pack 'n Play is in the living room; we can put him there."

She follows me there and gently lays him down. It doesn't seem to faze him. "Now what?" she asks me, just as I'm covering a yawn. "Never mind." She grabs my hand and leads me to the couch. "Lie down and get a few more hours of sleep."

"No." I refuse to miss a single second of my time with her today.

"Ridge, you're exhausted."

I pull her into my chest with the hand she's holding. "I want to spend the day with you," I say, my voice low.

"I'll be here."

"Not good enough. I'm not missing this time with you to sleep. I can do that later."

"No, you can't. You have a newborn, Ridge. You have to rest when he does. Don't be stubborn."

I yawn again before I can even answer her. I know she's right, but I'm fighting it anyway.

"What if I lie with you?" she offers.

That changes the game. I don't reply, just lie down on the couch and pat the spot in front of me. She shakes her head, wearing a small smile, and takes her spot. I pull the blanket we used last night off the back of the couch and drape it over us. My hand rests on her hip and she uses my arm as a pillow.

My girl, she's a smart one. This is the best idea she's had yet.

"You're making me sleepy," she says, stifling a yawn.

"You feel good." I slide my hand around to rest on her stomach. The T-shirt under her hoodie has ridden up, so my hand touches soft, warm skin.

"You're warm." She relaxes further into my hold. "Sweet dreams," she says, and that's the last thing I remember before sleep takes me.

✲✲✲

I HEAR THE soft sounds of Knox's babble, and I know I need to get up. It's not until I hear her sweet voice that my eyes pop open.

"Shh. We don't want to wake Daddy. Remember the plan? We need to let him sleep as long as we can." Knox babbles some more at her. "I know, tell me about it," she whispers. "You got your belly full and now you're ready to play, huh?

She's so damn gorgeous. Her hair is messy with not a stitch of makeup, and the sight of her in this moment will star in my every fantasy from here on out. "Hey," I say, my voice still thick with sleep.

"Hey, hope we didn't wake you?"

"Nah, how long has he been up?"

"About an hour or so. He had his bottle and a new diaper, so he's ready to go." The way she smiles down at my son lights a fire inside me that she accepts both of us.

"What time is it?" I sit up, rubbing my hands over my face.

"Twelve thirty."

"Shit. I'm sorry, you should have woken me up."

"I had just woken up, needing to use the bathroom, when this little guy started to stir. He and I talked about it, and we decided to let you sleep."

I stand and walk over to the loveseat and sit down beside them. "Is that how it is, little man? You ditch old Dad for a beautiful woman?" I ask my son, reaching out and letting him latch on to my finger.

"We made a deal. We'd let you sleep and then when you woke up, we'd pout until you took us to the park to go for a walk."

"Oh, really?"

"Yep." She puffs out her bottom lip in her best pouting face. It does nothing but make me want to kiss those full, soft lips of hers.

"Pouting isn't necessary. I will take you two anywhere you want to go." I lean in and kiss the top of her head. "Do you mind watching him so I can get dressed and brush my teeth? I need to kiss you."

She leans down to talk to Knox. "We got this, huh, little dude?" He smiles at her.

"Be right back." I dash up the stairs and rush through brushing my teeth. I throw on some basketball shorts and a T-shirt and call it good. My next stop is Knox's room. I grab him an outfit for today, some diapers, extra clothes, wipes, a blanket and an extra receiving blanket just in case. I shove it all in his diaper bag and carry it downstairs.

"I just need to make him some bottles for the road and I'm all set."

"Can we help?" she asks, standing to follow me into the kitchen.

"Actually, yes, you can." I stalk toward her. Two long strides has me standing in front of her, and I cup her face with both hands and bring her lips to mine. "It's been too long since I've done that." I release her, both of us wearing a grin, and finish making bottles.

"Let me load up the stroller and then we can go."

"Is this what you want him to wear? Does he get to sport is PJ's today?" She winks at me.

"Woman, you have me all flustered. No, there's an outfit for him in the diaper bag. A few of them, actually. We've had some accidents, so I want to make sure I'm prepared."

She sifts through the bag on the counter. I watch as she grabs a diaper, wipes, and a new outfit. "I got this one. You finish up whatever you need to do."

Twenty minutes later, we're loaded up and on our way to the park.

"LET ME GET the stroller." I hop out of the truck and grab it out of the backseat. *Now to just figure out how to open the damn thing.* I'm still struggling when Kendall joins me at the rear of the truck.

"Problems?" She laughs.

"How do you open this thing? Is it even safe?"

Again, she laughs. "It's safe, Ridge. Can I try?"

I step back and let her try. Apparently, you have to be smarter than the stroller, because she grabs the handle and next thing I know, it's unfolded and ready to go.

"What the hell? How did you do that?"

"The handle has a button underneath. I pushed it."

"Har, har, smartass. I pushed it too."

She shrugs and grins. "I guess I just have the magic touch."

I smack her ass, wearing a grin of my own, before quickly moving out of the way so she doesn't have the chance to retaliate. Opening the back door, Knox snaps his eyes open at the sound. "Hey, bud, you ready for your walk?" He closes his eyes again, and I grab his car seat and carry him to where Kendall is standing with the stroller. "Great, now how does this part work?"

"I think it just snaps in." She holds tight to the stroller while I settle the car seat, and sure enough it snaps right into place.

"Well, that was easy enough. I just hope we can get him out of it."

She chuckles. "I'll grab the diaper bag."

"Okay, baby, diaper bag, keys, cell phone." I look at Kendall. "Am I forgetting anything?"

"Nope. Want me to lock the truck?"

"Yeah." I wait for her to lock the door and then we're off.

"They have trails we can walk on, if you want," she suggests.

One hand on the stroller, I reach out with the other and pull her to my side. "What, you two didn't have this little excursion planned out?" I tease.

"We were thinking more of just rolling with it and seeing where the day takes us, right, bud?" She looks down at Knox. "I've lost my sidekick."

"I guess you'll just have to settle for me." I kiss her temple then release her to push the stroller.

Chapter 32

Kendall

The weather is beautiful; it's a warm high-seventies today, and the sun is shining. I don't know what made me think of the park; I guess I just wanted do to something that would include Knox. I know how Ridge feels about leaving him when he's with his parents so much during the week.

Looking down at the sleeping baby, I see the sun is in his eyes. I grab Ridge by the elbow to slow him down. "Hey, hold up." He stops immediately. I reach out and pull the canopy of the stroller over Knox, so the sun isn't beating down on him. I go to pull away and Ridge places his hand over mine.

"You're good," he says with a wink. I don't argue, leaving my hand where it is. The scene we create I'm sure is an intimate one, one of a new family. My heart hurts for Melissa, and for Ridge and Knox.

"So, why a nurse?" he asks out of the blue.

"I've just always liked helping people. And I love kids. I worked at a pediatric hospital before moving home."

"You're good with them."

"I think maybe it's because I was an only child. Whenever little cousins came around, I was always begging to hold them or playing with them." I pause for a second before turning to him. "What about you? Always want to take over the family business?"

"Yes. I grew up idolizing my father. He worked hard and still had time for the three of us. I knew I wanted to be just like him."

"And kids? Did you see yourself being a father?" I don't know why I ask that. It's not like he has a choice in the matter, but I want kids. If this is really going anywhere or leads to more, that's important to me.

"Yeah, I did. I assumed I would find the one, just like my dad talked about with Mom. Still to this day, anytime he's gone, even just to the store, before he leaves and as soon as he's back, he has to kiss her." He stops as if remembering, a small smile tipping his lips. "Dad used to tell us as kids that he knew from the moment he met her that she was his future. I wanted that. I still do." He looks over at me, slows his walk, bends down and kisses my temple.

I'm glad he insisted I hold on to him; otherwise, I'd be a puddle of goo, right here on the paved walkway of the park.

"My parents' have a similar story," I say, once I've composed myself. "They met in college, fell hard and fast, and they're still going strong today."

"Big shoes to fill," he replies.

"Yeah . . . Honestly, I had all but given up that I would ever find that." We stop to sit on a park bench beside the small lake. He parks the stroller so the sun isn't in the baby's eyes, then settles on the bench next to me. His arm rests across my shoulders, and he pulls me close.

"And now?" he asks, his voice low.

"Now." I stop to collect my thoughts. "Now, the dream of having what my parents' have is back in full bloom, I just. . . ."

"Just what?" he murmurs.

"Now I know who I want it to be." The words tumble out before I can stop them. His voice, his scent—he scrambles my brain. He's getting the real me.

His lips are close to my ear when he whispers, "Let it be me."

Holy shit! Is this really my life right now? Reaching down, I pinch my leg and jump from the sting.

"What are you doing?" he asks. I can hear it in his voice that he thinks what I just did is crazy.

"I had to know."

"Had to know what, sweet girl?"

I look up at him and get lost in his dark eyes. "I had to know if this was real. I was making sure you aren't just a figment of my imagination."

He chuckles. "No, baby, I'm not. I'm one hundred percent real, and I'm yours." He says it like there's no question. His statement is final.

"What does that mean exactly?" There I go again, not thinking before I speak. I look around to make sure no one's listening in on our conversation. It's just the three of us.

"That means exactly what I said. I'm yours. I want this, and I want you."

"But that means . . . what? We're dating? Ridge, this is all really fast and confusing and I—"

"We're more than dating. You're more than just someone I'm dating casually. Don't ask me to explain it because I can't. I just know it. There's this coiling deep in my gut and it constricts at the thought of us not being together. I'm trusting that to lead us into our future."

"Do I get a say in this?" I ask him.

He studies me for a long time before replying. "No. Not unless you say you agree with me. I don't give up easy and I won't now, not when it comes to you."

Swoon!

"You ready for some lunch? I'm starving."

"Yes."

We stand to leave. Ridge grabs my hand and places it back in the crook of his arm while he pushes the stroller. The walk back is quiet, like we're both taking the time to process what we just talked about.

"Okay, so how do we get him out of this thing?" he asks with a worried expression.

"Try the button on the handle," I suggest.

Sure enough, it works, and Ridge is able to free the car seat from the stroller. I manage to load up the diaper bag and fold down the stroller just as he reaches me on the other side of the truck. "I got that, babe." He takes it from me and lifts it effortlessly into the backseat.

"I probably need to look at getting another vehicle. An SUV or something," he says, shoving the diaper bag in the backseat as well.

"You could've put it in the bed of the truck," I tell him.

"Yeah, but what if it's raining and I need the stroller and we have a bunch of other stuff? We won't be able to use the bed of the truck."

"You could get one of those bed cover things," I suggest.

"I could, but this is a business truck. It's probably time I get something that doesn't have Beckett Construction sprawled down the side."

"That's who you are."

"It is," he agrees. "But I'm also a dad now."

"You're a good man, Ridge Beckett."

He reaches over and laces his fingers through mine, letting our combined hands rest on the center console. "I want to be, for you and for him. I want to be."

I don't know what to say to that. 'Thank you?' 'I'm falling for you hard and fast, and I hope like hell you catch me?' For once, I keep my mouth shut as we drive to the diner just down from my office.

"This okay?" he asks, motioning his head toward the backseat. "It's family friendly."

"Perfect." Just like him. This day has been one of the best, and I can only hope we have many more just like it.

Ridge grabs Knox, seat and all, tossing the diaper bag over his shoulder. I stand at the front of the truck, trying like hell not to drool. Six-two, broad shoulders, arm porn—as Dawn and I like to call it— tattoos running down his arm, his dark hair messy, and those dark eyes that seem to devour me anytime he's near. I want to pull my phone out and snap a picture of him. Not to mention he's holding a baby carrier, and from the look on his face as he stares down at his son, you know he sees him as the brightest part of his life. There isn't a female out there who wouldn't melt at the sight of him in this moment.

I snap out of my trance and walk toward him. He places his hand on the small of my back and leads me into the diner. It's a slow Sunday afternoon, so we find a booth in the back corner. The waitress is there bringing one of those stands we can set Knox's seat on. We thank her, order our drinks, and she disappears.

"What are you getting?" he asks.

"I'm starving, so it all sounds good."

"I think I'm going to get a steak hoagie and fries."

"I'm going with a turkey club and cheese sticks."

After we place our order, Ridge digs a diaper and wipes out of the bag and removes Knox from his seat. "I'm going to go change him."

Not a minute later, he's back looking frustrated. "There not one of those changing station things in there."

"There is in the women's. Let me do it." I stand and hold my hands out for the baby.

Ridge grumbles, but hands him over along with the diaper and wipes. He kisses me on the forehead then stalks to the counter to no doubt complain about not having said changing station in the men's room.

When I get back to the table, I give him the wipes and sit down, still holding Knox. He's such a good baby, and I know even though he won't admit it, it's nice for him to have a break.

"I can take him." He starts to stand.

"I got him," I say. Then it hits me that maybe he doesn't want me holding him. "I mean, unless you don't—"

"Stop it," he growls. "Anytime, Kendall. Anytime you want to hold my son, you do it. You are not some damn stranger off the street."

He read my mind. "Good." I smile.

The waitress brings our food and I start to eat with one hand. "I can take him," Ridge offers again.

"I know, but you eat faster than me. You finish, and then you can feed him while I eat."

"You eat first, and I'll feed him."

"No dice, Beckett."

He grumbles but doesn't fight me further.

"Well, isn't this cozy?" a leggy blonde asks, stopping at our table. Ridge immediately stops eating and glares at her.

"Stephanie," he greets her coolly.

"I see you found a stand-in mommy," she seethes.

"I told you I was done, now leave."

"What? Without an introduction to your little stand-in?"

"She's my girlfriend. Leave now, Stephanie," he grits out.

She laughs humorlessly. "Really? Well, you move fast, don't you? Did you know that his baby is a bastard? That he only wants you so he doesn't have to do it on his own? Is that really what you want?"

Ridge slams his fist down on the table, and I'm sure all eyes are on us. I reach out and place mine over his, his eyes immediately snapping to mine. I smile at him, hoping he can see that her words aren't affecting me and shouldn't get to him either. Once I see he's calmed, I turn and face Stephanie.

"If you knew him—*really* knew him—you would know that, up to this point, he's done it all on his own. You would know that I had to force him to let me hold this little guy while he ate. If you really knew him, you would know that he puts those he cares about first. Furthermore, if you knew me, you would know that I want them both. I know this little angel lost his momma, and I'm honored that I get to be a part of his life. As for you—" I stop and take a minute to look at her with disgust. "—if I ever hear you call this baby anything other than his name, you will answer to me."

"Listen, you little—"

Ridge stands. "Leave, Stephanie, now!" His voice is low. Lethal.

"Ma'am, I'm going to have to ask you to leave," our waitress says.

"Me? What about them?"

"Ma'am, this is a small establishment, and we've all heard what happened. You aren't welcome here."

"Whatever." Stephanie turns on her heel and stalks out of the diner.

"I'm sorry about that," the waitress apologizes.

"You have nothing to apologize for," I tell her.

She nods. "Can I get you anything else?"

I glance at Ridge and he looks . . . defeated. And angry. "No, just the check please." Turning to Ridge, I push his plate toward him. "Eat."

"Kendall, I can—"

"Eat, Ridge. This little guy is going to be hungry soon. We had a plan, remember?"

"Dammit, Kendall, we need to talk about this."

"And we will, when it's just us, without half the town listening in."

"I won't lose you over her," he says emphatically.

I reach across the table and he grabs my hand immediately. "You won't. Just eat. We're going to finish our lunch, and I promise we can talk after."

He nods, bringing my hand to his mouth for a soft kiss before releasing me. I finish off my cheese sticks just as Ridge finishes eating. I pass Knox off to him so he can eat too. I try to focus on my lunch, but it's rude to not make eye contact when talking and Ridge . . . Well, he's sexy and distracting. He's currently still brooding, this big tough guy holding this tiny baby. It's an image that will forever be engrained in my memory.

Chapter 33

Ridge

As soon as we walk out of the diner, I run into Mr. Williams and his wife. The guys and I just built them a new home a few months back.

"Ridge, hi! Good to see you," he says, holding out his hand for me to shake. "You remember my wife, Nancy."

I nod to his wife. "Good to see you."

"You too. Who is this little one?" she asks, stepping closer to peer into the car seat.

"This is my son, Knox, and this is my girlfriend, Kendall," I introduce them.

"He's adorable," Mrs. Williams says. She stands and addresses Kendall. "You have a beautiful family."

My girl doesn't miss a beat. "Thank you," she says politely.

She could have made the situation awkward as hell, but she didn't. Instead, she claimed us, me and my son. It takes everything in me not to pull her to me and kiss the hell out of her.

"Well, we won't keep you. Good to see you, Ridge," Mr. Williams says, holding the door open for his wife.

As soon as the door closes, I look over at Kendall. "You don't know how bad I want to kiss you right now."

She inches closer and stands on tiptoes. "What's stopping you?"

I close the distance and kiss her. It's not how I want to, but it serves the purpose of calming me the hell down. I've never wanted to hit a woman, not until today. Not even when Stephanie showed up at the hospital. That day, I was just done. I knew she wasn't someone I could see going the distance with, and after she opened her mouth I knew it was over. Bet or not, I never wanted to see her again.

Today, though? Today, I wanted to hit her. She called my son a bastard and disrespected Kendall. I was barely controlling my anger when her hand slid over mine. Just the simple touch of her skin against mine made it better.

"Where are we headed?" she asks once we're back on the road.

"Home."

She doesn't say anything, and it probably has to do with the fact that I snapped the word at her. I'm still mad as hell over Stephanie and, even more than that, afraid Kendall's going to walk. That I'm going to have to spend my time convincing her that she's what I want, instead of kissing her. I reach over and grab her hand, lacing our fingers together. She doesn't pull away, and I take that as a good sign.

Once we make it back to my house, I grab Knox while Kendall insists on taking the diaper bag. As soon as the seat hits the couch, she goes to work unbuckling him. He stretches his little body, and I fight the urge to pull out my phone and take a picture.

"How about some play time?" Kendall sits him on the floor under this baby gym thing Mom brought over. I watch as he stares up at each object while Kendall either moves them or squeezes them to make noise. He's fascinated.

Needing to be closer to them, I lie on the floor behind Kendall, sliding in close and pressing my body next to hers. I hold myself up with one arm while the other rests on her hip.

"Cuteness overload," she says when my boy smiles up at the bear that crackles every time she touches it.

Not able to help myself, I kiss her shoulder. "I'm sorry about today, with Stephanie."

"Not your fault."

"It is. I was kind of dating her when Knox was born."

She looks over her shoulder at me, and her face has this 'are you kidding me' expression.

"It was a bet," I ramble on, and then feel her stiffen. "Let me explain, please."

She nods, but continues to stare down at my son. I tell her how the bet came about, how Stephanie was never my match, and admit that I was with her for the wrong reasons. I tell her about the day Knox was born, how Stephanie showed up at the hospital and started spewing shit about not wanting to be a fill-in. I tell her how I ended it right then and haven't thought about her since. "I know how it sounds, and I'm sure you don't think too highly of me right now."

She's quiet and lays her head down, using her arm as a pillow, resting her other hand on Knox's belly. I remain silent, giving her the time she needs to process everything I've just told her. She's still here in my arms, so that gives me hope.

"I would've never expected that from you. The way you are with Knox, the way you are with me . . . I'm having a hard time seeing you as the guy who plays with someone's emotions for a simple bet."

She's right. "It was wrong. I realize that now. I was so caught up in just taking the bet that I didn't think about how it would end."

"And the guys. I'm just . . . disappointed, really."

Shit. "We didn't do it to harm anyone, and Stephanie isn't without her faults as well. Not that that excuses what I did, of course."

"Did you win?"

"No. I still had a month to go when Knox was born."

"So, if Melissa hadn't been in that accident, if Knox weren't here, I would've never met you? Well, we might have crossed paths, but you would be with her."

The way she says "with her" tells me she's not taking this very well.

I lift her hair off her shoulder and rest my chin there. "I would like to think that, no matter what my situation was at the time, when I met you I would've still been smart enough to realize you were what I wanted."

She offers her finger to Knox and he latches on. "So this little guy, not only is he your gift, but he's mine too."

I'm not sure what she means, so I wait patiently for her to continue, all the while saying a silent prayer that she doesn't kick my sorry ass to the curb.

She removes her hand from his grip and turns to look at me. I back up so she has room to lie on her back. Propping myself up on my elbow, I look down at her. I want to kiss her, to tell her she never has to worry about me playing games with her, but I need her to come to that conclusion on her own. No matter how long it takes her to get there, I'll give her that time. Not having her in our lives is not an option at this point.

I'm too far gone.

"He brought you to me. I was convinced that I was finished with relationships. Cal had left a wound so deep I never thought it would fill."

Needing to touch her, I trace her jawline with my index finger. She shivers at the contact.

"Knox brought you to me."

She closes her eyes, and I want to demand that she open them. I can't get a good read on what she's thinking, what she's feeling when those baby blues aren't looking at me.

When she finally does open them, there's a sea of emotion staring back at me. "Not only are you filling the wound, you're healing my soul. I will admit that what you've told me about your relationship with Stephanie, it bothers me. However, you've never once made me feel like I was any less than everything in your eyes. Call me crazy, but I'm not willing to give that up. It's a feeling I'm quickly becoming addicted to."

I place my lips next to hers, and this time, I let her take the lead. She doesn't disappoint, her tongue tracing my lips, silently asking me to open for her. I do. Hell fucking yes, I do, in every way possible. My heart, my head, my soul, and my mouth to taste her. Everything I am is open for her.

Just her.

My sweet girl.

She slides her tongue against mine and I grip her hip, pulling her closer to me. I just can't seem to ever be close enough to her. I want to fucking devour her, but I don't. I hold back, letting her show me how far she wants to take this. Whatever she wants, she gets.

"Ridge," she says, pulling away.

"Yeah, babe?" I kiss down her jaw, tracing her neck with my tongue.

"There's someone at the door."

"Don't care," I mumble against her neck.

"Ridge." She laughs, one so carefree I vow to hear it daily.

Burying my face in her neck, I sigh, defeated. "Fine, but I'm not done with you." I kiss her lips one last time before climbing to my feet, adjusting my hard-on to answer the damn door. "This better be good," I grumble as I pull it open.

"Hey, man," Kent greets me.

I try hard not to scowl at him. "What's up?"

"Dad called and he's got the tractor stuck down over the hill. Wanted to see if you had time to help me pull him out. Mom said she would keep an eye on Knox."

"Come on in." I hold the door open and once he's inside, I head back to the living room. Kendall is on all fours, smiling down at Knox and making noises that I'm sure have some pretty crazy faces to go with them, but her fine ass waving in the air is distracting me from finding out or even laughing at her antics.

"Hey, Kendall." Kent chuckles.

She turns to look behind her and laughs. "Busted, little man." She sits back on her butt and picks Knox up, settling him in her lap. "Hi." She takes Knox's hand and waves at Kent.

This girl.

"Babe, Kent's dad got their tractor stuck, and he needs me to help him get it out. I'm sorry."

"Of course. This little guy and I will just hang out until you get back." She stands from her sitting position on the floor, as if she needs to stand tall for me to let her keep my son.

I stand there watching her. I didn't expect her to offer to keep him, but then again, I should have. That's just Kendall. "You don't have to. Kent's mom—"

"Tell Daddy we got this, Knox." Her blue eyes look up at me. "We'll be here when you get back."

A vision of coming home to her every day flashes through my mind. Her force, whatever it is, pulls me to her.

I wrap my arms around both of them. "I'll hurry." I kiss Knox on top of the head. "You be good for Kendall," I tell my son, who doesn't have a fucking clue what I'm saying. "And you, I'll be back soon."

She tilts her head up and I take my chance to kiss her. "Be safe," she whispers.

Reluctantly, I release her and follow Kent out the door.

Chapter 34

Kendall

"Well, it's just you and me, kid," I say to Knox. I decide to use my time wisely to help Ridge out a little bit, so I climb the stairs to Knox's room and grab him a sleeper. It's already almost five, so bath time and PJ's it is. I set out his clothes and walk across the hall to the bathroom. His little lip quivers as soon as I pour water over him, and he also pees in it. I turn the water back on, double-checking the temperature, and begin to bathe him. I work quickly, and luck is on my side because he cooperates—plus no more accidents.

"Look at that little lip. I'm sorry. Let's get you some warm clothes on." I carry him back to his room, drying and dressing him quickly. I open his closet to find the hamper and see an infant wrap still in the package. It's never been opened. I smile, thinking of Ridge walking around the house with baby Knox wrapped up and close to his chest. I open the package and read the instructions. This thing looks like a puzzle, but I finally figure it out and soon have Knox strapped to my chest.

Downstairs, I decide to clean up, Knox snoozing away as if this is a normal occurrence. Once I finish with the living room, I head into the kitchen, thinking I could make dinner for Ridge, but his cupboards are that of a bachelor for sure. He has the base for the car seat in his truck, so going to the store is out.

Digging a little deeper in the freezer, I find some frozen lasagna and garlic bread. That will have to do. I break the lasagna into little pieces, spray the bottom of the Crock-Pot I happened to find with non-stick spray, and add the pieces of lasagna. I don't know what time he'll be back, so this will ensure it cooks and stays warm for him.

Dinner established, I decide to go sit in the gazebo. I grab my purse and pull out my e-reader and phone then remember seeing a smaller diaper bag in the bottom of Knox's closet so I run upstairs and get it. I toss my things in, adding a blanket, bottle, and binky for Knox—not that we're going to be far, but being prepared is just me. I guess Ridge and I have that in common. I slide into my shoes and decide I should write Ridge a note on the dry erase board on the fridge, in case I don't hear him come home.

Daddy,

Kendall took me down to the pond.

Love,

Knox

I giggle when I read the note. I'm sure Ridge will get a kick out of it too. I grab the small diaper bag I just packed and head to the gazebo.

It blocks us from the sun, and there's a small warm breeze once we're settled onto the wooden bench. Peeking down at Knox, he's still snoozing away. I take a minute to just close my eyes and let the breeze blow through my hair. It's so peaceful here.

I feel lips press against my forehead, causing my eyes to pop open.

"Hey, Sleeping Beauty," Ridge says softly.

I smile. "Hey, get everything taken care of?"

"Yeah, I've been back for about ten minutes or so."

"Did you see my note?" I hope he wasn't worried.

He tucks a strand of hair behind my ear, only to have the wind whip it right back out. "I've been watching you sleep."

"Creeper." I smile.

"Beautiful," he murmurs, bending to kiss me.

I blush. "What time is it?"

"After seven. Let's get you two inside." He stands and offers me his hand. Once he pulls me up, he grabs the diaper bag and we walk back to the house, arms wrapped around each other. "You made dinner," he says, closing the door behind us.

"Well, not really. I put frozen lasagna in the Crock-Pot. It was slim-picking and you had the base of the car seat, so I was kind of stuck." Not that he would've wanted me driving around town with his son.

"We need to get you one," he says casually.

"One what?"

"A base for his car seat."

Okay then. I guess I got my answer. "I just need to put the garlic bread in the oven, and it'll be ready in about ten minutes."

"I got it. You want me to take him?"

"No, he probably needs changed, and he hasn't eaten since the diner. I took a bottle with us down to the pond, but he never woke up to eat."

"Where did you find that thing?" He points to my chest.

"In the bottom of his closet. I gave him a bath so you wouldn't have to, and I was looking for the clothes hamper and just happened to find this."

"Little man has all the luck." He smiles.

"Oh, yeah, and what makes you say that?"

"He got to sleep on your chest all afternoon."

Again, I feel the heat creep across my cheeks.

"Charmer."

"I speak the truth." He winks.

I manage to get Knox out of the wrap without harming either one of us. As soon as I do, he starts to fuss and I know he's hungry. A quick diaper change and he's having dinner.

"I can feed him," Ridge says, looking over at me from the back of the couch.

"It's fine, Ridge. I don't mind helping. This little guy is easy to fall for."

"Oh, yeah? And what about his daddy?"

"Jury's still out," I tease.

He laughs and kisses the top of my head. "It's ready. I'll bring plates in here. What do you want to drink?"

"Just water."

I insist on Ridge eating before me while Knox finishes his bottle. The two of them play on the floor while I eat and watch them.

"I thought spending the day with you would help this craving I seem to have where you're concerned."

I just about choke on my garlic bread. I cough, chew, swallow and take a drink of water before asking, "And?"

"Not even close. I hate that you're going home soon."

"Hey, you'll see me tomorrow though, right? Knox has his one-month appointment."

"Yeah, it's first thing. That way, I can just take him to Mom after then head to work."

"Good plan. Then your parents are having their Memorial Day cookout this weekend. Reagan invited Dawn and me, but. . . ."

"I want you there, Kendall. Not as a friend of Reagan's, but as my girlfriend. And that's not until Saturday night. No way in hell am I going from spending the day with you today to a quick visit at your work and then not again until Saturday. No way. I need more time with you."

"I'm home most days by five, unless I'm covering for one of the girls. You let me know when you have time."

"Every night after five." He laughs. "All the way through until . . . What time do you leave for work?"

"That's a lot of time." I smile at him.

"I don't know if any amount of time with you will ever be enough." He says it almost as if he's talking to himself, all the while looking at Knox. Someone walking in on our conversation would think he was talking about his son, and he very well may be, but I also know those words are for me.

I stay long enough to help him clean up the kitchen, and then head home. He walks me to my car and gives me a good-bye kiss that I won't soon forget, with a promise from me that I'll let him know I make it home safe.

❦❦❦

RIDGE AND I have been official for over a month now. I met his parents at their Memorial Day cookout, and he met mine when they showed up at my grandparents' house to check out all the work. Ridge promised me that they didn't say anything to embarrass me.

This is a short workweek, today being my last day since Saturday is the Fourth of July. My office is closed on Friday in observance of the holiday. Gotta love three-day weekends.

Ridge and I are going out tomorrow night, just the two of us; Reagan's going to watch Knox at his place. I'm excited and nervous. We've spent every day together this past month, since each night after work, I stop by his place and we have dinner together. It's just easier with Knox and all his stuff being there. It's a lot to travel with a baby to anticipate what you might need.

Normally, I would feel guilty leaving Dawn at home so much by herself, except that's not the case. She and Mark really hit it off and have been spending a lot of time together. I'm happy for her.

> **Me:** *Leaving work now. Have to stop by the house and change. You home yet?*
>
> **Ridge:** Yep. The boys and I took off early today.
>
> **Me:** *Lucky. See you soon.*
>
> **Ridge:** Be safe, babe.

I place my phone in the cup holder and pull out of the parking lot. I'm ready for this weekend, and excited for tomorrow night with Ridge.

Dawn is staying at Mark's, so we'll have my place to ourselves, if that's where the night leads. If our make-out sessions are any indication, or Ridge's vow that I'm killing him, I would say the chances are good.

Chapter 35

Ridge

I let the guys off early today. I've been ramped up on excitement, surprising Kendall with a night away. I've antagonized over leaving Knox, but Reagan will have him at my house. He'll be in a familiar setting, and regardless of how she pouts when Kendall's around, he loves his Aunt Reagan. He also loves my girl.

I've been taking things slow with her physically. I know my bet involving Stephanie worried her; I could see it in her eyes. I wanted to make sure she knew she's what I want, not just what she can give me—not because she loves my kid, but because of who she is. I've found willpower I didn't even know I had. She's stayed over a few nights and it was hard as hell—literally and figuratively—to hold her next to me all night and not know what she feels like from the inside. Tonight, I plan to change that.

I need her. It's way past want; I literally feel like I need her to breathe. I'm falling for her. Every day, something will happen that has me giving her another tiny piece of my heart. From the way she sends me messages out of the blue, just to say hello, to the way she seems to melt into me every time I touch her. She's great with Knox and my parents,' sister, and friends all adore her. They're not the only ones. My son lights up when she walks into a room. I should be worried that he's growing attached to her. Hell, he's only two months old, but you can see it when he hears her voice. He loves her. I'm not worried though because, like my son, I'm well on my way.

Mark gave me Dawn's number and she packed a bag for her. He brought it to me to work this morning. I waited for him or the guys to ride my ass about it, but surprisingly none of them said a word.

I'm just finished putting away the groceries Reagan requested when I hear Knox waking up from his nap over the baby monitor. I rush upstairs to get him. "Hey, little man. You have a good nap?"

He coos and flaps his little arms. "You remember what tonight is, right? Aunt Reagan is going to have a sleepover while Daddy and Kendall have one as well, just not here close to little ears."

I change his diaper and grab his binky before heading downstairs. We settle on the floor under his baby gym, which he loves. That's how Reagan and Tyler find us twenty minutes later.

"Hey, you two," Reagan says, taking a seat on the couch. Tyler follows behind her.

"Hey, man," I greet him. Not sure exactly what he's doing here, because he knows I'm leaving with Kendall tonight.

"This one forgot to put oil in her car and it wouldn't start."

That explains it. "Sister, I told you to get your oil changed weeks ago."

"I know, I know, I just forgot. Don't worry, Mom and Dad said they would bring me one of theirs in case there's an emergency."

I panic slightly at the thought of there being an emergency involving my son while I'm away having what I hope to be a magical night with my girlfriend. Reagan must see it on my face.

"Chill, Daddy. He'll be fine. It's just better safe than sorry."

"I'll be around, man. Don't stress. You've been looking forward to this," Tyler says.

"Thanks. It's just . . . I've never spent the night away from him."

"And if it were for anyone other than Kendall I'd give you shit for it, but it's her, man." He says it as if just her name explains it all. I guess it does.

Reagan tries to take Knox from me, but I hold him tight. We sit around and talk for the next twenty minutes or so until I hear her pull up. "She doesn't know," I remind them. "Just play it cool."

Tyler throws his head back and laughs. "Dude, it's not us you need to worry about. You're a wreck."

"Hello," Kendall's sweet voice calls as she enters the house. "Hey, didn't expect to see you two." Leaning down, she hugs Reagan and kisses Tyler on the cheek. I glare at him, which causes him to laugh even harder. "What did I miss?"

"Nothing, just your man being jealous," Reagan tells her.

"Hello, handsome," she says, leaning toward me. Only her lips connect with Knox's forehead.

"Kendall," I growl. She knows I need those lips first thing.

She giggles and places a tender kiss on my lips. "I missed you," she whispers.

Gone.

G.O.N.E for this girl.

"Missed you too, sweet girl," I whisper back.

She takes the seat beside me. "Gimme." She holds her hands out for Knox, and he smiles.

I hand him over, partly because I want them both in my arms and it's easier if she's holding him, and partly because I know she's attached to my boy. As soon as I have Knox transferred to her arms, I reach behind her, grip her hips, and lift them onto my lap. She doesn't even yelp in surprise anymore; she expects my caveman antics. It's not something I can control, or have even tried to. I want them close, always.

"So, what are the two of you into?" she asks Tyler and my sister.

"I asked them to stop by," I say, rubbing circles on her legs.

"You all want to do dinner?" she asks.

"Actually, babe, I have a surprise for you."

She looks at me over her shoulder. "You do?"

"Yeah, Reagan is actually going to keep Knox, so I thought we could go away for the night."

She looks down at Knox, and I can see that she's also struggling with leaving him. She does at night, but it's always with me. "We have a date, just us, tomorrow night," she reminds me.

"I rented us a cabin, up at Thompson Lake."

"Seriously?" she asks.

I think it's finally starting to set it. "I don't have any clothes. We have to stop by my house." She looks at Reagan. "Are you sure you can keep him? We can take him with us."

My sweet girl.

"It's all good, Kendall," Reagan assures her. "I've known for a couple of weeks."

Kendall hugs Knox closer. "When do we leave?"

"As soon as you feel like you've had enough loving from the little man. I had Dawn pack you a bag. It's already in the truck."

"Hey, bud, you get to have a sleepover with Aunt Reagan," Kendall continues to talk to my son. He may not understand her, but he hangs onto every word. His eyes follow her as she talks, never looking away.

"You be a good boy," she tells Knox, and her voice breaks.

"You okay?" I whisper in her ear.

"Why am I upset? He's not mine. I mean, it's . . ." She stands against my attempt to keep her on my lap, hands Knox to me, and walks out of the room.

I stand to follow her and Reagan holds her hand up. "Ridge, stop. She loves him; this is a hard situation for her. Let her have a minute."

I take a step toward the hall and Tyler stands too. "She needs a minute, Ridge. Think about it. She's been with you since he was, what, a week or so old? She's here all the time." "She leaves him with you at night, but no one else. She wears her heart on her sleeve, that one," Reagan adds.

I wait as long as I can stand it before I hand Knox to Reagan and go in search of her. I knock lightly on the bathroom door and she opens it slowly, silent tears rolling down her cheeks.

"I'm sorry. I know I have no right, and I'm trying to control it, I just . . . I'm sorry. I'm excited about going away, I am. I want time with you."

I step into the small half bath and close the door behind me. Hands on her hips, I lift her to sit on the counter. I pull a tissue out of the box on the back of the toilet and wipe her cheeks.

"You love him, Kendall. I get that. Hell, it causes all kinds of emotions to swirl inside me. He's a part of me."

"I do and he is, but he's such a sweet baby, and I miss him when I'm not with you. I miss you when I'm not with you," she says, looking down at her lap.

"Baby, look at me." I wait for her sad blue eyes to meet mine. "We miss you too. Both of us. We love you." Shit! This is not how I wanted to tell her. I had it all planned out for tonight—to tell her I've fallen in love with her, make love to her, candles, a bottle of wine, all that. I had it all planned and I blurt it out in my bathroom.

Real smooth, jackass.

I need to fix this. I cup her face in my hands so she can't look away. She hasn't said a word, and that scares the hell out of me. "I'm in love with you. All of me, every second, every hour, every day that I spend with you, that love grows, and I ache until I can see you again." Her silent tears continue to fall, but she remains silent. "It gets me here," I say, holding our combined hands over my heart. "Seeing you with my son. The way you love him."

"I do," she says, her voice soft. "I love both of you so much, and it's been fast and perfect, and I wouldn't change it for anything. I'm just scared that it's going to go away. That the universe will fight against me, against us being this happy."

Not gonna lie, I'm choke up. "You love me?" I ask her.

She laughs. "You caught that, did you?"

"I did." I kiss her tear-covered lips then rest my forehead against hers. "This is real, Kendall. This is me and you and that little boy in there, living life. Who cares if it was fast or what others might think, even the universe? It's ours, and that's all that matters."

Chapter 36

Kendall

I am such a baby. I know he's not mine, but God does it feel like he is. I love that little boy with everything inside me. If I lose Ridge, I lose Knox, and I think that's what threw me over the edge. It hit me that those two have become my world in such a small amount of time.

I wouldn't come back from losing them.

"I'm sure they think I've lost my marbles," I say into Ridge's chest. He's holding me close as I sit on the small counter in his bathroom.

He chuckles. "No, they don't. They get it. They told me to give you time, but I couldn't stand the thought of you hurting and me not being there to hold you through it."

I slip my hands under his shirt and feel the defined planes of his back as he holds me. I told him I loved them, both of them, but it's more than that. It's as if I'm no longer me without them. Nothing makes sense in my life without seeing the two of them as a part of it. Part of me is fearful Ridge would think I am trying to take Melissa's place. Don't get me wrong, it would be an honor to have that little man call me Mom, but that choice will be up to Ridge. Maybe one day in the future.

I would never want to take her place. I like to think that she's looking down on us, and she's happy that Ridge found someone who loves them the way I do. I think about my parents' and my childhood. If it were me looking down on those I loved, I know it would bring me peace.

"You love me?" I ask him, needing to hear it again.

He chuckles. "I more than love you, Kendall. I just don't have the words to explain it. It's all-consuming, fierce, and I promise you it's forever."

Pulling back, I look up at him, a slow smile spreading across my face. "Let's go say good-bye to little man and head to the cabin."

His lips touch mine. "Love you, sweet girl." He steps back and lifts me from the counter.

I follow him downstairs, dreading seeing Tyler and Reagan after the way I acted, but I should've known better. Reagan has Knox, and as soon as she sees us she walks right past Ridge and stops in front of me.

"You okay?" she asks, her voice low. I nod and offer her a teary smile. She surprises me when she pulls me into a one-armed hug. "He loves you. They both do. Embrace it, Kendall."

I want to tell her that he told me. That I just shared one of the best moments of my life in that little half bath, but I don't have time before she's pulling away and handing Knox to me.

"Hey, buddy," I say, my voice cracking. He grins up at me, and I can literally feel that grin tugging on my heartstrings.

"We're going to take a minute." Ridge places his hand on the small of my back. I don't question him, allowing him to guide us upstairs.

Chapter 37

Ridge

It only took us another twenty minutes before we were loading up and on the road. Kendall and I took Knox up to my room and just cuddled with him. The way she loves my son makes my heart feel as though it's going to beat right out of my chest. I want to tell her that she has nothing to worry about, that she's it for me and she'll never be apart from us, but I don't want to scare her away.

She's in my soul, and nothing is going to change that. I want her now and always, and she fucking loves me. I didn't want to tell her like I did, but in reality it was perfect. She knows it was unplanned, that my love for her bubbled over and I had no choice but to tell her. The fact that she said it back is the cause of the permanent grin on my face.

The two-hour drive to the cabin is quiet. I reached out for her hand as soon as we were in the truck and she latched on, her grip tight the entire trip. I know my girl, and she's processing tonight and earlier. The fact that we said "I love you" just hours ago.

"Is this it?" she asks.

"Yep, this is it. Have you ever been here?"

"No, although I've heard good things. Dad actually brought Mom here for their anniversary one year."

"Smart man," I say with a wink. That brings out her blinding smile.

"I think so. My parents' are amazing."

"Of course they are. They raised you, didn't they?"

"Charmer." She grins.

"Only for you, sweet girl. Only for you." I grab our bags with complaint from Kendall that she can carry hers. Yeah, not gonna happen. Instead, I hand her the key to the cabin, and she unlocks the door for us.

"Ridge . . ." She stands in the center of the room and turns in a circle. "This place is great. It's not at all what I expected."

I laugh at that. "What exactly did you expect?"

"Something more . . . rustic."

"I didn't really want to rough it this trip. I have plans that all the amenities will be needed for."

"Oh, yeah? And what might that be? Painting each other's toenails?" she sasses.

I drop our bags and stalk toward her, throwing her over my shoulder. "Not even close," I say, smacking her ass and carrying her off to the bedroom. I toss her on the bed and she's laughing so hard she can hardly catch her breath.

"Caveman." She giggles. "My cabin. My woman," she says, attempting a manly voice.

"Not my cabin," I lean down to kiss her neck. She tilts her head, giving me full access. "My woman." I trace the length of her neck with my tongue, until my lips reach her ear. "My everything," I whisper, and she shudders. I'm not sure it's from my words, my touch—hell maybe both. Not that it matters, of course. I have her right where I want her. Two months. Two fucking long-ass months without knowing what it feels like to be inside her. That changes tonight.

I pull back from the kiss and search out those baby blues. What I see surely matches the reflection in my own—passion, want, lust, and love. Tonight has been a long time coming.

Standing to my full height, I lace my fingers through hers and guide her off the bed. She doesn't hesitate. Once I have her standing before me, I kiss her again.

Slow and steady wins the race. As much as I want to rush through this, to push inside her now, I won't. I'm going to savor her, cherish the gift of this amazing, beautiful woman.

"Lift your arms," I whisper against her lips. Again, she doesn't hesitate, her arms slowly rising into the air. My fingers slide under her shirt, and she shivers when my fingers trace up her bare stomach. I run my hand underneath her bra, tracing a line across her chest against the lacy material. Her eyes are closed, her teeth clamped onto her bottom lip. I'm not only driving her crazy, but me as well. I drag my hands down her soft skin and grip the hem of her shirt. Quickly, I pull it up and over her head. This isn't the first time I've seen her, but this is the first time I know she's mine, know she loves me, and I'll get to feel her heat wrapped around me. Reaching down, I adjust my hard cock.

Tilting my head, I latch onto one of her perfectly pert nipples through her bra.

"Ridge," she moans, and I have to remind myself to go slow.

"Yeah, babe?" Her eyes pop open and glare at me. I wink at her before crossing over and pulling the other tight bud into my mouth. Her hands grip my shoulders, and I welcome the pain of her nails as they dig into my skin. This is real. She's real, and this is happening. I will gladly bear the markings of our night together.

Dropping to my knees in front of her, I lavish her with kisses, tasting her skin everywhere my lips will reach. When I reach the waistband of her jeans, I unsnap them and slowly slide the zipper down, the sound echoing into the quiet room. The only other sounds are our breathing and my lips against her skin.

"Hold on to me," I tell her. My voice is raspy and filled with want. All for her.

When her hands land on my shoulders, I grip her jeans and pull them over her hips then down her long legs. I'm so lost in her I forgot I had to take her shoes off. "Sit down, babe." She falls to the bed as if her legs can no longer hold her up; I grin because I did that. I make quick work of removing her shoes, her jeans immediately following. Looking up, my girl is lying back on the bed, propped up on her elbows, wearing nothing but her sexy-as-fuck black lace bra and panties. I take a minute to memorize her in this moment, burning the image of my beautiful sweet girl in my brain to last me a lifetime. When we're old and gray and watching our grandkids run around the yard, I want to remember this moment, the entire fucking day. The day we pledged our love for each other, both through words and actions. Because that's what I'm doing— I'm showing her how much I love her through touch. I'll be fucking her, but there will never be a doubt in her mind that it's not the result of the love I feel for her.

I stand and as if she can read my mind, she moves back to fully lie on the bed. I rip the shirt over my head, kick off my shoes, and quickly discard my pants, taking my boxer briefs with them. Bending down, I pull off my socks, reaching up to grab hers as well. She giggles when I swipe my finger up the center of the bottom of her foot.

"Love that fucking sound, sweet girl," I say, climbing on the bed to lie beside her.

"I'm ticklish."

"Hmm, I'll have to store that for a later day." I kiss her sweet lips.

"What about you?" she asks when I finally release her mouth. "Are you ticklish?"

"Nope," I lie.

She studies me, her blue eyes trying to determine if I'm telling the truth. I work my arm around her to unhook her bra, needing her naked. She surprises me; once I have both arms around her, her hands trail up my sides and she tickles me. She didn't think it out too well because I have my arms around her; even though I'm laughing, I'm able to grip her hips and lift her over me. As soon as her hot center lands on my hard cock, she stops her assault. She rocks her hips and I throw my head back on the pillow, letting the feel of her heat wash over me. Only a thin piece of lace is separating us, and I want it gone.

"Kendall." Her name is a plea falling from my lips.

She rocks against me again. Her bra, which I successfully unsnapped, is hanging off her arms. She slowly removes it, one strap at a time, and tosses it over her head.

"Fucking gorgeous," I say, sitting up to kiss her. I'm barely able to press my lips to hers when she pushes me back down on the bed. She rocks against me again, throwing her head back, her long dark hair cascading down her back.

"Feels good," she murmurs.

Fuck this! The panties need to go. "Lift for me," I say, tapping her thigh. She does as I ask. I grip her panties and tear first one side then the other, careful not to mar her perfect skin in the process.

"Those were my favorite," she pouts.

"They were in the way."

She sits back down and her wetness coats my cock. She again rocks her hips, and a slight shift would have me sliding home, inside her heat.

Flipping her over, I land on top of her. "I'm clean," she says out of the blue. "I mean, I'm on the pill and . . . it's been a while and after Cal, I was tested . . . I mean, I have been several times since him, just you know, wanted to be sure. We always used protection, but I just . . . Yeah, I'll shut up now," she rambles on.

God, I love this girl.

"Me too, babe. I've never gone without, but that doesn't mean it's not possible. I mean, that's how I got my son, after all."

Her panic softens at the mention of Knox. "He's a miracle baby." She smiles.

"He is," I agree. "I've been tested since Stephanie, but it's a risk, Kendall. Apparently, my boys are good swimmers." I wink to try and lighten this conversation. Not to mention it's killing the mood.

She nods. "It is, but it's one I'm willing to take with you. I don't want anything between us."

I grip the sheets by her head. It takes all my will power and strength not to thrust my hips and slide inside her, but I hold off, much to my cock's disappointment.

"It's your call, sweet girl." The thought of her carrying my baby does something to me; it's the same feeling I get when she tells me she loves me.

As if she's reading my mind, she says, "I love you, Ridge."

I nod. Decision made. Less talking, more kissing.

I crush my lips to hers, sliding my tongue past her lips. Hers duals with mine. She wraps her legs around my waist and tries to pull me closer, whimpering when I hold steady.

"Please," she begs against my mouth.

I pull away and smirk at her. "We have all night," I remind her.

She huffs out a breath in frustration, but when I latch onto a bare nipple and suck it into my mouth, it turns into a low moan, deep from the back of her throat. I take my time, giving each of her perfect tits equal attention. I could spend hours doing just this, but not tonight. Tonight, I want to experience all of her.

Releasing her nipple with a small pop, I move down her body, not pausing until I reach her belly button. I trace it with my tongue and her hands land in my hair. It's actually kind of perfect because of where I'm headed next. Even though this isn't the first time I've tasted her, it feels like it is. Every touch, every caress, every joining of our bodies feels more intimate to me because she knows I love her. She knows this is more to me, that it's everything. That *she* is everything.

Tonight, all night, one hour at a time, I'm going to show her over and over until every part of my soul is infused with hers.

With her hands buried in my hair, I dip my tongue into her hot center and she tightens her grip. That slip of control from her has me losing mine. I devour her, adding one finger then two, humming my satisfaction as I bury my face deeper. She lifts her hips trying to get me closer, chasing her release. What my girl wants, she gets. I increase my efforts, nipping, licking, sucking, and humming, all the while working my fingers in and out of her. Not a minute later, she's calling out my name.

"Ridge!" she screams as she holds my mouth tight against her. I don't stop until I feel her slump against the bed.

Chapter 38

Kendall

I slump against the bed, releasing the death grip I have on his hair. My body feels like Jell-O, my limbs are weak, my heart is racing and the delicious ache between my thighs tells me I want more—more of Ridge, more of his mouth, but most importantly, all of him. I need to feel him inside me, to have that connection with him that we've been fighting since day one.

At first, I thought he didn't want to sleep with me—that was until he started rounding the bases. However, no matter how hard I tried he wouldn't slide home. He said I needed to understand that he wanted to be with me for more than that, and waiting was the best way to prove it. It's not until I heard him mumble something that sounded like "you're more than a fucking bet ever could be" that I understood his hesitation. After that, I let him have control. I knew we would be here eventually, and I have to say, the months of foreplay have my senses on high alert.

Ridge lifts his head and wipes his mouth on the back of his hand.

This time was different; he was relentless, working me to orgasm as if he needed it just as bad as I did. From the feel of his hard cock against my thigh, I'd dare to say I'm right.

"I need you." I whisper the words, but from the flare of heat in his eyes, I know he heard me.

Slowly, he slides his hard body up mine, until our lips are once again fused. I can taste myself, and although it's not my favorite thing, no way in hell am I stopping. When I said I needed him, I wasn't exaggerating. I need him to breathe.

He rests his elbows on either side of my head, holding the majority of his weight off me while he runs his fingers through my hair. "You're beautiful, Kendall," he says, his eyes holding mine. I can feel my face heat.

"My sweet girl," he murmurs as he kisses each cheek, my chin, my nose. Finally, his lips land on my forehead, and he holds them there.

I run my fingers through his already mussed hair. It's sexy on him. Of course, Ridge could make anything look sexy. Leaning up, I trace the star tattoo just above his left pec with my tongue, and he hums his satisfaction. I love his ink. I've spent hours tracing them, memorizing every line, every angle of each one.

I wrap my legs around his waist and lock my ankles behind his back. Lifting my hips, I show him what I want, what I need.

"I've never done this," he whispers as he nips at my earlobe.

I'm confused at first, because he has an adorable little boy.

"Not without protection. That's a big deal, Kendall. For the chance that I totally sound like a woman right now, I need you to tell me this is what you want."

"Yes." I don't hesitate. Is it my smartest decision? Probably not, but I want it.

He rests his forehead against mine. "You unman me, baby."

Reaching down with one hand, he grabs his erection and slides it through my folds. I

whimper at the contact. This is a first for us—the first of many, I can only hope.

I place my hand on his arm. My intent is to help him guide himself home, but I notice the slight tremor in his hand. "You're shaking."

"Yeah." He chuckles, but then his face grows serious. "When we do this, you're mine, Kendall. I need you to know that there's nothing that will take you from me. That's it, we seal the fate of our future."

If I wasn't wet before, I am now. "Yes" is my answer, the only word I can seem to push past the emotion clogging my throat.

A slow smile tips his lips. Lowering his head, he whispers in my ear, "I love you, Kendall."

Then he pushes inside.

I sink my teeth into my bottom lip to keep from crying out—not in pain, but in relief. He's had me on edge for weeks. Sliding my arms under his, I hug him as tight as I can, my nails digging into this skin. He moans and thrusts a little faster. It fuels him, my need for him, so I sink my nails in deeper and hang on for the ride.

"So." Thrust. "Fucking." Thrust. "Sweet." Thrust. His hips move in shorter, faster strokes, and I can feel myself start to fall. It's been well over a year for me, and it's Ridge. I have no restraint when it comes to him.

"So close," I pant, lifting my hips and tightening my legs that are still locked around him.

"I'm with you, baby. Let me hear you," he grits out as he unleashes.

I hold on, digging my heels in his ass and my nails in his back as I just feel. Feel all of him. "Now."

He does this move with his hips that hits just the right spot, and I'm doing exactly what he says as I scream out his name. "Ridge!"

Falling into me, he buries his face in my neck as his orgasm works through him.

We lie there, both of us utterly spent. I run my hands lightly over his sweat-covered back.

"Shower."

I chuckle because I couldn't agree more. "Please," I answer him.

"It's not nice to laugh at a man after sex, sweet girl," he mumbles into my neck.

I playfully slap his shoulder. "Not at you, the situation. It's messy." I curl up my nose.

I can feel his chest bouncing with his silent laughter. "That it is, baby. Let's get cleaned up, and we can throw some steaks on the grill." He slowly pulls away from me.

Once he's on his feet, he helps pull me to mine and leads us to the shower. It's a huge walk-in big enough for ten people, but it's just the two of us. "You're dirty," he whispers in my ear as he runs his fingers through my folds.

"You make me dirty," I reply, tilting my head, giving him better access. I'll let him get me dirty any second, any minute, and any hour of every damn day.

"I like it," he says, kissing me neck.

"Oh, yeah?" My voice is all breathy from the way his lips against my skin make me feel. He consumes me.

"Mmhmm." He reaches around me for body wash, and it's the exact kind I use. I don't ask how he got it in here. Our bags are still at the door where he dropped them, but I know Ridge—he's always prepared.

He pours a huge glob into his hands and slowly runs them over every inch of me. I stand still, enjoying the feel of his rough, callused hands as they tenderly roam over my heated skin.

"Your turn," I say once I'm rinsed off. I return the favor, taking my time, running my hands over every muscle, tracing every tattoo. That's my favorite thing to do, but I think doing it in the shower tops all other locations.

We stay there until the water turns cold. Ridge hops out and grabs a towel, wrapping it around me. "I'll go get our bags." He kisses me quickly, grabs a towel for himself, and pads out the door, dripping water everywhere.

By the time he's back, I'm dried off with my hair up in a towel. "Do we have to wear clothes?" he asks, roaming his eyes up and down my body.

"Nah, I'm sure the neighbors won't mind me flashing my girly bits as we grill our steaks," I say casually.

"Fuck that." He digs in his bag, pulls out one of his T-shirts, and hands it to me. "This should cover everything."

"I have clothes, right?" I ask because, honestly, I'm not sure. He said he had Dawn pack me a bag.

"Yeah, but you don't need them when you have mine." He pulls on a pair of boxer briefs and a pair of jeans that are ripped, worn, and sexy hell. Just seeing them on him makes me wish he were taking them off, not putting them on.

"I'm going to start the grill." He pulls me in for a quick kiss and then he's out the door.

Considering he wants me in nothing but his T-shirt, I don't bother too much with my appearance. I quickly brush my hair, dig in my bag for a hair tie, put it in a topknot, and call it good.

I find Ridge in the kitchen, pulling out the makings for salad. Standing behind him, I place my hand on his back. "Can I help?"

"Yep." He turns, lifts me up, and sits me on the counter. "You can keep me company."

"How do you think they're doing with the little guy?" I ask.

He smiles up at me. "I was just thinking the same thing."

"Can we call her?"

Drying his hands, he reaches across the counter, grabs his phone, and dials Reagan. Putting it on speaker, he hands it to me with a quick kiss before going back to the salad.

"Hello," Reagan answers, laughing.

"Hey, sister," Ridge says. "How's our boy?"

Our boy.

"Adorable. Tyler is making these crazy-ass faces and his grin is cracking us up. He's talking up a storm."

Ridge lifts his head and he's smiling from ear to ear. "That's great. Let us talk to him."

"Sure, hold on a second. Hey, Knox. Daddy and Kendall want to say hi." I hear rustling, and then his little baby babbles come over the line.

"Hey, buddy. Daddy misses you," Ridge says into the phone.

Knox coos and babbles some more.

"Say hi," he whispers to me.

"Hey, little man. Hope you're being good for Aunt Reagan." I wait to hear his baby talk back to me, but there's nothing.

"Hey, who was just talking to him?" Reagan's back on the line.

"Kendall," Ridge says.

She laughs. "You should have seen him. He was looking around everywhere, like you were going to be hiding behind him or something. Here he is again."

"All right, bud. You be good. Daddy and Kendall will see you tomorrow," Ridge tells him. Greeted with silence.

"Same thing. Kendall again?" Reagan asks.

"Nope. It was me."

"You two have this little guy spoiled rotten." She laughs. "All's good on the home front. He's getting ready to have his last bottle for the night before we put him down."

I wait for Ridge to ask if Tyler is staying too, but he doesn't. I'm sure once it hits him he'll be wanting answers. It *is* one of his best friends and his little sister, after all.

"Sounds good. We'll be home early afternoon, in time for the cookout at Mom and Dad's," Ridge tells her.

"Gotcha, brother. You two kids behave," she says, and the line goes dead.

"He sounded happy," I whisper.

"He is happy. He's loved." Ridge kisses me slowly. "I need to go check on the steaks."

Chapter 39

Ridge

I could not have asked for a better trip. Kendall and I spent the entire time wrapped in each other's arms, exploring each other's bodies. It's a night that I'm sure to never forget.

We left a little earlier than what I planned, but when I woke up this morning with my girl in my arms, something was missing—my son. It's like she could read my mind, because she asked if we could leave a little early to get back and beat traffic. I knew the real reason why.

Mom and Dad are having another cookout for the Fourth. They love to entertain and now that Dad is retired, Mom doesn't mind it as much because he's there to help her. I have one more surprise for Kendall this weekend—I called her parents and invited them. They made up an excuse when she asked them their plans. I want both of our families together. Family is important and she's a huge part of mine, and I want her parents to be involved in that.

"I almost forgot to tell you." She turns to face me in the passenger seat of the truck, as much as her seatbelt will allow. "I got Knox the cutest little outfit for today." She stops. "I mean, if you want him to wear it today."

"Hey." I reach over and grab her hand. "Yes, I do. It's fine, babe. I love that you love him," I tell her honestly.

She grins. "It's the cutest little pair of jean shorts, and a red shirt and blue tank top. I even got him a matching fisherman's hat and a pair of sunglasses."

Seeing her excitement over an outfit for my son makes me smile. She's such a sweet person with a heart of gold. I'm a damn lucky man that she chose us.

"We'll have to make sure Mom gets a picture of the three of us. Not that we'll need to ask her, since she always has her camera at the ready at these things."

Ten minutes later, we're pulling up outside my house. Kendall's car's in the drive, and so is Tyler's truck. I make a mental note to ask him if there's something going on with him and my sister.

Kendall meets me at the front of the truck, and I hold my hand out for her. She doesn't hesitate to lace her fingers through mine as we head into the house.

"We're back!" I yell as soon as we step into the entryway.

"In the living room," Tyler calls out.

Reagan is asleep on the couch, and Tyler has Knox in the crook of his arm, watching the sports channel. "He was up three times last night. She's exhausted." He points to my sister.

"Did you stay here with her?" I ask him.

He hesitates. "Yeah, fell asleep on the couch. She didn't wake me."

I look around my living room and see a pillow and blankets that my sister is using. His story seems to add up.

I reach down and take Knox from him. "Hey, bud. You kept Aunt Reagan up?" He coos and smiles at me. "We missed you," I say, reaching out to snag an arm around Kendall's waist, pulling her into me.

"Hey, Knox," Kendall coos, and I swear he lights up. "We're going to Grandma and Grampa's for a cookout," she tells him, tickling his little foot.

"He had a bath," Reagan says, eyes still closed. "He shit all over himself at six o'clock this morning."

"Aww, did your belly hurt?" Kendall asks him.

He grins. My boy.

"Tyler, take me home. I have to get ready." Reagan literally rolls off the couch. After climbing to her feet, she walks toward me and gives all three of us a hug. "I'm proud of you, Ridge." This time, her voice is serious. "You do this on your own, and never once complain."

"He probably just missed me, that's why he didn't sleep well. Usually, he sleeps at least six, sometimes eight hours, straight."

"He missed you guys. Look at him, all smiles." She chucks his chin. "See you in a few hours."

"You need a ride?" I ask her.

"Nah, man. She's on my way, so I'll swing by and pick her up."

I watch as my sister and Tyler wave over their shoulders as they drag ass out the door. "Something's going on there," I tell Kendall.

"Hmmm."

"What do you know, woman?"

"I know she's your sister and she's amazing. I know Tyler must be a great guy because he's important to you. I know you should stay out if it, and if there *is* something going on, let them figure it out."

I smack her on the ass. "Go shower and get ready. We men don't take near as long."

She stands on tiptoes and kisses my cheek, then gives Knox one on his as well before grabbing her bag and running up the stairs.

"She's special, Knox." He babbles. "I'm glad you approve, because Daddy wants to make her a permanent part of our lives." He coos and moves his little arms. "She loves you too, little man. She loves you too."

I spend time with my son, trying to pull every smile from him I can. That's how Kendall finds us, lying on the floor, me acting a fool just to see him smile.

"My boys look happy." I can see in her face she didn't mean to let that slip.

Grabbing Knox, we stand to greet her. "Your boys think you look beautiful." She does. She's wearing red shorts with a white and blue layered tank top. She's also wearing a blush from my words. Will she ever get used to me telling her, stop blushing? I hope not.

"My turn." She opens her arms for Knox. "Let's get you ready while Daddy takes a shower."

I kiss her, getting lost in her, in us, until she says "Ow!" Looking down, Knox has her hair tight in his fist. "Guess he was jealous." I laugh and help free her from his grip before dashing off upstairs.

The driveway is full by the time we make it to my parents.' I'm glad; maybe she won't notice her parents' car. I don't look for it, because I already know they're here. Dad texted me just as we were leaving the house.

I grab Knox, seat and all, drape the diaper bag over my shoulder, and reach for her hand. "I have to carry the food." She laughs.

"No, leave it. I'll come back out and get it."

"Ridge, that's silly. I can carry it."

"No, I want you with me. Come on." I tug on her hand to pull her away from the truck. "Let's say hello, and I'll come back out and get it." She shakes her head, but doesn't say anything else as she laces her fingers through mine and we head inside.

We take all of Knox's things to his bedroom, as Mom calls it. "You're gonna have the ladies drooling," I tell my son.

"He looks so cute. Here, don't forget the glasses." Kendall hands me a mini pair of Aviators. Where she found them, I have no idea, but they make him look cute as hell.

Knox in one arm and the other around Kendall, we head out to the back deck.

"What?" She turns to me, mouth hanging open as soon as she sees her parents. "How did you . . . ?"

"I wanted our families to get to know each other. This is us, sweet girl," I whisper in her ear just as her parents approach us.

"Hey, you two." She grins, giving each of them a hug. "I'm glad you're here."

"It was all Ridge." Her mom turns to me. "Thank you for the invite."

I put my arm back around Kendall and pull her to me. "You're family." I can see recognition in her eyes from my simple statement.

Yeah, I love her and this is permanent.

"Can I hold him?" her mom asks.

I nod and transfer Knox to her arms. He's good for a few minutes, until his little lip juts out. Kendall is next to him in a flash. "Hey, bud. It's okay," she says softly. His eyes follow her voice and then he grins when he finds her.

"Like father, like son," her dad says, coming to stand next to me.

"She's amazing," I tell him.

"That she is, just like her mother."

"You're a lucky man." He is if her mother is anything like her.

"So are you," he replies.

"I love her."

"I know. I can see it. You remind me of me."

"Then you know what I want."

"I do. She's my baby and she's not had the best of luck with men, so take care of her."

"With everything in me."

He laughs. "Good talk." He squeezes my shoulder and leaves me to join my dad back at the grill.

The rest of the day is filled with family and friends, and lots and lots of food. Mom always makes way too much. I keep Kendall and Knox close, touching her every chance I get.

"Hey, I'm going to go check on Knox and help them clean up," she says, trying to move off my lap. I hold tight.

"He's fine. Mom is in the house, and I have the monitor." I point to where it's sitting on the patio table.

"Ridge." She laughs. "I'm going to go help your mom." Her voice is final, so I kiss her shoulder and let her go.

"You haven't let her out of your sight all day." Dad says, taking the seat beside me and handing me a beer.

I wave my hand, declining. "Can't. I'm driving home, and I have Knox tonight. Already had my two for the day," I tell him.

He nods, a look of approval on his face. "I'm proud of you, son. You're a damn good father." He takes a long pull of his beer. "I like her." He points his bottle to where Mom and Kendall are standing in the kitchen. Her parents left a couple hours ago.

"I love her," I tell him.

He laughs. "You always did know what you wanted."

I don't say anything, because he's right. I've always gone after what I wanted, and Kendall is no exception.

"Hold on to that, Ridge. I can see she cares for you too. It takes work and a hell of a lot of love, but I promise you if she's the one, it's all worth it."

"She's worth it," I assure him.

He nods and that's the end of that. A man of few words, my dad, but when he does talk, you listen. He always has something profound to say.

Today, he didn't tell me anything I didn't already know.

Kendall is everything.

Chapter 40

Kendall

It's Monday and I'm back at work. The long weekend was amazing, and I'm sporting a permanent smile on my face. Dawn has reminded me of the fact every time she comes into my office. The last time she stopped in, she needed a paperclip. I threw it at her and told her to stop making excuses to razz me and get her lazy ass back to work. She laughed all the way down the hall.

Trying to keep focused is proving difficult today, after the weekend. My phone vibrates and I sigh in frustration, knowing it's probably Dawn. I'm never going to get through this report at the rate I'm going. Pulling my phone from my scrub pocket, the frustration leaves as I see Ridge's name light up my screen.

> **Ridge:** Mom and Dad are taking Knox to my aunt and uncle's. They won't be back until after dinner. You and me, mini date night?

I smile.

> **Me:** *Mini date night?*
>
> **Ridge:** Dinner, just the two of us. By then, Little man will be home.
>
> **Me:** *Yes. Where? Should I meet you?*
>
> **Ridge:** Anywhere. I'll be at your place at six.
>
> **Me:** *See you then.*
>
> **Ridge:** Love you, sweet girl.

My heart melts.

> **Me:** *Love you too!*

Looking at the clock, I see it's only one. Four more hours before I can rush home and change to get ready for my mini date with my man.

"Hey, Kendall," Dawn says from my office doorway.

"Really?" I ask, laughing.

"Hey now, this time, I have a reason. And it's not just to tell you you're glowing." She smiles knowing her description gave her the opportunity to tell me yet again. "Mark just texted and wanted to know if you and Ridge—and Knox, of course—wanted to grab dinner tonight."

"Ridge just texted me. His parents are going to have Knox until later this evening, and we're going to dinner," I tell her.

"Seriously?" She laughs.

"Let me call him." I grab my phone from my pocket, pull up his name, and hit send.

"Hey, beautiful," his deep voice answers. I try like hell not to let Dawn see how easily he affects me.

"Hey, Dawn wants to know if we want to do dinner with her and Mark."

He chuckles. "Mark just asked me the same thing. I was getting ready to text you. I'll leave it up to you, babe."

"It'll be fun," I tell him.

"Sounds good, sweet girl. We'll be at your place at six or a little after."

"Perfect. I'll let Dawn know."

"Sounds good, baby. Love you."

My face floods with heat. "Love you, too," I say, ending the call.

"What? You're telling him you love him and didn't tell me?" she asks.

"It was over the weekend. It just happened, and I haven't seen you. You were with Mark, remember?" I remind her.

She blushes too. We're a mess. "So, the guys will be at our place around six," I tell her.

She holds up her phone, showing a text from Mark probably saying the exact same thing.

"Come on, five o'clock." She grins as she leaves my office for what feels like the hundredth time today.

At four fifty-nine, Dawn is standing in my doorway, tapping her foot.

"This has been the longest day in history," I say, shutting down my computer.

"It really has. The patients were even slow. I didn't think five o'clock would ever get here."

"I know. The long weekend ruined me."

We drove separately this morning, since she stayed at Mark's last night. Ridge begged me to stay, but I had laundry to catch up on. He offered to go pick up every piece of clothing I owned and bring it back to his place. Crazy man. Needless to say, after a very tempting goodnight kiss he relented, and I went home. It was hard to sleep in my own bed after being in his for the past several nights.

"Where are we going?" I ask Dawn once we're home. We both took up residence on the couch, but we need to be getting ready so the guys aren't waiting on us.

"I suggested that new steakhouse. Mark said he doesn't care."

"Ridge is the same way. Sounds good to me."

We start to talk, getting caught up with what's been going on in our separate lives. She and Mark are really hitting it off. She confessed that she's falling hard, and she thinks he is too.

"I'll have to grill Ridge later and see if he can give me any insider info."

She laughs. "You don't have to do that."

"Hey, we girls have to stick together," I say.

My phone vibrates in my pocket.

Ridge: Headed your way.

"Shit! It's ten till. We need to get ready." We both scramble off the couch and race to our rooms.

"We need a girls' night!" Dawn calls out from her room across the hall. "I miss my bestie."

"Plan it!"

A loud knock sounds at the door. "Shit," I say, as I hear Dawn yell for them to come in. Ridge must have been closer than I thought. I slide my tank over my head and meet Dawn in the hallway. I'm buttoning my shorts, not paying attention, when she stops in front of me.

"What the hell are you doing here?" Her voice is filled with anger. Hatred.

Looking up, I see Cal. My ex Cal, standing in my living room. My first thought is that it took long enough. But then I remember that Ridge will be here anytime, and he knows about Cal and how he pushed me around. He looks sober now, but you never know with an addict. What I *do* know is that Ridge is not going to be impressed.

"What are you doing here, Cal?" I ask, stepping around Dawn and joining him in the living room. He's standing just inside the door.

"I miss you, Kendall."

"Really? It's been almost a year since I left, and not even a phone call from you." I cross my arms over my chest, not buying his bullshit.

"I got clean," he says, his voice low. "When we got home and your apartment was cleaned out, I went on a bender. Ended up thrown in jail, mandatory rehab for three months. I've been clean ever since."

"What the fuck ever," Dawn mumbles under her breath.

"That's great. If it's true, then I'm happy for you. But I've told you time and time again that it's over between us."

"I can make it up to you, Kendall," he pleads.

I open my mouth to answer when there're another quick rap of knuckles before the door opens and in walks Ridge and Mark.

I move toward Ridge, lacing my fingers with his and pulling him to stand with me behind the couch. Mark makes his way toward Dawn.

"What's up, babe?" Ridge asks.

Taking a deep breath, I introduce them. "Ridge, this is Cal. Cal, this is my boyfriend, Ridge." He stiffens beside me, drops my hand and places his arm around my waist, pulling me into his side.

"Boyfriend?" Cal seems more defeated than angry.

"Boyfriend," Ridge repeats.

"Kendall, can we just . . . go somewhere and talk?" Cal asks.

"Not happening, my man. You have something to say to her, you say it from where you are," Ridge tells him.

"I didn't ask you," Cal says through gritted teeth.

Ridge throws his head back and laughs. "I don't give a flying fuck who you ask. I'm the one who's telling you it's not going to happen."

Cal turns to me. "You let this guy boss you around?"

"What? Like you pushed her around and cheated on her?" Ridge asks. His anger is growing, if the sound of his voice and the grip he has on my hip in any indication.

I wrap my arms around his waist and rest my head on his chest, trying to help diffuse his anger. "Cal, I've told you it's over. If you really are clean, then I'm proud of you. I wish you the best of luck, but it's over."

"It's *been* over," Dawn adds from behind us.

Cal hangs his head in defeat. "I miss you," he whispers.

Ridge growls.

"Cal, you *think* you miss me. I was in your life before the drugs. You need to find something positive to focus on. Even if Ridge weren't in the picture, I wouldn't be coming back to you," I say gently.

Ridge kisses my temple.

"We can work through this," Cal pleads.

"Enough!" Ridge says, his voice raised. "She's told you that she's not interested. There is nothing here for you."

"I love you, Kendall," Cal says, sadness in his eyes.

"Out!" Ridge roars.

"Ridge." I grip his shirt, and he looks down at me. "I love you," I tell him.

He squeezes my hip.

"Cal, please go. I'm proud of you for getting clean, but it's time for you to move on."

He looks up at me, and I can see in his eyes he truly thought I would come back to him. My heart hurts for him, but it's too late for us.

"Are you happy?"

"Yes," I say without hesitation. The man holding me tight against his side will guarantee that I am.

"Okay." He reaches into his pocket and Ridge steps forward, as if he needs to protect me. Cal pulls out a white envelope. "This came to your old address, but they delivered it to mine. I've had it for a while now. I wanted to find a job before I came back for you. Wanted you to see I've changed." He sets the envelope on the coffee table. "You're going to want to read it," he says, his sad eyes finding mine.

"Good-bye, Cal."

He stares at me for what seems like eternity, and it's uncomfortable for everyone. Finally, he says, "Good-bye, Kendall. For what it's worth, I'm sorry for everything that happened between us." Then he looks at Ridge. "Take care of her."

Ridge doesn't acknowledge him. Cal gets the hint, offering a sad wave before he leaves, the door clicking softly behind him.

"You okay?" Dawn asks.

I nod against Ridge's chest; he has me crushed to him. He lowers his head to whisper in my ear. "I love you, Kendall." Those four words pull me out of the sadness Cal brought with him. I meant what I said, that I'm proud of him, but Ridge is my heart.

"How about we order in?" Dawn asks.

"Yeah, that's a good idea," Ridge agrees.

"Pizza?" Mark suggests. "You girls like the place just down the street, right?"

"Perfect." Dawn grins at him. "We'll go pick it up, give these two some time."

"Thanks," Ridge says to them.

When they're gone, he leads me to the couch and pulls me onto his lap. "You good, sweet girl?"

"Yeah. I mean, I'm surprised he showed up after all this time, but I don't want him. You're where I want to be."

"I know that." He kisses my bare shoulder. "I also know that seeing him again probably brought up a lot of those old memories."

"Yeah, but I'm good, really. I feel bad for him, I do, but there was never a choice to make, Ridge. I'm in love with you."

"I know that, but I still love to hear those words fall from your lips." He kisses my shoulder again. "So, what do you think's in the envelope?"

"Honestly, I have no idea. I guess I should look." I stand and walk to the table by the door, grabbing the envelope. It's addressed to me at my old apartment, but there's no return contact information. Not sure what I'm going to find, I sit on the opposite end of the couch as Ridge. I see his face fall, but he doesn't push me. Mr. 'I need to touch you at all times' knows I need a minute to see what's inside.

"It doesn't have a return address," I tell him.

"You want me to open it?" he offers.

"No, it's probably a letter from him, trying to convince me. Honestly, I have no idea what else it could be."

"Pizza's here," Dawn announces, setting the boxes down on the coffee table. "I'll grab plates and napkins. What do you guys want to drink?" she yells from the kitchen.

I laugh at her, place the letter aside, and help her gather everything we'll need.

Two large pizzas later, we're all groaning that we ate too much. It was so good, though.

"So, what was in the envelope?" Dawn asks.

I shrug. "Don't know, haven't opened it yet."

"What are you waiting for?" she asks.

I laugh at her, reach for the envelope, and tear it open.

Kendall,

It's taken me a while to find you, as adoption papers are sealed pretty tight. I'm your sister, Melissa. We're twins, not sure if you knew that or not. I was told by the private investigator that I hired that you know you were adopted. I wanted to make sure my contacting you didn't shatter your world.

Anyway, not sure how much you know about our mother. She was sixteen and gave us up with the hopes of a better life. We were both adopted, but my first adoptive parents didn't turn out so great. They got messed up with drugs and God only knows what else, and I was placed in foster care. Don't be sad though. A few years later, I was adopted by an amazing family. I will forever be grateful for everything they did for me. About four months ago, I lost them. It was tragic and unexpected, and left me once again all alone in the world.

I've thought about you a lot over the years, and well, losing my family has me putting myself out there, reaching out to my sister.

I'm actually going to be in your hometown in a few weeks. That's a story in itself. You see, I had a one-night stand——a first for me——with a guy who lives there. I didn't stick around after, running off in the middle of the night. Turns out our little rendezvous created a miracle. I'm pregnant, and even though I'm scared as hell to raise this baby on my own, I want him. More than anything, I want him. I've gone back and forth about whether or not I should track down the father and tell him, but I figure he has a right to know. So in a few weeks, I'm making the trip. I've written him too, just in case I chicken out. You might know him, since he's close to our age. His name is Ridge, and he works for Beckett Construction.

If you're around, I'd love to meet and have lunch. If you would rather not, I get that too. I just wanted to send out that olive branch if you ever decide you'd like to meet me. I hope you're happy and life is treating you well. I've enclosed all my contact information just in case you want to meet up, now or in the future.

Best wishes,

Melissa Knox

I let the letter fall into my lap, tears falling from my eyes and dripping onto the paper. I feel tight arms around me and realize I'm in Ridge's lap. I was so zoned out from her letter I didn't even notice.

"Baby, you're scaring me. Please tell me what's wrong," Ridge pleads.

Shit.

Ridge.

Knox.

Melissa.

I jump off his lap, the letter falling to the floor. Ridge grabs it before I can. "Baby, I won't read it if you tell me what's wrong. If you don't, I have to. I have to know what's causing you to be so upset." He steps toward me and I take a step back.

"Ridge," Mark says, cutting him off, placing a hand against his chest.

"Get off me." His voice is menacing. "I have to hold her," he tells Mark.

"Give her a minute, man. Just let her process whatever it is she read."

"Kendall." His voice cracks. "Baby, tell me what's wrong so I can fix it."

Dawn comes to me slowly and wraps her arms around my waist. I hug her back because I need my best friend. My entire world just came crashing down and I'm going to lose him, lose both of them. As soon as he finds out I'm Melissa's sister, he's going to be done with me. Won't he?

"Sweetie, can we read it?" Dawn asks. "Can we read the letter?"

My eyes find Ridge, and although he's blurry as I try focus through my tears, I can see the anguish on his face. I nod and he sighs with relief.

He plops down on the chair, opens the letter, and begins to read.

Chapter 41

Ridge

My fucking heart is about to beat right out of my chest. Something in that envelope has her emotionally a wreck, and I want to know what the fuck it is. How am I supposed to fix it if I don't know what it is? I just need to hold her. Once I have her in my arms, I can get her to tell me, I know I can.

When Dawn asked her if we could read it, and she agreed, I returned to my seat. I read it once through and then again, thinking my mind is playing tricks on me.

Is this real life? Have we not been through enough already? Did she know she was adopted? I didn't know that about her. Is that why she's so upset? I need to hold her.

"Kendall, baby, can I please hold you?" I ask her. My voice is thick with the emotion I'm fighting back.

She just stares at me, silent tears rolling down her cheeks.

"Please, baby." My voice cracks again. I don't take my eyes off her and I'm thankful, because she gives a slight nod. That's all the encouragement I need before I'm on my feet and wrapping her in my arms. She begins to sob against my chest, and I can feel my own emotions welling up in my throat. She's breaking my fucking heart right now and I can't fix this. I need to fix this for her.

I hear Dawn gasp, and I know she and Mark have just read the letter.

My phone vibrates in my pocket. I assume it's my parents.' I dig it out and toss it to Mark. "Check that. If it's my parents,' text them and let them know I need them to keep Knox a little longer, and I'll explain later." He nods and his fingers begin flying across the screen.

I don't move, just hold her as close as I can, running my fingers through her hair, continually kissing the top of her head. I'll stand here in this spot and hold her for as long as it takes.

"Kendall, sweetie, why don't you guys sit down? I'll get you something to drink," Dawn suggests.

Kendall doesn't move, and neither do I. "I got you, sweet girl," I murmur in her ear. She grips my shirt tighter.

I don't know how long we stand there. Seconds, minutes, hours, days—I've lost complete track of time.

"Baby, you want to sit?" I ask her. She gives a slight nod so I pull away, intending on carrying her, and she latches on.

"Don't leave me," she cries.

Fuck me.

"Shhh, I'm not going anywhere." Bending down, I lift her into my arms and carry her to the couch. She curls into my chest and buries her face in my neck.

I run my hands up and down her back, trying to soothe her. "Kendall, baby, I need you to help me here. There was a lot of information in that letter, and I don't know what's spooked you the most. Can you talk to me?"

No response.

"Hey, man, your mom's not feeling well. I'm going to meet them and take Knox back to your place," Mark says, his voice low.

"No." Kendall lifts her head. "Bring him here." She looks up at me. "Please?"

I nod to Mark. "Okay, babe, he's going to bring Knox here."

"I'll go with you," Dawn tells Mark.

I'm thankful to have a minute with just us—hopeful is more like it. Maybe I can get her to talk. "Baby, please talk to me."

"I'm adopted," she finally says.

"Did you already know that?" I ask her. "I mean, I know what the letter said, but was she right? Did you know?"

"Yeah, I was a baby, a newborn. My birth mother, she was just a kid. She did what was best for me, and I've lived an amazing life," she says through more tears. Her voice is sad.

"Did you know you were a twin?"

"No."

Okay, well, we're starting to get somewhere. "That's a shock, huh?"

"Yeah, but she was your Melissa, Ridge."

My Melissa. "She was Knox's mother, yes, but she was never mine, Kendall."

"I'm finally happy, happy with a man who makes my heart skip a beat every day." She sniffles. "And now I'm going to lose him."

Wait, what? "Kendall, look at me." She doesn't. I tilt her chin up with my index finger. "How are you going to lose me?"

"Because!" she yells. "My twin sister was your one-night stand. Knox's mom. I'll be a constant reminder of what you lost."

"Never," I say, shifting her in my lap so she's straddling me. I cup her face with my hands and make her look at me. "That's never fucking going to happen. You are my heart, and nothing—and I mean *nothing*—will take me away from you. Is that what you think? That I could just stop loving you?"

"I don't know," she whispers, her voice giving away just how bad this is hurting her.

"There is no choice, sweet girl. I'm no longer me without you—you and Knox. You are a part of me, Kendall Dawson. She was a girl I met in a bar, and we slept together. That night resulted in the miracle that is my son. What happened to her is tragic and sad. Finding out that she's your twin, that's news that rocks the foundation, shakes it up a little, but it doesn't crumble. Nothing ever will."

She continues to look into my eyes as silent tears coat her cheeks. So I keep going, knowing I will until she understands what I'm telling her.

"It's news that is unexpected, but that's life, right? Life is full of unexpected moments that lead you to find your way. Maybe Melissa sent you to me. Did you ever think about that? From the beginning, my pull toward you was something like I've never experienced. Maybe that was her pushing us together. I don't know how the universe works, but I can tell you that I thank God for you every day."

She's quiet for a long time. I don't say anything else, just letting her process my words, what I'm saying. That I will love her until the day I take my last breath.

"I love you. I love Knox, and the thought of not having either of you, it breaks me."

Oh, my sweet girl. "Won't happen, baby. It's you and me, remember?"

She nods and wipes her eyes.

"Can I kiss you?" I know it's not really the time, but I need something. I need to show her that nothing in that letter changes a damn thing for me. She's my heart.

She laughs. "You really want to kiss this mess?" She points to her face.

"Yes, you're my beautiful mess," I say, leaning in to kiss her salty lips. The door opening has me pulling away.

Mark is carrying Knox in his seat and sets him on the couch beside us. He sees us and babbles, moving his little arms and legs.

Kendall laughs and turns sideways in my lap, pulling him out of his seat. Immediately, she hugs him tight to her chest. The little bugger grabs onto her hair, and she smiles. "I love you, Knox Beckett," she says, kissing him on the forehead.

Is it possible for your heart to be too full of love and happiness and hopes for the future? Mine feels so full it could burst from my chest at any minute.

"We love you, Kendall Dawson," I whisper in her ear, hugging them both. She smiles through more tears, and that smile tells me we're going to be okay. We'll take it one day at a time until we learn to live with our unexpected reality.

THE LAST THREE months have been filled with tears and uncertainties. It took Kendall some time to process that she's a twin and that the man she loves and his son are connected to said twin. I also had some processing to do—I had to decide how long I needed to wait to ask her to marry me.

Knox will be seven months old in a week. It's hard to believe. He really is starting to look like my little man. It's been so much fun to see him learn new things and to be able to share that with Kendall. I'm ready for more, and Knox is too; he told me he's ready to be a big brother, in his own little babbling way.

I talked it over with Knox, and we decided tonight is the night. I called Kendall and invited her over, told her we were having a quiet night in. We are, just the three of us. Hopefully, by the end of the night she'll be my fiancée, and I can finally convince her to move in with me. I've been trying for the last two months, but she still turns me down. I know she's still leery, and in the back of her mind she feels like she has taken her sister's family, but she needs to see that we're *her* family, Knox and me.

I have everything set up. I bought the frozen lasagna and put it in the Crock-Pot just like she did that first day the three of us spent together. I have the same blanket we used down at the gazebo the night before, washed, folded and waiting for us by the back door. Nothing over the top, just us and how it all started.

I hear her pull in, so I quickly zip up Knox's hoodie and hand him the red rose, hoping like hell he doesn't try to eat it.

As soon as she opens the door, we're standing there, both of us holding a single red rose. I offer her mine and Knox mimics me. "Thank you, handsome." She leans in and kisses his cheek. He giggles. "And you." She stands on tiptoes and presses her lips to mine. Knox grunts and pulls on her arm. He's a little jealous when it comes to Kendall, not that I mind. I love that they've formed that bond—makes tonight's plans even sweeter. We're already a family; this will just change her last name, make it official.

"How was your day?" I ask.

"Good. It's been a long week. I was definitely ready for my weekend with my two favorite people," she says. Knox reaches for her and she beams as she takes him and settles him on her hip.

"We missed you." I kiss her temple. She stopped spending the night through the week, but from Friday after work until Sunday, she stays here. She still stops by every night, but she said during the week it was just easier with work to stay at her place. She seemed to always forget something—no scrub top, her stethoscope, something. I tried to convince her to move in, and this was her compromise. Hopefully that all changes tonight.

"So, dinner is in the Crock-Pot, and I thought we could take a walk out to the gazebo."

"That sounds like fun, huh, bud? You want to feed the fish?" She looks up at me. "It's actually fairly warm out still. We better enjoy it while we can."

I nod my agreement, grab the blanket, and hold the door open for them. I trail behind as Kendall points out birds and the leaves on the trees. Knox mimics her and points too. Once we reach the gazebo, I set the blanket on the bench and open the bucket of fish food we started keeping out here a few weeks ago. Knox loves to feed the fish. He gets more food on us than he does in the water, but his giggle is worth it.

"Hey, I have to show you the shirt I found for him," I tell her.

She smiles.

"He's actually wearing it," I tell her.

"Did Daddy buy you a new shirt?" she asks him. "He did? Can I see?" She sits on the bench and adjusts him on her lap. I kneel before her and grab his little hand so she can pull down the zipper. "Let's see the new duds," she says, pushing the jacket open.

I watch her face closely as she reads it. I see her confusion. Her eyes flash to me and that's when she sees the ring. "What's it say?" I ask her.

Tears well in her eyes as she places her hand over her mouth. Knox pats her cheek, seeing she's upset. "Will you marry us," she whispers.

I reach for Knox and he jumps into my arms. "We love you, Kendall. We want you to have our last name. We want Knox to be a big brother." She laughs through her tears. "Make our little family complete and marry us?"

Her smile is blinding. "Yes!"

Knox claps and squeals with delight, seeing Kendall smile. She launches herself at me. I wrap my arms around her, catching her in my embrace.

I will always catch her.

Chapter 42

Kendall

Did you know that in the fine state of Illinois a retired judge can marry you, as long as they weren't discharged for any disciplinary actions? Did you also know that my grandfather is a retired judge?

Today is my wedding day.

The night Ridge and Knox proposed, I immediately called my family, who of course already knew. I asked Grandad to marry us and he agreed. Ridge and I talked about when we wanted to get married. His only stipulation was as soon as possible.

So here we are, four weeks later, the week before Thanksgiving, and we're getting married. I've never been one for flare, so I wanted something small and intimate. We're actually at the lodge up at the lake that Ridge and I went to back in July. Our parents and grandparents, his sister, Dawn, and of course Kent, Mark, Seth and Tyler are here. That's it. Small and intimate, just the way I wanted it.

We decided that we wanted our parents to stand up with us. Odd, yes, but how do you choose from your friends? Not to mention that our parents have been married for years and are still just as in love. It's inspiring. Dad gets to pull double duty, as he's also walking me down the aisle.

"You ready, Kendall?" he asks.

"Yes!"

He chuckles. "Let's get you married." I link my arm through his and we head down the small walkway that leads me to Ridge and Knox. We decided that Ridge would hold Knox, because he's an important part of today as well. When we reach them, Knox reaches out for me and I feel the tears start to burn the back of my eyes. I hug my dad and he holds on tight. "I'm so damn proud to call you my daughter."

That does it, the tears starting to fall in earnest. "Love you, Daddy." I may be adopted, but it's never felt that way to me. I understand why my birth mother gave me up, and I respect her for that hard decision she had to make. I've never had the desire to seek her out, because I have my parents,' the man and woman who raised me. I hope I can be that person for Knox.

"K. K." Knox reaches his little arms out for me again, so Ridge laughs and hands him to me. This makes our little man happy, as he rests his head on my shoulder.

"You're breathtaking," Ridge says, his voice echoing throughout the room. He grins when the guys yell out about him being whipped, and the women "ooh" and "ahh."

I love our family, our friends, and this life we've made with each other.

Ridge and I opted for traditional vows. I don't need sweet words to know he loves me and is devoted to me. I feel it in my heart and in every touch. Every second, every minute, every hour, every day I feel his love for me.

"By the power vested in me by the state of Illinois, I now pronounce you husband and wife. You may kiss your bride," Gramps says.

Ridge grins and moves toward me. This catches Knox's attention, which lifts his head and points at Ridge. "No, no," he says.

The crowd laughs, as does Ridge. Reagan steps forward and holds up Knox's favorite stuffed teddy bear, and he reaches for her with a smile.

She winks at us and walks away with him. Before her back is even turned, Ridge pulls me to him for a soul-searing kiss. "I love you, Mrs. Beckett," he says against my lips.

Mrs. Ridge Beckett.

Holy shit! We did it!

※ ※ ※

THE RECEPTION WAS dinner with our loud boisterous group. Knox stole the show and of course ate up all the attention. He's actually going back home with my parents' tonight. Mom and Dad are both really excited about it. Ridge's parents offered as well, but he thought it was important that Knox get to spend time with both grandparents. Since his mom keeps Knox during the week, this was a solution that everyone thought was a good compromise. Not to mention his parents rented the same cabin they had a few years ago for their anniversary. Sounds like Ridge and I won't be the only Beckett partaking in extracurricular activities this evening.

"You ready to kick them out?" Ridge whispers in my ear.

"Yes," I say as he trails his lips up my neck.

"Good. Let's go say good-bye to our boy." My heart soars. From the minute he proposed, Knox became ours and I couldn't be happier. I couldn't love that little man more if I had given birth to him myself. I still go through periods of guilt over Melissa, my sister, sometimes feeling like I'm living her life. I can only hope that she's looking after us and knows I love both of them with everything I am.

We find our parents sitting in the sunroom. Knox is curled up on my mom's lap and looks to be close to sleeping. That is until he sees me. "K," he says, his little voice laced with sleep. He holds his arms out, and I don't hesitate to take him from her and pull him into arms.

"Hey, buddy." He lays his head on my shoulder, and I snuggle him close. "You're going to spend the night with Grandma and Grandpa." My parents' insisted that's what he calls them. Not that he can call them anything yet, but he will. They've accepted him as if he were mine, not that there was ever any question. Look what they did for me.

"Hey, bud, can Daddy get some love?" Ridge asks rubbing Knox's back. Sleepily, he leans into Ridge, who pulls him into his arms. "We did it, little man," he whispers to Knox. "We married Kendall. She's ours

281

now."

My heart can't take it. This man.

Ridge and I say good-bye to Knox and our parents, which just leaves our friends and his sister. I assumed we would drop subtle hints, but that's not at all what happens.

We enter the cabin from walking Knox and our parents out and Ridge simply says, "Out."

"Ridge!" I smack his chest.

He grabs my arm before I can pull it away and pulls me to him. "I want some time with my wife."

"I don't know, man. I thought we could hang out, maybe play some cards or something," Kent teases him.

"Yeah, you know, celebrate your nuptials and whatnot," Seth adds.

Mark and Dawn are curled up in a chair laughing. Reagan is in another and Tyler is sitting on the floor, leaned back against the chair leg. They haven't come out and said there's something going on, but any fool could see that there is. Not to mention Tyler's calmed down a lot. He only has eyes for Reagan, although I'll give him an A for effort in trying to hide that little detail from his best friend.

"Really? You fuckers wait until the day you get married. Payback's a bitch," Ridge pouts.

That has everyone laughing. Tyler and Mark stand, taking his words to heart I'm sure. They both seem to be ideal candidates for the next in line for holy matrimony. Seth and Kent stand to leave as well. Each of the guys gives me bear hugs and kisses on the cheek, which has Ridge growling at them. I also hug each of the girls, as does Ridge after the manly handshake/hug/pat on the back thing he does with the guys.

The door is barely shut when he bends and lifts me in his arms. "Now the real party begins, Mrs. Beckett." He kisses my temple and carries me off to the bedroom.

It's fitting to consummate our marriage in the same place we first made love. That's how I knew getting married here was the right choice. It's where we became one for the first time, and where we'll continue with the next phase of our future.

Chapter 43

Ridge

I can't get her to the bedroom fast enough, having barely held it together all night. I wanted to share this with our family and friends, but what I really wanted—what I *needed*—was to make love to my wife.

My wife.

She's mine. Forever, she's mine.

I carry her to the bedroom and set her on her feet next to the bed. Although we planned this wedding in less than a month, Kendall was able to find a dress that's kept my cock hard since the moment I first saw her in it. It's form-fitting like a glove around her curves and short, showing off those long legs of hers. And although she's a vision in it, I want it gone. I want to slowly peel it from her body and sink into her. The image of her today, when she appeared before me, will be one I will take with me to the grave. The moment she became my wife.

"You take my fucking breath away, Mrs. Beckett," I say, running my lips over her bare shoulders.

"You don't look too bad yourself, Mr. Beckett."

"Turn for me, baby." She does as I ask, and I stop her once her back is to me. She left her long hair down, so I sweep it to the side over her shoulder and kiss the nape of her neck. I trail my lips down her back until I reach the zipper. *Time to go.*

I slide it down. "Arms up, sweet girl," I say next to her ear. She complies and the dress falls to the floor. My mouth drops open when I see nothing but a white lace thong. "Mrs. Beckett, if I had known that was all you had on under that sinful dress, I would've kicked our guests out as soon as we said 'I do.'"

She chuckles. "Surprise." She turns to face me and I take in the beauty that is my wife, sweeping my eyes over every inch of her. When I reach the thong, my chest tightens as I see 'Mrs. Beckett' stitched into them in lavender—her favorite color, our wedding color, marking her as mine. I had intended to rip them from her body, but not now. I need these, not only as a memento of this day, this moment, but I like to see her labeled as mine. I make a mental note to find out where she got them and get her more.

Mrs. Beckett.

"You're wearing too many clothes," she says as she begins to unbutton my shirt. I grip the sides and tear it open; I need her, and this is taking way too long. She laughs as buttons flutter across the hardwood floor. She pushes the shirt off my shoulders as I unbutton my khaki pants and let them slide to the floor. Pulling my arms out of my sleeves and tossing the shirt behind me, she kneels before me and slides my boxer briefs down. When I kick them off, she looks up at me, blue eyes blazing with love as she takes the tip of my cock into her mouth. Reaching out, I have to grab ahold of the dresser to keep from falling on my ass. This woman.

"Not like this," I say as I feel myself getting closer, chasing the release that her warm mouth is pulling from me. "Not tonight. I need to be inside you." She slowly releases me with a pop and wipes her mouth with the back of her hand. I almost lose my shit at the sight of her.

My wife.

"On the bed," I tell her. She doesn't hesitate as she turns and climbs onto the big four-poster bed, her ass swinging, tempting the hell out of me. I follow after her and nip her right cheek.

"Gah!" She laughs.

Will it always be this way? Will we always be able to laugh in the bedroom? Will she always feel like what's keeping me centered? I sure as hell hope so. I will fight like hell every day to make sure of it.

She falls to her back, reaching out to run her fingers through my hair. She loves it, and I keep it a little longer for that purpose—whatever my girl wants.

I bend down and kiss her. "I love you, Mrs. Beckett," I say, slowly pushing into her.

"Love you too," she breathes as she takes all of me.

I lock my eyes on hers and slowly make love to my wife. I didn't think that this, being inside her, could ever feel better than all the times before, but it does. This time, it's different; I can't explain it, but I feel it. The way our bodies are joined as one, the way her back arches off the bed, her feet digging into my ass, her nails digging into my back. Her eyes, those baby blues that hold my stare as I continue to thrust in and out of her. It's all different, better, and I'm rocked to my core.

My sweet girl.

My wife.

"Ridge," she moans, and I thrust harder as we chase our release together as husband and wife for the first time. I feel her squeezing me, and I let go inside her.

Rolling over, I crush her to my chest, just holding her.

"That was . . . intense," she says when I finally release my death grip on her.

"Yeah," I agree. No other words are needed. Our connection that was already solid as steel somehow seemed to mold into something you could only ever experience with your true soul mate. She's mine.

We lie there for I don't know how long, her head on my chest, my hands running through her hair. It's not until I look over and see the envelope that I realize I forgot to give her, my wedding present.

I had to enlist my new father-in-law's help, and he was all too willing. "Hey, you ready for your wedding present?" I ask.

She lifts her head and smiles. "I thought we said no gifts?"

"We did, but mine isn't something I bought."

"Ridge. You promised."

"I know, but this is more of something we can all use."

She gives me the stink eye, but then her lips tip with a smile. "Fine, gimme," she sits up in bed, holding the sheet to her bare breasts.

I jump out of bed, grab the envelope, and hand it to her. Her face scrunches up in confusion. Climbing in the bed beside her, I pull her to me. "Open it."

Slowly, she opens the envelope and pulls the papers out. I can't see her face, and it's killing me not knowing what she's thinking.

"Kendall?"

"Adoption papers," she breathes.

"I had your dad draw them up. I know you're not ready, that you're still struggling with everything, but I wanted you to have them. I want you to know that in my eyes, you are his mother. Melissa gave him life, but you're raising him and I want nothing more than you to legally become his mom. Your dad hasn't filed anything yet. Instead, he gave me these. It's drawn up and all you have to do is sign it to start the process. You take as long as you need. Just know that I love you, and even if you never sign them, in my eyes you are his mom."

Her shoulders shake with silent sobs, and I kick myself in the ass for ruining our wedding night. "I'm sorry, baby. I don't want to upset you or ruin this night, but I need you to know."

"Ridge, this is the greatest gift. You are giving me the rights to your son. That precious little man." She covers her mouth. "I love him. I couldn't love him more if he were mine."

"I know that."

"I just—"

"Shhh." I hug her tight. "Take all the time you need to process it. When you're ready, sign them and give them to your dad. He'll take care of the rest."

She nods.

I slide the papers back into the envelope and place them on the nightstand. Kendall surprises me by climbing on my lap and straddling my hips. Her hands cradle my cheeks. "You are the most amazing man. I don't know if it was Melissa or just luck, but whatever brought you to me, I will be eternally grateful. I love you." She kisses me and it soon grows heated. The next thing I know, she's sliding home and I make love to my wife for the second time.

Epilogue

Kendall

After our wedding night, I decided to see a counselor. I wanted to be Knox's mom—in my heart, I felt like I was—but I just couldn't get past the guilt. Survivor's guilt is what my therapist's calls it. For the last several months, I've gotten better. I've come to realize that what happened to my sister was tragic, but I needed to keep living. That little boy who lights up my world every single day needs a mother, and I'm the lucky one. I have the adoption papers in my top dresser drawer. Ridge and my dad neither one has mentioned them. My husband is truly the most amazing man on the planet.

I've been thinking more about signing them and making our little family official. It wasn't until last week that I finally did. When Knox called me Mom, my heart soared and I knew in that moment that he needs what I had. I had two people who wanted a child and made me their own. They never treated me like I wasn't a part of them, and that's how I treat Knox.

So I signed the papers. I dropped them off to my dad at his office and he simply smiled and nodded. Here I am a week later, stopping by to pick up the copy of the official adoption petition to give to Ridge. It's little man's first birthday, so it's kind of a gift for both of them. Well, that and my other news. I've been feeling off the last couple of weeks, so I made a doctor's appointment this morning, and low and behold, I'm pregnant. I don't think I've stopped smiling since the second the doctor told me.

Luckily for me, Dad chalked it up to being happy about the papers, so he didn't question me. He wouldn't have been wrong, but to know I'm carrying a part of Ridge is surreal. And Knox . . . well, my little man is going to be a big brother. I need to tell Ridge first.

I think back to the way he proposed and I hop online to place my order. Overnight shipping is outrageous, but I'll be lucky to wait until tomorrow to tell him.

He's not going to be home until late tonight; he and the guys have started back up with card night. Reagan and Dawn are coming over and helping me decorate for Knox's birthday party tomorrow.

"What has you smiling like you won the lottery?" Dawn asks.

Shit. I can't tell them I'm pregnant, but I can give them a little something. "Did you know that Ridge gave me adoption papers for Knox as a wedding gift."

They both nod yes. "I signed them." I grin.

They both tackle me with hugs, and when I hear a squeal and little hands wrap around my legs, I know this is right. The girls back away and Knox seals the deal when he says, "Mom," and holds his little arms up to me.

"Oh, my God!" Reagan cries.

I pick him up and he gives me a sloppy kiss on my cheek. I look over my two best friends, and they both have silent tears running down their face and blinding smiles. "Don't tell Ridge. It's a surprise."

They both agree, and for the rest of the night, they fire off ideas of how to tell him. I bite my tongue and smile as I listen to their ideas. They are pretty inventive, but I like mine better. I just have to cross my fingers that overnight Saturday delivery comes through for me.

It better, for what it cost.

Ridge

Knox started walking a few weeks ago, and his little legs carry him all over the place. Kendall and I thought he got into everything when he was crawling, but those little legs are fast.

This past year has brought so many changes in my life, my son and my wife being the biggest. I can still remember the fear I felt when Melissa died. The fear of raising him on my own. Then fate stepped in— or Melissa, rather, because I know in my heart that she sent Kendall to us—and I found this beautiful, sweet woman to raise him with me. To share my life with.

Life is good.

Today is Knox's birthday party, and my wife seems to be on edge. I've chalked it up to her wanting everything to be perfect for his big day.

"Hey, babe," I greet her. She's in the kitchen stirring something in a Crock-Pot. "Is that our lasagna?" I ask, resting my hands on her hips and kissing her neck.

She laughs. "No, meatballs."

"Dada." Knox comes barreling into the room. Leaning down, I catch him and lift him into my arms.

"Hey, birthday boy." He gives me a sloppy kiss right on the lips and I laugh. Life has definitely changed, and I embrace it. I love our life.

"Mom." He points to Kendall.

I freeze. That's the first time I've ever heard him call her that, and I don't know how she's going to react.

She places the lid back on the Crock-Pot and turns to face us. "Hey, sweetie." She tickles his chin.

"Mom." He leans toward her, his arms held open wide.

"Come here, you." She takes him from my arms and bounces him on her hip. "Are you ready for your party?"

I watch in fascination as he just plays with her hair. I don't blame him; I love the feel of those silky strands sliding through my fingers. It doesn't seem to faze her that he called her Mom. I take a deep breath, wanting that for them, for her to give in and let herself believe that she's that person for him. She is already, but she fights it.

Hearing a car outside, her attention is drawn out the window. She sees the mailman and grins. "I got you and Daddy a present for your birthday." She looks up at me. "Can you call your mom and see if she can stop and pick up a bag of ice?"

"Sure, babe." I hold my hands out for Knox. "You want to come with Daddy?"

He leans toward me, but Kendall holds him close. "I kind of need him for the surprise I got the two of you." She smiles.

I chuckle. "Okay, then. I'll go call Mom."

She nods then rushes out to the mailbox. Her excitement is evident. I guess that's why she's been acting a little off today; she was probably just nervous that whatever it is she ordered wouldn't be here in time. I rack my brain for something that she could've bought that would be for both me and our son. I've got nothing.

The call with my mom takes longer than what it should have, as she rattles on about all the gifts she bought him. I assume my wife was banking on this, which is why she had me call.

I'm sitting in the living room when Knox comes tumbling in as fast as his little legs will carry him. "Dada!" He hugs my legs and climbs up on my lap. Kendall is laughing when she sits down beside me. Knox is playing with my beard when a small white envelope appears in my line of vision. Kendall and I haven't had the best of luck with little white envelopes, so I hesitate.

"Open it," she says, grinning.

I take that as a good sign, so I tear open the envelope. Inside is a single piece of paper from the state of Illinois.

'Official Petition for Adoption.'

I whip me head toward her. "You signed?"

Tears in her eyes, she grins. "I did. Counseling has helped, and last week he called me Mom. Something just clicked. I knew his situation is much like my own, and I want to be that person for him."

Wrapping my hand around the back of her neck, I pull her into a kiss.

"No," Knox protests, trying to pry us apart.

"He loves his momma," I say to Kendall.

She laughs as tears stream down her face. I lift Knox in the air. "Its official, bud." I throw him up and catch him, and his laughter fills the room. He grabs onto my shirt when I settle him into my lap, and that's when I notice Kendall changed him. I've never seen this one before; maybe that's what came in the mail. Moving his arms so I can read it, I freeze.

'I'm the big brother.'

I stare at it and read it two more times before turning to look at my wife.

"Surprise," she says.

"Are we . . . ?"

She nods.

I'm too overwhelmed to say anything, emotion clogging my throat, so I kiss her, long and hard. Then I grab them both in my arms and hold them tight.

Life has thrown me some curve balls, and there have been times when then unexpected changes have literally knocked me on my ass. I had to learn to live one breath, one second, one minute, one hour, one day at a time. I've learned that the best things in life are truly the unexpected.

I've embraced it and learned to live in my unexpected reality.

KAYLEE RYAN

Facebook:

www.facebook.com/pages/Kaylee-Ryan-Author

Goodreads:

www.goodreads.com/author/show/7060310.Kaylee_Ryan

Twitter:

@author_k_ryan

Instagram:

Kaylee_ryan_author

Website:

www.kayleeryan.com

Other Works
BY KAYLEE RYAN

With You Series
Anywhere With You

More With You

Everything With You

Stand Alone Titles
Tempting Tatum

Levitate

Just Say When

Southern Pleasure

Soul Serenade Series
Emphatic

Assured

Acknowledgements

I have the love and support of a wonderful family who stands behind me. Thank you for your understanding and your constant support and encouragement. None of this would be possible without you. I love you.

The entire Indie Community is a world of in itself that I am proud to be a part of. I've made life long friends on this journey and will be forever grateful for all you're the support I have received.

Sommer Stein, Perfect Pear Creative Covers, you nailed it, Cover Girl! The cover of Unexpected Reality is more than I could have hoped for it to be. Thank you for always being on point and making my vision come to life.

David Marineau, it's been great working with you. Thank you for being the face of Unexpected Reality. I wish you nothing but success.

Marc-André Riopel & Josee Houle this picture speaks for itself. It's amazing and your combined talent produced a beautiful image.

Tami Integrity Formatting, you never let me down. You make my words come together in a pretty little package. Thank you so much for making Unexpected Reality look fabulous on the inside!

Masque of the Red Pen, thank you for your amazing proofing skills.

Becca Manuel, yet again you have produced a trailer that captures the book perfectly! Thank you so much.

My beta team: Kaylee 2, Jamie, Stacy and Lauren you ladies have become family to me. I value your feedback and the friendships that we have created. No matter if it's a plot change, new story line, or even cover images, the four of you are there. Always. I cannot tell you how much your never ending support means to me. I love you ladies.

Give Me Books, thank you for hosting and organizing the cover reveal and release of Unexpected Reality. I appreciate all of your hard work getting this book out there.

To all of the bloggers out there . . . Thank you so much. Your continued never-ending support of myself, and the entire indie community is greatly appreciated. I know that you don't hear it enough so hear me now. *I appreciate each and every one of you and the support that you have given me.* Thank you to all of you! There are way too many of you to list . . .

To my Kick Ass Crew, you ladies know who you are. I will never be able to tell you how much your support means. You all have truly earned your name. Thank you!

Kaylee (2) Not much new I can say. You are a constant beam of support and the friendship that we have formed is something that I will always cherish. Thank you for being you!

Last but not least, to the readers. I truly love writing and I am honored that I am able to share that with you. Thank you for your messages and tags on social media. I love hearing from each and every one of you. Thank you for your continued support of me, and my dream of writing.

With Love,

Kaylee Ryan
AUTHOR

CPSIA information can be obtained
at www.ICGtesting.com
Printed in the USA
LVOW04s2313021016
507122LV00013B/120/P